"I used to be a babe," Deirdre sighed.

Ten years and twenty pounds ago.

"I was never a babe," Anne sighed, pale and slim, her wispy brown hair cropped short, androgynous in her corporate suit.

"I hated being a babe," said Juliette, who was still a major babe, in Deirdre's opinion, though she seemed to be doing her best to keep that under wraps, cloaking her still-slim figure in oversized knits, letting her long dark hair go gray and perennially yanking it back in a knot.

"I'm still a babe," said Lisa, smiling at the young waiter who'd been hovering near their table, crooking her index finger at him, which was all it took to make him rush over, order pad at the ready.

See, thought Deirdre, I want to be more like that.

MORE ADVANCE PRAISE FOR

BABES IN CAPTIVITY

"The truth at last about what happens after the happily ever after. Sassy Pamela Redmond Satran's new nov razor-sharp in its observations of marriag female friendships. It should be subtitled

Motherhood Made a Man Out of Me

"Here's the latest in the hottest subject in fiction: the secret world of suburban moms. A sassy, fun read."

—Danielle Crittenden,
author of *amanda bright @ home*

ALSO BY PAMELA REDMOND SATRAN

The Man I Should Have Married

Now available from Downtown Press

Babes in Captivity

A Novel

Pamela Redmond Satran

New York London Toronto Sydney

An *Original* Publication of Pocket Books

DOWNTOWN PRESS
1230 Avenue of the Americas
New York, NY 10020

ISBN: 0-7434-6355-2

First Downtown Press trade paperback edition July 2004

10 9 8 7 6 5 4 3 2 1

DOWNTOWN PRESS and colophon
are trademarks of Simon & Schuster, Inc.

Manufactured in the United States of America

For information regarding special discounts for bulk purchases,
please contact Simon & Schuster Special Sales at 1-800-456-6798
or business@simonandschuster.com.

In loving memory of my brother
Richard Redmond
1956–2003

Acknowledgments

My world of women friends offered support of every kind in the writing of this novel. Novelist friends Christina Baker Kline, Alice Elliott Dark, Rita DiMatteo, and Benilde Little were enormously helpful in helping me find the heart of this book along with ways to set it beating faster. A huge thank-you to my book group—Sharon Hersch, Paula Stark, Lori Field, Karen Cohen, Liza Asher, Patti Jordan, Karin Diana, and Murry Newbern (who got me in)—for reading an early draft of this novel and offering ideas that reshaped the fates of Deirdre, Juliette, Lisa, and Anne. My own wonderful mothers' group inspired me to write about how central these friendships can be to women's lives long after the kids scatter to their separate futures. Thank you Denise Rue, Margo Garrison, Marcella Vanwinden, Beth Albert, Lorna Giles, and Shelley Bedik Bloom.

Acknowledgments

I am the luckiest of novelists to have an editor, Amy Pierpont, who not only makes me want to be a better writer but shows me how. Thank you to Amy, along with Louise Burke and Megan McKeever at Downtown Press, as well as to my British publisher, Louise Moore at Penguin. An enormous thanks to my wonderful agents Michael Carlisle and Kathy Green in New York and Clare Conville in London.

A special thanks to my brother-in-law Chuck Fulkerson, who gave his train enthusiasm to Trey, and to Jane Fulkerson, who contributed one of the few erotic details not in my personal repertoire.

Thank you and love to my family: my husband, Dick Satran, my children Rory, Joe, and Owen Satran, and my brother Richard Redmond, whose death when I was midway through writing this book transported me to a deeper world of feeling and creativity.

CHAPTER 1

The November Dinner

"I hate my husband."

Deirdre Wylie hurled her overstuffed red bag onto the table at which her three friends sat drinking wine. She was half an hour late for their monthly dinner, and it was all Paul's fault. She'd reminded him at least twelve times today that he had to be on time because it was moms' night out, and still he was late. And she was drenched, from the storm that had been raging all day and was still driving pellets of icy rain against the dark windows of Cleopatra, Homewood's new French-Egyptian place. And then, she'd been in such a rush to get here that she'd hit a squirrel, sending its small furry body flying right over somebody's white picket fence.

"I mean it," she said, shaking the rain from her auburn curls and collapsing onto a chair. "I really hate him."

Lisa was the first one to start laughing. Then Anne, whose

lusty chuckle was always such a surprise, erupting from her lean body in its conservative business clothes. Last Juliette, who was her best friend in the group and usually tried to be supportive, even when Deirdre herself suspected that whatever tantrum she was having wasn't worthy of anyone's support, including her own.

"That Paul," Lisa said, obviously working to make her voice sound serious. "He's such a monster."

"You ought to divorce him immediately," said Anne, leaning back in her chair and stretching so that Deirdre caught a flash, beneath Anne's starched white business shirt, of a lace bra in a fierce red that matched her lipstick.

"I'll take him," said Juliette. "I love Paul."

Everyone loved Paul—all her friends, all her family. Okay, even *she* loved Paul, the sweetest, gentlest man on earth, the very opposite of the bad boys who had trampled her life from her teens straight into her twenties. Unlike those other men, Paul was someone with whom she could plan a wedding, weather in vitro, raise twins, take out a mortgage, drive a mini-van, program the TiVo, and clean out the refrigerator. Unfortunately, he just wasn't someone who turned her on.

Not like Nick Ruby, her old boyfriend, player of the upright bass, comrade in her now-defunct singing career, still-ranking holder of the title of Best Lover of her life. Nick Ruby, whom she'd read in the *Times* this very morning was playing in New York, where he'd recently relocated, which just so happened to lie a mere fifteen miles due east of the chair in which she now sprawled.

And that was the problem, wasn't it? It wasn't that Paul was late, or that she'd hit the squirrel, or that Zoe had thrown up in the car, or that the dentist had told her she needed three crowns and a root planing, or that the roof had sprung a leak. The problem was something that didn't, at first glance, seem like a problem at all: the idea that a more exciting life, a life she had once had and might still have again, was coming to town.

"Nick Ruby's moving to New York," she blurted out.

The name meant something only to Juliette, who sucked in her breath. "The Berkeley guy. The musician."

"Mr. Sex," said Deirdre, nodding while draining the bottle of wine into her glass.

"Oh, God," whispered Juliette. "I'm nervous already."

"Why are you nervous?" said Deirdre. "You're not the one who's thinking about having an affair."

Although she was focused on Juliette, out of the corner of her eye Deirdre saw Anne and Lisa exchange a quick glance.

"See, that's why I'm nervous," said Juliette, a tremor in her voice.

"Are you actually thinking about having an affair?" asked Anne.

Was she thinking about it? Sure, she was thinking about it. Would she really do it? That was far more questionable. Affairs were so time-consuming. So messy—all that showering, all those changes of underwear. All that *lying*.

The itch she was feeling seemed at once vaguer and larger than simply a sexual one.

"Maybe what I want isn't him," she said. "Maybe what I want is to sing again."

She'd given up her musical career as precipitously as she'd

ended her relationship with Nick, turning down a starring role in the touring company of *Cats* to go to graduate school in social work, her first disastrous foray into the helping professions. After social work—she and Paul were already married by then—she'd tried being a stockbroker (except she kept trying to talk people out of buying stocks), a decorative painter (until she began telling her customers that faux finishes were tacky), and a nursery school teacher (her very briefest career of all).

Why didn't she ever try singing again? she wondered. She'd had a passion for it she'd never found in either the worthier or the less pressured professions she'd tried. And she missed the person she'd been back then, the sexy girl who wore see-through shirts onstage, the better to show off her lush breasts, who drove alone in an old Cadillac convertible from California to New York, who was never afraid, never doubted herself.

"I used to be a babe." Deirdre sighed. Ten years and twenty pounds ago.

"I always wanted to be a babe," said Anne, pale and thin, her wispy pale brown hair cropped short, androgynous in her corporate suit, her bright lips the only obvious flag of her sexuality.

"I hated being a babe," said Juliette, who was still a major babe, in Deirdre's opinion, though she seemed to be doing her best to keep that under wraps, cloaking her still-slim figure in oversize knits, perennially yanking her long dark hair back in a knot.

"I'm still a babe," said Lisa, smiling at the young waiter who'd been hovering near their table, crooking her index finger at him, which was all it took to make him rush over, order pad at the ready.

See, I want to be more like that, thought Deirdre, admiring

Lisa's confidence, her certainty. Lisa was not beautiful—Juliette was the truly gorgeous one of their group, and even Deirdre herself might, given time and effort, have Lisa beat in the beauty department. But Lisa kept herself in impeccable shape, her stomach taut after four pregnancies, her skin and teeth flawless, her straight blonde hair so even at the bottom it might have been cut in one clean chop, as with a guillotine.

"The lamb is the thing to order here," said Lisa, snapping her menu shut. "That's what I'll have. Rare, of course."

Juliette and Anne, always reluctant to counter Lisa's dictates, ordered the lamb too, and Deirdre was about to follow suit. But then she thought: I don't want lamb. I do not want the fucking lamb. I'm not even hungry. Waiting for Paul to come home, growing more agitated by the second, she'd gobbled chips and olives and cheese, and now she didn't feel like eating anything at all.

"I'm just going to drink," she told the waiter. "Can you please bring another bottle of wine?"

The other women looked shocked. "But you have to eat *something,*" said Juliette.

"No," Deirdre answered. "I have to lose weight. Come on, ladies, don't you ever want to throw off all the rules of our suburban lives—the three square meals a day, the fresh sheets every Friday—and go a little wild?"

But what was wild by the definition of their circumscribed world? Juliette thought a new rug for the living room might provide the satisfaction Deirdre was looking for. Anne suggested a job, something steadier and more lucrative than singing. Lisa mentioned a new Power Pilates class at the gym, which would burn off a lot of energy, though Juliette wondered whether yoga, the calming kind, might be a better idea. Deirdre kept drinking wine and shaking her head.

"Maybe what you need is a Pocket Rocket," Lisa finally suggested.

Lisa had been promoting the Pocket Rocket, a miniature vibrator, for several months now, as enthusiastically as she'd recommended using toothpaste as silver polish (Deirdre didn't own any silver, and if she did she wouldn't polish it) and putting your kids to bed by seven o'clock (good luck: Zack and Zoe, though mere first graders, were usually wide awake playing video games long after she and Paul had conked out).

"I'd rather have a good penis, thank you," said Deirdre. "If only I knew where to find one."

"Penises aren't very efficient," Lisa said, "whereas the Pocket Rocket guarantees you an orgasm—zip zip zip—every time."

"I don't think that thing would work for me," said Juliette.

"It works for everyone," pronounced Lisa.

"Even if you've never had an orgasm?" asked Juliette.

"You've *never* had an orgasm?" said Anne, her face registering real shock. "Not even by yourself?"

Juliette blanched. *"Especially* not by myself."

"I guarantee," said Lisa. "Use this thing, even with Cooper—even with Paul, Deirdre—and you'll have the best sex of your life."

That Deirdre could not buy. "I don't believe a mechanical device could give me better sex than I had with Nick Ruby."

"I've got to admit," said Lisa, "I think the best sex of my life happened without electronic intervention too."

Just then the waiter appeared bearing plates of lamb, his

cheeks as pink as the meat. Deirdre suppressed a grin and raised her eyebrows at the other women, who sat back and refused to meet her eye. They were all, she could tell, trying to keep from laughing. As soon as the waiter retreated—very reluctantly, Deirdre guessed—they all leaned back in to hear Lisa's story.

"Okay," she said, slicing into her meat. "It was when I worked on Wall Street, when I was a money trader, and this other trader and I had been flirting for weeks. He was this fabulous-looking guy, hugely confident, dated models, that kind of thing. Anyway, late one afternoon after the markets had closed, we were standing by the coat rack talking, and on impulse I reached out and grabbed him. I mean, *grabbed* him. Neither of us said anything. Everyone had already left the office, so we did it right there on a desk, with our clothes on."

"Weren't you embarrassed when you saw him the next day?" Juliette asked.

"Embarrassed? Ha!" Lisa cried. "I loved knowing I had this secret power over him, that I could have him whenever I wanted."

Anne sighed deeply. "That's the way I feel about Damian."

A woman who was still dreamy about her husband, after ten years of marriage? Given that Anne's husband, Damian, a long-haired and languid British filmmaker, was sexier than all the other husbands combined, Deirdre could just manage to buy it. But that didn't mean she wanted to hear about it.

"Husbands don't count," Deirdre told her.

"Okay, okay," said Anne. "Before Damian, my best was in a gondola. The ski type of gondola, in Zermatt—we're talking the Matterhorn, all the way up. Two Austrians. Rolf and Wolf."

7

"You're kidding," said Deirdre, though the blond massive-
ness of Rolf and Wolf had already taken sweaty form in her
mind.

"I'm kidding about Rolf and Wolf—I never did get their
names."

"Didn't you feel"—Juliette seemed to be searching for the
right word—"squished?"

"Precisely," said Anne, smiling. "What about you, Juliette?"

Juliette shook her head. "No orgasms, no great sex."

"But still," said Anne. "There's got to be one time, one person that stands out."

"All right, then I'd have to say my first boyfriend, when I was
seventeen," said Juliette. "My mother and I had just moved to
Paris, so I was still this young American girl, very naive. He was
French and—well, you know about French men."

"Not really," Deirdre said. Though the article this morning
had said that Nick Ruby had spent a couple of years in France.

"French men, when they're in love, devote everything to
pleasing the woman."

"And yet . . . ," said Anne.

"Sometimes even a French man can't do enough," Juliette
said. "But still, I was so in love. He made me happy that my
mother had dragged me to France. He even made me stop longing for my father."

They all knew the basics of Juliette's story: handsome
American actor father marries beautiful French mother and
installs her in his tiny Pennsylvania hometown with their new
baby while he leaves for months on the road. Parents penniless
but madly in love until Juliette's mother gets sick of being pen-

niless and decamps with the by-then-teenaged Juliette for Paris. Father disappears into the maw of Hollywood; mother bitter and alone, but at least back in France.

"So what happened?" asked Deirdre.

"My mother engineered the breakup. He was an art student and that scared her. She'd married my father for love and felt that had been a huge mistake. She talked me into going to New York, to FIT, for a year. By the time the year was up, of course he had found someone else."

"That's awful," said Deirdre.

"No, I actually ended up thinking my mother was right," Juliette said. "She said I should marry for security, and I think that was smart in a lot of ways."

"But what good is security," said Anne, "if you can't have orgasms?"

What good is security, thought Deirdre, if you had to be married to Cooper Chalfont to get it? Deirdre loved her friend, but she couldn't stand Juliette's stiff of a rich husband.

"You won't need Cooper for security," Deirdre said, "once you get your therapy degree."

Juliette, whose son, Trey, had Asperger's syndrome, a form of autism, was thinking of applying to graduate school in occupational therapy at one of the programs in the city for next fall.

But now she said, *"If* I get my degree."

Deirdre frowned. Not that she was any big career dynamo— Anne was the only one of their group with a serious full-time job—but she disapproved of Juliette's seemingly total lack of ambition. It only gave Cooper more of a hold over her, Deirdre felt, and the occupational therapy idea had at least seemed to offer her friend some future that didn't depend completely on her husband.

"I can't believe you're having doubts again," Deirdre said. "I thought you'd decided you really wanted to do that."

"Yeah, but I'd give it up in a second if I could have another baby." Juliette looked around the table, her large hazel eyes resting on each of them in turn. "That's what I really want."

"You do?" said Deirdre. Since they'd met over six years ago, as sleep-deprived first-time mothers pushing carriages zombielike down the main street of Homewood, Lisa had gone on to have three more children, but the rest of them had held fast. Deirdre had had so many problems getting and staying pregnant the first time, that when she had twins there was no reason to risk another pregnancy. Anne and Damian, both with demanding careers, had decided to limit it to one. And Deirdre had always assumed that Juliette, whose son had so many problems, wouldn't even consider chancing another child.

"I thought," she said now, "because of Trey . . ."

"Trey isn't what's stopping me," Juliette said. "I haven't worked up the nerve to ask Cooper."

"What does Cooper have to do with it?" Lisa asked, neatly cutting the last slice of her lamb in two and popping half of it in her mouth. "With me and Tommy, money and work are his domain, and house and kids are mine."

"Yes, but," Juliette said, looking even more rattled than she had during the Pocket Rocket discussion, "anything significant, Cooper insists that I consult him."

Lisa shook her head. "If I wanted another baby, I might give Tommy a heads-up, but then I'd just go ahead and have one."

Juliette shuddered. "Cooper would be really upset if I did that."

"I have to say I agree with Juliette," Anne said. "I can't imagine doing anything important without discussing it with Damian, and vice versa. We're partners in everything, which is how I want it."

"But there must be something you want, just for you," said Deirdre. "Something that isn't necessarily first on Damian's list."

Anne pushed away her half-eaten food and looked around the room. "I'd like to own this place," she said. "That's my version of having another baby, opening a restaurant of my own."

"You never told us that," said Deirdre. Anne seemed to have an endless capacity to surprise, with her sexy lingerie hiding beneath her straitlaced suits, her brainy demeanor masking her passionate heart.

"It's always seemed so unattainable, since I'm the big breadwinner, the one who's got the health insurance," said Anne. "I'll do it someday, when one of Damian's films hits it big."

"You can't put everything off for someday," Lisa said. "I learned that when my mother died." Lisa had been only sixteen when her mother died of cancer; Anne too had lost both her parents when she was still in college.

"I agree," Anne said, "but I really think someday's coming soon. Damian's finishing up his new film, and I think this could be the one."

They sat there silently for a moment and then Deirdre said, "What about you, Lisa. What's your goal?"

"I don't have one," Lisa said, managing to make it sound as if not having a goal was the smartest plan of all.

"Oh, come on, there must be something you want." Deirdre

was in awe of Lisa's confidence, except when it veered toward smugness. "How about running a multinational corporation? Or becoming the first woman president?"

"No. Really. My life is exactly the way I want it."

"You're too perfect," Deirdre teased. "You obviously have to die."

"You haven't declared a goal either," Lisa said.

Hadn't she? It was just that she wanted so much, it was hard to narrow it down to any one item.

"I want to be a babe again," she said finally.

"Not exactly a full-time job," Anne pointed out.

"Being one isn't a full-time job, but *becoming* one might be, at least for a while," said Deirdre. Undoing six years of chocolate chip cookies was going to take a lot more than skipping a single dinner—especially if she drank the calories instead.

"I can give you a diet and exercise plan," said Lisa.

"Um, no thanks," Deirdre replied. Whatever regimen Lisa prescribed, Deirdre knew, would almost certainly be too healthy and rigorous for her. "I also want to go see Nick Ruby at one of his club dates, and I was thinking you could all come with me. We could do it for our next dinner."

Her friends traded glances. Doubtful glances.

"Come on, you guys!" said Deirdre. "If you're there, you can keep me from getting into too much trouble."

"All right," said Juliette, looking at Anne and Lisa. "We'll go with you."

Deirdre took a deep breath. "And I think I want to try singing again," she said.

At that moment, a piano sounded across the room. She

hadn't noticed the black baby grand when she swept into the restaurant in a tizzy over Paul's lateness. And then she'd been so involved in conversation, she hadn't spotted the twins' nursery school teacher and her old boss, Mrs. Zamzock, her hair tightly curled and her lips colored her trademark magenta, taking her place on the piano bench.

"Oh my God," she said, ducking into her sleeve. "It's Mrs. Zamzock from Duckling Academy. This is so embarrassing."

"What's so embarrassing?" asked Juliette.

"Maybe you should get up and sing with her," said Lisa.

"If you want to be a singer," said Anne, "you could start now."

"I don't want to be a lounge singer in New Jersey!" said Deirdre, horrified. "I want to be a star!"

They all looked at her. Had she actually said that? Did she actually mean it?

"Don't you dare laugh," she warned them.

"We weren't going to laugh," promised Juliette.

"All right, let's make a pact," said Deirdre. "By the time we all meet next month, let's each do something to get closer to what we want."

"Maybe we should make it a race," Lisa said. "Make it more interesting."

"A race?" The word alone made Deirdre's pulse quicken in a queasy mixture of excitement and—what was that? Oh right: fear. A race would mean she'd have to stop spouting off and actually do something.

"Yeah," said Lisa, leaning forward as if she were already at the starting gate. "Don't worry, I'll think of some challenge for myself, something major. What do you think, ladies?"

"I could introduce the baby idea to Cooper," Juliet said, giving a little shiver she didn't even seem aware of.

"Bring it up after sex," Anne advised, reapplying her lipstick, "or even better, during. That's my plan with Damian and the restaurant discussion."

Deirdre felt a vibration that seemed to originate in her chest and up through her neck and lips and brain, shooting right out of the top of her head. She felt electric with the sense that everything was about to change, not just for her, but for all of them. She had provoked it, she reminded herself; she had wanted it. And now she had no choice but to scurry to keep up.

CHAPTER 2

Juliette

A baby. Now that she'd said it out loud to her friends, now that she'd allowed herself to imagine it could be real, Juliette wanted it so badly she could almost feel her belly swelling and the baby's miniature feet tickling her from somewhere deep inside.

It could happen tonight. She was ovulating, she knew: she could feel the telltale twinge in her side, the creaminess between her legs, even a little blip in desire. A very little blip.

She stood before the mirror in the master bathroom and removed one of the long bobby pins from her hair, and then another, and another, and unwound the black elastic that bound it tight. Then she raked her fingers through its length and studied herself for longer than her usual second or two. Her husband wanted her to wear her hair loose like this all the time, she knew. He wanted her with dark eyeliner accentuating her eyes, with artificial pink enlivening her cheeks and lips. "You have a gorgeous figure—you should show it off," he said. But she didn't want the attention, not from the world, not from him. She fingered the long loose white cotton nightgown that hung from the hook on the back of the door. She'd forgo this tonight; tonight, she'd appear in only a bra and panties.

She hated having to ask Cooper for anything, especially when she suspected he might not readily give it to her. In their marriage, there was the veneer, of course, that they were equals; anything less would have shamed Cooper's good idea of himself and his life. But the truth, as she saw it, was that he held most of the power. Most of the money, most of the power. She dealt with this by flying beneath the radar, by not putting his dominion to the test.

And, of course, another reason she kept delaying the baby discussion was that, if he said yes, they'd have to have sex, and sex was something she preferred to avoid.

Now she couldn't avoid it—the talk with Cooper, the sex that might follow—any longer. Though she was ten years younger than Cooper and he treated her perennially like a youngster, she was turning thirty-five in January, and thirty-five was the age at which everything involved in having a baby changed, when the tests were not just optional but required, when the risks ballooned. And those were just the ordinary risks, not the extra ones that applied to her, whose only child had Asperger's, which that might have a genetic basis. Assuming she managed to conceive at all.

"Cooper," she said, flicking off the bathroom light and stepping into the bedroom. She'd meant to put on lipstick, but she'd forgotten. Maybe he'd be so astonished to find her standing there in her white lace-edged underwear he wouldn't notice.

Cooper was standing by the bed, already wearing his pajamas, Brooks Brothers navy-and-white-striped broadcloth that he counted on receiving from his mother every Christmas. Pajamas for Christmas, a shirt and tie for his birthday, a place setting of the Wedgwood for their anniversary. They'd received their tenth place setting in June, and Juliette, in a rare fit of irony, had said, "I don't know why we'd ever need more than ten." Cooper had started to point out that dishes might very well get broken through the years, and that at some point the duty of hosting family holidays would fall to them, until Juliette interrupted him and gently explained that she had been joking.

He raised his eyebrows and took in her underwear in an exaggerated way, as if she'd just announced she was heading out of the house this scantily dressed.

"What's going on?" he said.

"Nothing."

She hesitated. Should she go over to him? Put her arms around him, act as if she wanted him? But that would not be entirely honest.

"Cooper," she said again, taking a step closer. "I've been thinking."

He laughed nervously. "Always dangerous."

She wanted to stop right then. Pretend she'd been about to say something else—"Maybe we should repaint the living room"—and go change into the billowy white nightgown.

But were things going to be different, better between them

next month? Next year? Was this ever going to get any easier? Did she really want to get pregnant, or not?

"I want another baby," she said.

And then stood there holding her breath.

Her husband turned away, busied himself picking up a dirty polo shirt from the Hitchcock chair that sat beside the dresser and folding it into thirds, then thirds again.

"Did you hear me?" she asked finally.

He sighed, still not looking at her. From the back, you could almost mistake him for an old man, with his white hair and his saggy pajamas. But when he turned around, he looked more like Richard Gere than James Coburn—Richard Gere playing one of his soft-spoken tiger-poised-to-spring businessman types. Suddenly, their bedroom felt more like a corporate office than the muted cream-and-white retreat it had been designed to be. Juliette wished she had something, preferably iron-plated, to cover her bare skin.

"I thought the baby issue was off the table," he said.

His voice was so well modulated Juliette thought she was probably one of the only people in the world who would find what he said frightening. Well, she and anyone who'd ever been his business adversary.

"It was never off the table," she said, trying to control the tremor in her voice. Her hands were moist with nervousness. "We actually never talked about it."

"I thought we agreed that Trey was going to be it for us."

There had been no such agreement. When Trey was three, around the time the mothers of so many of his nursery school classmates were getting pregnant and having their second babies, they first realized something might be wrong with him. That whole year, and the next, were taken up with tests and evaluations and diagnoses, so many of them wrong. By the time all the experts agreed that Trey's problem was not wheat allergies or ADD, not autism or shyness, but Asperger's syndrome, he was five. Then there had been the time involved in learning about the illness—he was highly intelligent but prone to obsessive interests and hopeless at relating to other kids—and figuring out the treatment options and finding the best teachers and the right therapists, which took them up to just about tonight.

"Right from the beginning," Juliette said, "we always talked about having more children, three or even four. I always made it clear I didn't want to condemn any child to being an only like I was."

But Cooper wasn't really listening, she could see that; he was already framing his rebuttal, shaking his head, pursing his lips, and staring at the lambswool carpeting.

"Given Trey's problems, the amount of time and energy involved in caring for him . . ."

"Not yours," Juliette mumbled.

"What was that?"

She raised her head and met his eyes squarely.

"I said it's not your time and energy."

"No, but it's my money," said Cooper.

A chill seized her as instantly and absolutely as if a window had blown open to the November night. She wrapped her arms around herself and moved to get her robe from the closet.

"You know, Cooper," she said, knotting the sash and yanking it tight. "That was really low."

He made a face she interpreted to mean: maybe it was. But I still meant it.

"And it isn't even true," she said.

There had been no prenup. She had been willing to sign one, happy even. She wanted him to know that the money itself wasn't important to her. What she wanted was to be a full-time mom, to have lots of children and the financial freedom to stay home with them, to lavish them with all the advantages—art lessons and summer camp, cool sneakers and ice cream every night—she'd never had growing up.

"Listen, baby," he said, reaching out to touch her arm. "This is getting out of hand."

She wrenched away. "Please don't touch me."

"I'm sorry," he said.

That was unusual. So unusual it could not be ignored.

"I don't care about the money," said Juliette, intending to reassure Cooper that his fortune was still his own, though in truth she did care about the therapy that money could buy for Trey, the substantial way it could purchase him a better future. For that, she'd be anybody's whore. "I care about our family."

"I care about our family too," said Cooper, "but our family also includes you and me. Our marriage."

The other unexamined subject.

"I want more time with you, Juliette. You know I've been wanting that ever since—well, really, since before Trey was born. And I was thinking now that he was in school all day, maybe you'd be freed up to think a little bit more about me."

From early in her pregnancy, it was almost as if Cooper was in competition with Trey, and of course, in Cooper's view, the baby always seemed to come out the winner. It was for the baby that she wore maternity clothes instead of the fitted little Chanel dresses Cooper loved, that she stopped drinking expensive wine and staying out late at client dinners. And over time, Trey had only absorbed more and more of Juliette's attention: all the specialists, all the therapies, the time she spent working with him one on one. She had help, at Cooper's insistence—Heather the nanny, the oldest of eight from a dairy farm in Shropshire—but still, with Trey, there was so much Heather couldn't do: consulting with his teachers, making sure that his responses were appropriate in all the home drills. There was so much that only Juliette could do, and wanted to do on her own.

"You have me, Cooper," she said, knowing as she said it that even she didn't have much hope that he would buy it. "I'm right here."

Cooper shook his head. "I don't think so," he said. "Not the woman I married."

"I'm the same woman, Cooper, just ten years older."

But she couldn't help but wonder how the beautiful bride, stepping into what she thought would be a fairy-tale life, could really be the same woman as the mother of a child who talked for hours on end about freight trains. Who hugged children he was trying to befriend with such enthusiasm they ran away screaming in terror. Who was so baffled and disheartened by his inability to connect that he'd told her, last week, that maybe the world would be happier if he wasn't in it.

"Listen, Cooper," Juliette said. "I know Trey takes a lot from me. But I thought you wanted that too. I thought you liked it that I could be with him."

"But now it's not just him. Now you want to go to school."

"Is that what's bothering you?" Juliette asked. This afternoon, when she'd resolved that this would be the night she'd broach the baby subject with Cooper, she'd bundled the graduate school catalogs into the back of a third-floor closet, along with her summer clothes. "Because that—I'd gladly give that up, if we were having another child."

Cooper sighed hugely and came at her, his arms outstretched. She had no choice but to let him engulf her. But standing there, nose to broadcloth shoulder, breathing in the scent of his evening tennis game and the cigarette she knew he sneaked every day after work, she felt herself pull back, but so slightly only she could feel the shift.

"I want us to be together," he said into her ear. "In love. Like we used to be."

Had they ever been in love? There was a picture of them, in Paris when she took him to meet her mother, that to her had always seemed to distill their relationship: His arm solidly around her, gripping her shoulder, smiling as if to say, Look at this beautiful girl I've won. He was romantic back then, sending huge bouquets of orange roses to the designer's studio where she worked, hiding jewel-like Tiffany boxes beneath her pillow. What she'd felt for him hadn't been passion and it hadn't been drama, thank God, but some steadier sort of thrum that suggested real staying power. Here is a man, she'd thought, who'll always take care of me.

"I may not want a baby," he murmured, "but I'll be happy to try making one."

"I'm serious about this, Cooper," she said, barely able to keep the anger out of her voice as she pulled away from him.

Tears sprung to her eyes and she swung away, unwilling to let him see that he was making her cry. Blindly, she stalked toward the bathroom and barricaded herself inside, muffling her sobs with a towel. She didn't want him to know how she was feeling, she didn't want him to comfort her, and she especially didn't want him to make love to her.

What if he had said yes, of course, let's have another baby? Would she feel differently then, more open, more loving to him? Huddled in the bathroom crying, she didn't want to be having these thoughts. She wanted to believe it was all his fault, that the only thing wrong was his resistance to her desire for another child. If she could only make herself keep believing that, she thought, she could also keep believing that their problems had a solution.

CHAPTER 3

Anne

Anne tiptoed out of her sleeping daughter's room, her heart quickening. After her long days at work, she relished her evenings with her child, but the moment she looked forward to the most was this one, when Clementine was finally asleep and she and Damian were alone. Anne flicked off the hall light and stepped into their bedroom, shutting the door tight behind her.

Damian was sitting in bed, under the covers, marking a script with an orange highlighter. He looked up at Anne, and she pulled her sweater over her head, smiling at him and shaking her hips, as if she were doing a striptease. He pushed his straight brown hair, longer than hers, back from his face and returned her smile. She whipped off her T-shirt and shivered. She was not wearing a bra, and it was so cold her nipples poked out even farther than they normally did, the closest she got to having curves.

Damian held out his free arm. "Come to bed."

Still quivering, she stepped out of her jeans but decided to leave on her sheer black thong. She hurried to get under the covers, snuggling close to him. His chest was as narrow and thin and pale as hers, but he was warm from the bed. She kissed his chest, her lips grazing the sharp edge of his nipple.

"I know what I'm getting you for Christmas," he said.

"A pony?" This was an old joke between them. As a child, she'd dreamed, every Christmas, every birthday, of waking up to find a pony in her living room.

"That," he said, "plus a really spectacular pair of knickers."

Even after a decade away from his native England, he still clung to words like *knickers* and *nappies* and *lift*.

"More spectacular than the ones I've already got?" she said.

She reared up and straddled him, the blankets tented across her back. He was wearing pajama bottoms—never a good sign—but she pushed herself playfully against him until his penis stiffened and poked from the buttonless fly.

"You don't have anything like these," he said. "They've got leather laces up the side, and a kind of slit down below. I've got a special secret source."

"Oh, really," she said, still teasing but feeling a bit hurt at the same time. Lingerie had always been one of his things, and she thought she'd done a good job of keeping him titillated. She believed she'd scoped out every lingerie shop in Manhattan as well as the suburbs. "What's your secret source?"

"It's a place in London called Agent Provocateur," he said, touching her hip with one hand, though he still gripped the script with the other. "They have things nobody has here."

"They do mail order to the States?" she said, leaning down and licking, very lightly, the ridge of his nipple. She was thinking that maybe she'd find the Web site or get a hold of the catalog and order something provocative for both of them herself.

"Uh, I'm not sure," he said. "I thought I'd do some shopping when I was over there for the final part of my shoot."

She stopped moving then. "I didn't know you had to go back to London."

"I told you," he said lightly, his attention back on the script. "You forgot. It's only for two weeks."

"Two weeks. When will you be back?"

"Not until right before Christmas, I'm afraid." He lowered his hand and she felt the script resting against her back. "The twenty-third."

"Oh," she said, thoroughly deflated. She'd been hoping to raise the issue of the restaurant tonight, but this news had left her feeling like she wouldn't have the heart to press forward. She hated when he went away on shoots, hated sleeping alone and spending her evenings alone after Clementine was asleep. And then there was the matter, especially at this time of year, of how she was going to juggle her work schedule with the inevitable holiday events at Clementine's school. Although they still employed Clementine's babysitter, Consuelo, full-time although their daughter was in school—Damian's schedule was too erratic for him to reliably plug any child-care gaps—there were occasions when only a parent would do. It was often easier for Damian to rejig his schedule to attend the choral pageant or the class party, and even though Anne would have gladly traded places with him, right now she was bound by the demands of earning her steady corporate paycheck.

"I'm sorry, doll," he said. "I'm afraid it can't be avoided."

"But couldn't you schedule it for after New Year's?"

"Not given the budgetary pressures we're under, you know that."

Damian was an independent filmmaker, one whose movies won prizes and were shown on the Sundance Channel but did not yet receive the financial backing of the big Hollywood studios.

"With any luck," he said, "I'll finish shooting a day or two early, squeeze in a quick visit with my family, and then when I get back be able to shut down for all of Clem's school holiday. I thought maybe I'd try to start her skiing this year. What do you think? Think she's ready?"

Anne turned her head so that her ear was pressed to Damian's chest, where she listened to the pulsing of his heart, as soothing as the ocean. When he was gone, she could never quite get warm enough in bed and often woke with her arms wrapped around his pillow.

Suddenly she had an idea. "I know," she said, rising up with the excitement of it. "What if Clementine and I went over to London? Met you there and then stayed on for Christmas with your family?"

She couldn't believe she hadn't thought of it earlier. She'd always dreamed of celebrating a Christmas in England and would love for Clementine to spend the holiday surrounded by grandparents and aunts and uncles and cousins, as opposed to their lonely little threesome here. Their past visits had all been in the summer, never for a traditional family holiday. With Anne an only child herself, her parents both long dead, it seemed more important than ever for Clementine to connect with Damian's family in Britain. His parents, along with his two much-older siblings and their seven enormous children, were the only extended family Clementine would ever have.

But Damian was already shaking his head. "God, there's nothing I'd like better, but I'm going to be working night and day, not a moment for pleasure."

"Oh, come on, Damian, you wouldn't have to spend a lot of time with us. We could wait to come over until right before Christmas, when Clem's vacation starts. Then you'd be just about finished shooting anyway."

There were some great new restaurants in London, she'd heard, and she'd love to visit them for fresh ideas. Maybe they could even shoot over to Paris for a few days at the end of the trip, eat some fabulous meals, and deduct the entire venture as a business expense.

"Come here," he said, letting the script and the marker drop to the floor. She leaned toward him, and when she was almost lying on top of him, he reached up and ran one hand up the back of her neck, lifting her hair from her neck while he slid the other hand in a caress down the length of her spine.

The first time he did this, it made her realize what they had was more than a fling. They met when she was living in London for her first job out of business school, and he was working as a bartender in The City, near her office. He was so handsome, with his long dark hair contrasting with his pale skin, his sharply chiseled features accentuating the fullness of his mouth. The first time she saw him, she stood staring, assuming he'd never be interested enough to look beyond her flat chest and her cropped mousy hair and her conservative business clothes to what she knew was her most thrilling feature: her mind. And then when they did go to bed together, she figured it was an affair, fling, nothing serious, never love. Until he lifted the hair from her neck with one hand while tracing her spine with the other.

"I don't know why you're so against us going to London," she mumbled into his chest.

"It's not you, doll," he said, beginning to stroke her hair. "I'd adore having you there. But every time we take Clem abroad, she's miserable with jet lag for an entire week, you know that. And then there's the Santa issue—having to transport all the gifts in one direction or the other. And then there's the three of us crammed into my parents' guest room."

She sighed. His mother was sweet, and for a few days Anne always enjoyed being fussed over and luxuriated in feeling like somebody's child again. But by the end of the week, she knew she'd have a renewed appreciation for the pleasures of independence. After a visit with his family, she was always at least as itchy as Damian to reclaim their own big private bed, their own quiet house, free from any requirement to discuss the weather or watch televised snooker.

"You'll see," he whispered, enveloping her in his arms. "We'll be together again before you know it."

"I'd love to see you shoot the wedding scene," she said, with the same kind of longing as if it were to be the real wedding of an old friend. It was to be the climactic scene of the film, the wedding between the British heroine and the African-American hero, a basketball player, who rescues her from a life of turning tricks at the Smithfield meat market. Damian was especially excited about having secured St. Bartholomew's, a twelfth-century church in a charming mews near the market, as the location for the scene.

"Well, the thing is, the wedding doesn't exactly go off anymore."

She sat up again. "What are you talking about?"

"I've decided that Sarah and Jeff aren't exactly going to get married. I mean, they're still going to be in the church and all, surrounded by all her tart friends and his teammates, but at the last moment a fight's going to break out between the best man and the tart of honor, and then there's going to be this massive rumble."

Damian looked extremely pleased at this turn of fictional events, but Anne's heart did a nosedive. This was the latest in a long line of changes to the story. When Damian initially decided to make Sarah, his heroine, a prostitute instead of a pastry chef, Anne had thought fine. There was a precedent for big mainstream movies with prostitutes as female leads, so that alone wouldn't make the film less commercial. Then, when his hero morphed from white to black, banker to basketball player, Anne had cheered him on: modern, artistic, and politically correct at the same time. But having the story end with a fight instead of a wedding seemed to all but guarantee that this film would join Damian's others as a charming, quirky, financial failure.

"This was supposed to be the one, Damian," she said. "The breakthrough project."

"And what precisely are you saying, Anne: that you don't think it will be?" His voice sounded stiff and cold, telltale signs of his British anger.

"I think you keep making it more artistic and less commercial."

"I'm an artist, Anne. If all I wanted was to make money, I'd be in LA making Will and Bloody Grace. Is that what you want for me?"

"No," she reassured him. "Of course not. But while you're creating art, I'm spending sixty hours a week running the operations department at Baker & Little. Is that what you want for *me?*"

He took a deep breath and shook his head, looking pained. She hated to make him look pained, but her own pain, her impatience to do what she wanted with her life, was growing more intense every day.

"We were supposed to have switched roles by now," she said. This blunt statement was far from the sweet sleepy exchange she'd imagined, but still, she was relieved to have the subject in the open.

That had been the deal, after all, when she worked right up to the moment she went into labor with Clementine. When she agreed they'd have no more children, despite her own eternal and irremediable loneliness over being an only child herself, over having no other family beyond their cozy circle. When she hauled herself back into her Times Square office when Clem was barely six weeks old, and continued to work forty-nine weeks a year through what was now her daughter's entire early childhood.

"I know," he said. "I know! I want that to happen too, you know that. But I've come so far doing this my way, Anne. And I have this new idea."

"New idea?"

"The one I told you about—the bloke who changes bodies with his ex-wife."

"Oh, right." She'd liked that one but had hardly let herself believe he'd actually pursue it.

"Well, I've been working on the treatment," he said, a grin starting to spread across his face. "I guess I was inspired by being around all those mums waiting around at the school gate for Clem this fall."

"And?" She felt herself growing excited, as she often did when he was starting a project, when the air was full of artistic possibilities. She'd often wished she had pursued a creative field herself, but finding herself utterly dependent on her own resources after her parents died, she switched majors from art history to business and then invested her entire inheritance in a Harvard MBA.

"I think this may be it," he said. "I can't wait to show it to you. I was hoping you'd have a chance to read it over Christmas, and then I was thinking I'd take it out to LA and pitch it right after the first of the year."

"Wow," she said. "That soon?"

"Assuming you think it's ready."

She was always his first reader, the one whose opinions guided most of his early decisions about which projects to pursue and how to shape his characters and stories. She enjoyed this position of power and influence, loved working with him and exercising this side of her talents.

But now she was increasingly eager to invest some of this creativity in her own career. She didn't want to come at him with an ice pick if she'd already made her point, but she also wanted to be sure he understood that it was time for him to take on the breadwinning, while she became the one launching an exciting if unsteady career.

"I thought after the holidays I'd start looking at spaces," she said.

"Spaces?"

"Restaurant spaces. The moms and I went to this new place last time, and all I kept thinking was how much better I could make it." Not only could she create a place that was more beautiful with more delicious food, she thought, but she was even more confident that she could turn a profit.

"Running a restaurant can get incredibly expensive," Damian pointed out.

"Like making a film."

"You'd be gone a lot of nights."

"But I'd be home a lot of days."

He hesitated, considering, she guessed, whether he wanted to keep up their verbal volley. When it came to a battle of wit and strategy, it was Anne—agreeable and loving, yet intensely intelligent to his mere cleverness—who triumphed every time. Every time she wanted to, that was.

This was one of those times when she didn't want to, not yet. She was still, after more than a decade, madly in love with her husband. She was well aware of his imperfections—his ineptness as a moneymaker, a focus on his art that others might consider self-absorption—though she chose not to examine them too closely. What she wanted, above all else, was to stay married, to stay in love, to keep her little family close and together. And that meant accommodating Damian's weaknesses as well as savoring his strengths, just as he did for her. If she wasn't as glamorous as he, if her profession was not as thrilling, well—their passion was on an even plane in the bedroom.

"I can wait," she said, as much to herself as to him. She turned so that her nipples, stiffening once again, grazed his chest. "The important thing is you and me."

"You and me," he echoed. There were his hands again, one lifting her hair from her neck, the other meandering down her back.

This was enough for now, she thought as she edged upward and then moved back down, fitting him inside her with a quick and expert grace born of all their years together. She closed her eyes and began to move, telling herself she could delay her own dream a little bit longer, in favor of the dream of their love.

CHAPTER 4

Lisa

Lisa got out of the shower, drying herself briskly as she walked through the bedroom. The kids were downstairs, finishing their breakfast—the rule was they got dressed as soon as they were up, and then ate while Lisa took her shower—and Tommy was still in bed. It was a Friday, his late night at Reed Jeep-Honda, the family car dealership he managed, and he always slept late on Fridays.

Except he wasn't asleep. He was lying there watching Lisa walk across the room.

"Come on, babe," he said. "Come on back to bed."

"I have to get dressed," said Lisa. She was, in fact, already getting dressed, already stepping into her black cotton panties.

"Come on, baby," Tommy said. "A quickie."

"The kids are downstairs."

"Put them in front of the TV."

She gave him her look, the stony one that meant "Of course I'm not going to put them in front of the TV and you should know that."

In response, Tommy flipped back the duvet to show her that he was naked and already hard.

"Tommy," said Lisa. "I have to go to the doctor this morning and I don't want to have to take another shower."

"You don't have to take another shower to go to the doctor."

"The gynecologist."

"Oh," he said.

He seemed to wilt a little. "Everything okay?"

"Fine," she said. "Just a follow-up." So annoying, some Pap smear screwup, the kind of incompetence that drove her crazy.

"Then come on, honey," he said, laying a little groan over his voice so she would know how badly he wanted it. "Come back to bed."

One of Lisa's beliefs was that it was important and healthy in a marriage to have frequent and energetic sex. Of course she didn't always feel like it, didn't always *adore* it, any more than other wives did. But she did it anyway, and she felt her marriage was stronger for it.

"All right," she said. "Let me just check on the kids. But it's going to have to be fast."

By her calculation, she had to be out the door in fifteen minutes if she was going to drop off all the kids and make her appointment on time, which meant she had to be finished with her shower in eight and starting it in six. Which gave her a minute tops to dash downstairs, settle the children, and get back up to bed.

The four of them were sitting, just as she'd left them, around the kitchen table, laid with a white tablecloth printed with red turkeys for Thanksgiving. Each of the children was eating oatmeal from an identical but different-colored bowl: Matty, who was six, had a blue bowl; Will, five, a red bowl; Henry, who was four, a green one; and Daisy, the only girl and, at nearly three, the baby of the family, a pink one to which she had affixed Barbie stickers she refused to remove. Under the table the border collie Laddie, whose training had presaged that of the children, lay thumping his tail.

"Okay, kids," Lisa said, trying to think of what she could do that would keep them distracted without violating her rules. "Who wants strawberries?"

They all looked at her without interest.

"All right." She glanced at the clock and noticed a full minute had already ticked by. "How about ba-na-nas!" She widened her eyes and shook her head for emphasis, but still, nothing.

"Okay," she said, desperation beginning to set in. She crossed to the pantry, unable to believe she was actually doing what she was about to do. She told herself to remember her long-term goals, her major priorities. Taking care of her health by getting to the doctor as scheduled, maintaining the closeness in her marriage, while staying calm around the kids, were more important than one little dietary variation. "Cookies!"

The children cheered, thrilled and startled by their extraordinary luck.

All except Henry, who was looking at her in a worried way.

"Cookies make holes in my teeth," he said.

"We'll brush later," Lisa assured him.

He looked even more frightened and reached for Lisa's hand. "Mommy," he said. "Help me brush now."

He was so sensitive, so tender, Lisa didn't know how he'd popped up in their family, much less as the third child of a closely spaced four.

She gave him a hug, but a brisk one so he would know that she couldn't be coaxed to let him climb onto her lap. None of the other kids, not his older brothers or his little sister, had ever seemed to crave this kind of contact, and sometimes Lisa had to admit it felt delicious, letting go for a few moments and just sitting there, feeling him nestle against her. But it was so impractical and put her schedule behind for the entire day.

"We're not going to brush now," she said, giving his hand what she hoped was a reassuring little shake and then letting it go. "Mommy's got something she's got to do real quick upstairs. Now you be good kids down here and we'll be leaving in just a few minutes."

She ran up then, figuring she was down to barely three minutes with Tommy. Whipping off her robe, she set the kitchen timer—the one she used to keep on schedule with everything from her showers to the kids' room cleanups—that sat on her dresser. Luckily he was ready to go.

"Do you want to be on top?" he asked.

That was code for, Did she want to have an orgasm? But there was no time for that. She could always turn to the Pocket Rocket later, after the gym but before the kids got home from school.

Shaking her head, she lay down on her back, and he moved on top of her, entering her instantly and moving in a rhythm familiar from their tennis games: lively and ambitious. Still, she refused to let herself get too involved. As soon as the timer went off, she had to be ready to hop. She ran through the morning ahead: switch the order she dropped off the kids because that would be better for getting to the doctor's, then squeeze in half an hour at the gym before running to the board meeting at St. John's.

Just thinking of the board meeting made her sigh in frustration. She'd taken on these volunteer activities because it drove her crazy to see these organizations run inefficiently, had agreed to sit on the boards of not only the church but also the nursery school and the women's soccer league, but they were proving more infuriating than satisfying. Sitting around drinking coffee, talking about kids, never getting anything really important done: she thought she was going to jump out of her skin. Her energy needed a more worthy focus, something like a job, but not a job. Something entrepreneurial, that she could work around her already well-honed schedule with the kids, something she was already talented at so she wouldn't have to waste time building up her skills to the point where she could earn meaningful money. She needed a worthy goal for her race with the moms, something she would enjoy but also something that would dazzle everyone else.

As Tommy's pace quickened above her, it came to her in a flash, the thing she wanted to do: she wanted to write a book. It would be called *How to Live*. Never mind that she'd never written anything longer than a letter before: the most successful books, the ones that got all the attention *and* all the money, were about the idea, not the writing. If she had an entirely free week to herself, she could probably write the entire thing, but of course she would never have that kind of concentrated time, so it would probably take a bit longer. The whole book would be lists, on a series of How to topics, everything from How to Get Your Kids Out of the House in the Morning to How to Have Fantastic Sex Even When You Don't Feel Like It.

It would be a huge hit, she knew it would. She supposed there were other books in this vein around, but the thing that would make hers different was that she really knew what she was talking about. She'd spent her entire life figuring out how to do things more neatly, more efficiently . . . better. Even as a kid, she'd voluntarily done all the laundry and cooking for the family and worked out an elaborate efficiency system for running the household. Lisa's mother would look up from where she sat reading Jane Austen and smoking her Lucky Strikes while the younger kids ran screaming around her and say, "Sit down, sweetie. Relax." But relaxing was the last thing Lisa could do in all that chaos.

She was so excited about her book idea that she wanted to tell Tommy, but she realized he was too involved with what he was doing to listen. Never mind: she'd show him the manuscript when it was finished.

The timer went off and still Tommy labored on, oblivious.

"Baby," she whispered.

He continued to sweat, breathing fast and hard in her ear while from downstairs came an incredible racket that was only now reaching her consciousness.

"Tom," she said, poking him in the ribs. "Jesus!"

She tried to wiggle out from under him, but he was not to be deterred. In the kitchen Laddie was yapping wildly, and Daisy let out one of her trademark high-pitched squeals that usually indicated she was doing something deeply thrilling that she knew she was not supposed to do.

"Tommy!" Lisa shouted, pushing him hard against the chest.

"Huh?" he said, rearing up.

"Get off! Something's going on with the kids."

She jumped out of bed and pulled on her robe with a rising sense of panic. Hurrying along the hallway, running down the back stairs, she knew this feeling of panic was irrational, neurotic even. But she didn't need a shrink to analyze her fears. It was a short step from her mother's slipshod housekeeping to her passivity in getting herself to a doctor until months after she first noticed her symptoms. By then it was too late; six weeks after the diagnosis of ovarian cancer, Lisa's mother was dead, leaving Lisa in total charge of the house, her alcoholic and largely absent father, and three younger siblings.

The first thing Lisa saw when she reached the door to the kitchen was the three boys still sitting at the table where she'd left them, but with their chairs pushed back. They were all looking toward the kitchen counter, their mouths open and laughing and their eyes shining and wide. Will kept throwing his head back and cackling toward the ceiling, and Matt, the oldest, was shaking his head and slapping his thighs. Only Henry looked toward where Lisa stood, freezing in midgiggle, casting one last frightened glance toward the counter, and then bursting instantly, inexplicably, into tears.

She followed Henry's gaze. There was Daisy, atop the counter, still oblivious to her mother. The little girl's diaper was in the sink, curled like a cast-off turtle shell, and her purple dress had somehow fallen over Laddie's head, contributing to the dog's frenzy. Daisy, completely naked, her mouth caked with cookie crumbs, was laughing wildly and striking fighting poses like the characters in her brothers' rationed TV cartoons. In each hand she held a long carving knife, and these she was brandishing toward the boys as she cried, "Hi-ya!"

Daisy saw her mother now and froze. She flashed a look to her brothers, as if to ask them what she was supposed to do now, but they looked even more confused and scared. Lisa could not let them see that she was confused and scared too.

"Give me the knives, Daisy," Lisa said, reaching toward her daughter and trying to convey to her children the sense that she was totally in charge here. How to Disarm Your Toddler, she thought. Step one: ask calmly, but in a confident and forceful tone of voice, that the child hand over the weapon or weapons.

But instead of handing over the knives, Daisy brandished them at her mother, crouching on the counter and warbling one last high-pitched hi-ya.

The truth was Lisa had not a clue what to do next. In her entire experience of motherhood, in all the years she'd largely raised her younger siblings, she'd never encountered anything like this. Oh God, what would Juliette do, or Anne? Undoubtedly hug the little devil. And Deirdre would probably laugh, just like Lisa's own mother would.

So she did the only thing she could think of, the thing she swore she'd never do but the one dictated by her every instinct: she grabbed her squirming daughter off the counter, snatched the knives from her hands and hurled them into the sink, and then, with her free hand, slapped the little girl squarely across her naked bottom.

CHAPTER 5

Deirdre

Deirdre kissed the twins good night—first Zack, who had started pretending he didn't like to be kissed at all, and then Zoe, who treated every good night as if she were sailing away on a voyage that might take months—and retreated to the bedroom, leaving Paul to handle Harry Potter duty. It was the Sunday after the long Thanksgiving weekend, and she was exhausted from all the cooking and the company and the endless days with the kids at home. At the same time, she felt bereft that this family idyll was nearly over, and that come morning she'd be alone again with no excuse for further delaying the launch of her future.

Switching on the light in her closet, stepping out of the comfortable clothes she'd worn throughout the family holiday, rooting around for her coziest nightgown, she encountered the dress. The dress that she'd found in the trunk in the attic when she was searching for her grandmother's crocheted tablecloth.

The silk charmeuse, bias-cut dress in a color formerly known as eggplant, vintage even back in 1989, when she'd worn it to sing onstage with Nick Ruby's band.

She reached out now and laid a finger on the tissue-y fabric, soft and frail as the skin on Paul's grandmother's cheek. Finding the dress, when she did, had strengthened her resolve to maintain her diet through the Thanksgiving weekend. She had not so much as licked the mashed potato spoon. What discipline! But it scared her, this laser focus, because it seemed to indicate that she really might intend to follow through on all of her fantasies.

Did she? Shutting her eyes, she raised the dress above her head and sucked in her breath as she let it fall over her body. It slid down smoothly over her shoulders, over her torso, coming to rest at her hips where a little wiggle encouraged the skirt down too. Deirdre opened her eyes and looked in the mirror.

Oh my God, there she was: Deirdre the babe. She looked up, meeting her own eyes, and then quickly looked back down again. There was too much judgment, too much experience in those eyes. Better to focus on her body and its power to draw her back to who she used to be: curvy, brave, bursting with sexuality.

"Aaa-aaaat last . . . ," she sang, running the tips of her fingers up the sides of her body from her hips to her breasts and then flinging her arms into the air in a gesture that was pure diva.

"At last what?" Paul asked, sounding amused.

She spun around in embarrassment and alarm. She'd been certain she'd heard him doing his best Ron Weasley voice just a moment before. Although he was tall—six foot six, so tall that everyone asked him whether he played basketball, which he didn't—Paul had a surprisingly soft step.

"Nothing," she said, feeling her cheeks color, the redhead's curse. "I was just . . ." What? Looking at herself in the mirror? Imagining she was living a different life? " . . . singing."

"You sound fantastic."

"Really?" she said, relief filling her chest. "I mean, I hardly sang anything, and I'm so out of practice, but you really thought I sounded okay?"

"As good as ever." He smiled. "Maybe better."

Paul had always loved her singing. They met, after all, when he was doing his residency at the university hospital in San Francisco and happened to have dinner at a restaurant in the Haight where she was singing jazz standards solely because it was the only paying music job she could find. This was after her Nick Ruby days, after her grunge period, after she had already turned down the role in *Cats* and decided to go to graduate school to the delight of her parents.

But what was this "maybe," she wondered, instantly reminded of one of the big reasons she'd stopped singing in the first place. She felt that old sense of insecurity slam into her like the mighty gust of a hurricane, and instantly all the good feeling that had filled her when she looked in the mirror was blown away, replaced by utter emptiness and despair.

"I've lost it," she said.

"I don't think so," he said, reaching out, oh so slowly, until the tips of his long fingers grazed the silk at her torso. "What's this you're wearing?"

"It's really delicate," she said, her hand coming up protectively. "I found it in a trunk in the attic."

"Whose is it?" he asked.

"It's mine. I mean, it used to be mine. I wore it onstage."

Paul raised his eyebrows. "Sexy."

Deirdre looked back in the mirror. She *did* look sexy, something she hadn't thought about herself in a long time. Sexiness was something she'd bartered away in exchange for her children—no, further back than that, in exchange for her marriage to Paul. You want this nice, kind, involved, considerate man? This *doctor,* of all things? Good choice, he's all yours, just hand over your sexiness. That's right, put it right there next to your freedom.

She'd always worried that maybe there was something wrong with her. Why could she get turned on only by the impossible men, the difficult and unavailable men, men like Nick Ruby? And then when someone wonderful like Paul came along, she went dead below the waist?

Well, not dead, but it took a lot more effort. And after going through months of infertility treatments, followed by months of bed rest to prevent a miscarriage, and then a near-crushing bout of postpartum depression and the early years of caring for two babies, she felt as if her already-flagging sex drive was on life support. Given a weekend away from the kids, fourteen straight hours of sleep, a large steak, and a bottle of excellent red wine, she might be able to summon some sexual energy. But in everyday life, with her everyday husband, she rarely felt the urge. Rarely even believed the urge existed.

Except when she thought about Nick. Except when she remembered how she used to feel, singing in a club late into the night, the spotlight hot on her skin, wearing a dress that made her feel naked, going home with a man who would never help her do the dishes. A man who had no dishes.

"I've been thinking about singing again," she told Paul now.

Paul sat on the bed, leaned back on his elbows, stretched out his long legs.

"That's a good idea," he said.

"I loved it, when I was doing it," she said.

"You didn't love it by the time I met you."

Actually, remembering that juncture now, Paul was always encouraging her to take gigs, mainly for the pleasure of sitting on a barstool in the dark back of the room, watching her. It was she who couldn't wait to stop, who finally went to work as a dentist's receptionist rather than continue.

"I was young," she said. "I let myself drop out because I thought *Cats* was a tacky show, because I thought I'd be lonely on the road, when taking that show could have made me a star."

"But then you wouldn't have met me," he said.

And that would be—a bad thing? Of course that would be a bad thing, she chided herself. Paul had given her the kind of love and security she'd never known, not with any of her hot but unreliable lovers. She hadn't even felt it with her lefty lawyer parents—her father was a Northern Irish Catholic, her mother a Chicana—always running off to bail someone out of jail or find someone a home. Eamon and Anunciata, as their children had been instructed to call them, had been more concerned with the global disenfranchised than with the kids left at home with the hippie nanny.

"What would I sing?"

He grinned. "Something that matches that dress."

She closed her eyes. She used to sing for Nick, alone in his room. It would be the middle of the afternoon, and they'd both have just woken up after a late gig and they'd be naked, and she'd stand at the foot of his bed in his all-white room and sing Billie Holiday or Janis Joplin—Take it! Take another little piece of my heart, now, baby. . . .

She couldn't sing that for Paul, couldn't imagine feeling comfortable wailing those desperate words in front of him. Looking at his sweet trusting face, she tried to imagine what she could sing that he would find sexy, when he said, "Sing that song, 'It's in his kiss.'"

"The Shoop Shoop Song?" Deirdre asked incredulously. "You think the Shoop Shoop Song is sexy?"

"I don't know," Paul said, looking confused. "I guess."

No wonder she found it so difficult to get turned on with him.

"Oh no, that's not the way," she sang jokily, thinking he would get the message.

But he broke into a delighted grin. "That's the one!"

She wagged her finger at him in a parody of a girl singer, warbling the lyrics about how it wasn't in his face or in his arms but in his kiss.

"That's great!" he cried. "Really great!"

She found she was smiling in spite of herself. "The audience isn't supposed to comment," she chided Paul, "however positively, after every line of the song."

Paul frowned. "I'm sorry."

"That's okay," she said, crossing the room and perching on the bed. "I'm glad you like it. Now I just have to figure out what to do with it."

"With the kids in school all day," he said, running his hand over her back, "maybe you could find a voice teacher, look for a group out here to sing with."

"Out here?" she said, aghast. "I was thinking about going into the city. I wasn't thinking of this as some little thing I could do on the side."

"Well, what exactly were you thinking?" His voice was still gentle, curious.

She sighed hugely. It wasn't like she had a plan: Step 1, Go to audition (if she could even find out where auditions were). Step 2, Become star. Step 3, Acquire cooler (much, much cooler) life. The hosting of Thanksgiving had given her a very convenient excuse for not getting it together, planningwise. Who could think about the rest of her life, after all, when she had a turkey to stuff?

But the holiday was over, and next Friday night, the usual night of the moms' group dinner, Nick Ruby was playing at a club in Tribeca.

"There's this guy," Deirdre said.

Was she really going to tell Paul about Nick? Yup, those seemed to be the words coming out of her mouth.

"This bass player I used to sing with. Upright bass, you know."

"Nick Ruby."

Wait a minute.

"We have that CD," Paul reminded her, evidently noticing the surprise in her eyes. "The one you found in the sale bin at Wal-Mart that fall we went to Vermont. You were telling everybody how crazy about this guy you used to be."

Was there any detail she'd neglected to divulge over the past decade? Anything Paul failed to remember? Juliette, Anne, even Lisa complained that their husbands couldn't seem to recall whether they took cream in their coffee or what size bra they wore. Not Paul. Paul, alone among the husbands, kept track of such minutiae as Deirdre's mother's maiden name (Ruiz), the type of stuffed animal she slept with until she went away to college (pink bunny, with black metal eyes), her age the first time she kissed a boy (fourteen, shamefully old).

"Right," Deirdre said weakly. "He's playing in New York. I thought I'd go hear him."

Paul nodded. "We could do that."

We? Oh my God, not we.

"I mean with the moms," she said. "Next Friday night."

"Oh." Paul nodded, his thin lips pressed together, his expression, which always hovered between benevolent and sad, veering toward the sad side. Would this be one of the handful of times in their entire relationship when Paul would get upset?

"I'm thinking of this as a career, Paul," Deirdre explained. "I can't go around with my husband holding my hand, taking care of me."

"I understand," Paul said, though he sounded dejected. "Sure, of course."

The problem with having such a sympathetic husband was that then you had to feel guilty. And indeed, that seemed to be guilt working at her stomach: guilt over her lingering attraction to Nick, guilt over her desire to see Nick for more than purely professional reasons. Did she even want to sing, she wondered, or was this revival of her musical ambition just a convoluted excuse to pursue Nick Ruby?

Deirdre flung herself back onto the bed beside Paul, gazing at the ceiling.

"Maybe I should just forget the whole thing," she said. "It sounds like you don't want me to go see him."

"No, no," Paul said, turning onto his side, staring down at her, and then reaching out and laying his hand on her stomach. "You should go. I want you to go."

"Because if I do this," she said, "it's going to be hard. You're going to have to be here a lot more, come home on time at night to take over with the kids and the house."

"I know," he said, his hand moving across her abdomen. "I want to do that for you, Deirdre. Really. Please."

So now he was practically begging her to go out into the world and become a singer again. Did he really mean it? Or was he just saying what he thought she wanted to hear? Part of her longed for him to tell her to forget about it, that he and the kids needed her at home, that it was time for her to give up this dream she already rejected a long time ago. If he were more of a take-charge guy, he could save her from her own worse impulses, the desires that were threatening not only her own well-being but that of the entire family.

But no, the only thing Paul would insist on was being kind and supportive. The only thing he would demand was that she be happy, and keep loving him.

Which he seemed to be indicating by inching his hand toward the hem of her silk dress.

"The kids," she said, looking toward the still-open bedroom door.

"They're asleep."

"I'm so wiped out," she said. "That was such a long week-end."

"You were great. Everything was great." He leaned down and kissed her cheek, and then moved to her neck, then up to her lips, kissing her softly—too softly. Maybe this was the basic problem? It's in his kiss, she thought, closing her eyes—or in this case, it's *not* in his kiss. Maybe if the kissing were better, everything else would follow.

Too late to worry about that now. Paul was already upping the ante, reaching down now to raise the hem of her dress as his lips headed breastward. Mayday! Mayday!

"I have to take off this dress!" she cried, leaping from the bed and pulling the dress over her head. She laid it carefully on the little leopard-upholstered chair in the corner before returning to where Paul lay wiggling out of his own clothes. She avoided catching his eye: she did not want to see him admiring her body, because she could not bring herself to admire his—his narrow shoulders, his long thin limbs, all bones—in return. Instead, she climbed on top of him, straddling him, placing her hands on his chest and rubbing against him. He was already hard. She loved him, she really did. But she closed her eyes and, moving so that he could enter her, imagined as thoroughly as she could that he was Nick Ruby.

CHAPTER 6

The December Dinner

It was the darkness. It was the little lamps on the tables and the velvet chairs and the smell of old smoke and spilt booze and the sound of musical instruments being tuned somewhere out of sight. Juliette had not been to a place like this in years, not since long before she met Cooper, but she was overwhelmed by memories and feelings as soon as she walked into the club where Nick Ruby was playing tonight. Anne and Lisa and even Deirdre, who had been atwitter throughout the drive in from New Jersey, all seemed completely normal now that they were inside the place, but Juliette felt as if she would fall in a drooling heap to the floor.

It was just that this kind of place, ancient and urban and exhausted yet vibrating with the possibilities of each new night, was the scene of so many of the highest points of her girlhood.

Usually, there was not enough money for Juliette and her mother to travel to a place where her father was performing, but sometimes it was close enough to home, or expenses were included that they were able to make the trip. Her mother always created a fantastic new dress for Juliette for the occasion, copying a design from Lord & Taylor's children's department and scouring the Lower East Side for the highest quality fabric at the lowest price, and Juliette would perch, careful not to disturb her pristine skirt, on the edge of the velvet chair, sipping at the free Shirley Temple that had to last the night. And then, her father would appear onstage, so handsome, his voice so deep and strong, like a movie star but better, because he was real, and because he was hers.

Thinking of this now, her heart began to beat faster and she felt a flutter of excitement in her stomach. These weeks of stalemate with Cooper, the forced cheer of the holidays when all she felt was depressed, had made her not want to come here tonight. But now, she was glad, as always, to be out with her friends, and doubly glad to be in this place that reached back to the happiest memories of her childhood.

"I shouldn't have worn this short skirt," Deirdre said, leaning in across the table. "I look like a hippo."

"You look great," Juliette assured her. Besides the short skirt, which was bright purple and looked amazing on Deirdre's womanly yet ever-slimmer body, Deirdre was wearing high-heeled suede boots, enormous earrings, and actual makeup. Anne, who had come directly from work, had enlivened her conservative gray suit with a lime green silk shirt, and even Lisa had upgraded to a curvier cut of khaki. Juliette suddenly felt self-conscious for not having thought to change out of her usual Mom Wear—a cozy, long, knit sweater over loose pants in a blackish brownish color, with her hair tied back and tortoise-shell glasses in place of special-occasion contacts.

"Do they have food here?" Lisa asked, surveying the crowd. All the tables were full, and people lined the walls three deep.

"I don't think any of these people eat," said Anne.

In fact, Anne and Juliette herself, who might have been the two thinnest women in Homewood, looked nearly plump in this crowd of hollow-cheeked low-slung leather pant and midriff-top-wearers.

"Let's just drink," Deirdre said, signaling for the waitress. "If we're going to start hanging out at places like this, we're going to have to give up food."

"Start taking drugs," said Anne.

"Smoke cigarettes," said Juliette, breathing deeply. No one was allowed to smoke in here anymore, of course, but the dark air was still tinged with the smell of decades of smoke. Juliette could almost see the smoke curling from the end of her mother's precious Gitanes, a treat she reserved for nights like this.

"Speaking of illicit pleasures," said Lisa. "I have your Christmas presents." She brought a brown paper shopping bag out from her black leather tote.

"It's only the first week of December!" Deirdre cried. "I haven't even begun to think about what I'm going to get you guys."

"This is a timeless gift," Lisa assured her, passing the boxes, wrapped in shiny red paper and tied with plaid ribbons, out to each of them. Fancy shampoo, Juliette guessed, from the size and heft of it. Or maybe cologne.

A moment later, she sat staring at the white cylindrical object in the clear plastic box she held in her hand.

"What is it?" Juliette asked.

Anne was smiling and shaking her head, and Deirdre whooped with laughter.

"You are such an innocent, darling," said Deirdre.

Juliette looked at Lisa.

"It's a Pocket Rocket!" cried Lisa. "I bought you all Pocket Rockets! Really—no woman should be without one."

Juliette remembered the Pocket Rocket conversation, but this didn't look the way she expected the Pocket Rocket to look.

"It's so small," she said, baffled.

"You don't . . . insert it," Deirdre said.

"Not intended for internal use," said Anne.

"You . . . apply it," said Lisa.

Deirdre leaned in. "She's talking clit."

Anne nodded. "I've got to confess, I already have one of these, and it's great. During sex, it provides some strategic friction."

Deirdre pulled back and looked at Anne. "During sex? I've never used a vibrator during sex."

"Why not?" said Anne.

"Well, I guess because it would be . . . embarrassing."

"But how else do you come during sex?"

"I don't come during sex," said Deirdre. "To me, sex and orgasms are no longer related. It's like the separation of church and state."

"It's easy to come during sex," said Lisa, "if you get on top and rotate your hips in a counterclockwise direction—I don't know why counterclockwise should work and clockwise shouldn't—but it does, making sure that with each revolution you make contact—"

"Stop!" Juliette cried. "Stop." Her cheeks were flaming.

"Okay," Lisa said. "Sorry. The point is that this little bugger"—she brandished the Pocket Rocket—"is like the Cuisinart of sex. It's like making pie dough. By hand it takes hours, but you turn this on and a few minutes later, the job is done."

Juliette looked with new interest at the Pocket Rocket. It was intriguing, the idea that this unprepossessing little device could give her a real live orgasm in less time than it took to microwave popcorn. Intriguing, she told herself, but impossible.

"You girls are bad for me," Juliette said, slipping the Pocket Rocket into her purse, careful to keep her tone teasing. "You put these ideas in my head, and then when they don't work out, I feel worse than before."

"I know what you mean," said Anne. "After last month's dinner, I went home and told Damian I thought it was time he started making more money so I could quit and open my restaurant."

"Wow," said Deirdre. "How'd he take it?"

"Let's just say I doubt I'm going to be the one who wins this competition."

"Can we not make it a competition?" Juliette said. "It's too much pressure."

"I'm sure I'm going to be the one who wins anyway," Lisa said, making it sound as if she were joking, though Juliette could tell she wasn't.

"Hey, I might jump up onstage and start singing tonight," Deirdre said. "What did you decide your goal was, teaching all of us how to have better orgasms?"

"Nothing that base," said Lisa. "I'm going to write a book." They all laughed at that.

"Well, if Madonna can do it," said Deirdre.

"I'm going to write a real book," Lisa said. "An advice book."

"That could take as long as my opening my restaurant," Anne pointed out.

"Oh no," said Lisa. "I'm sure I could polish it off in a week, if I only had more time. Once my holiday party is over, I'll be able to focus."

"Which reminds me," said Anne. "When is your party this year? Damian's in London shooting and he's going to be there until right before Christmas."

"It's not until whatever that Saturday is right before New Year's," Lisa said.

"Oh, good," said Anne. "Actually, I wanted us to go with him and spend the holidays over there this year, but he thought it would just be too much with Clementine."

"You should go on your own," said Juliette. "For a short visit before the holidays."

"I'd love to," said Anne, "but I've got work, and Clem, and Consuelo's husband doesn't like her staying the night."

"Clem can stay with me," said Juliette.

"No, no, that's too much bother."

"No, really," said Juliette, beginning to get excited about the idea. "Trey would love it, and I have Heather to help me. It would be our pleasure, no trouble at all. If Cooper won't let me have another kid of my own, I'll just have to start taking in yours."

"What do you mean, Cooper won't let you have another kid of your own?" Deirdre asked.

Juliette took a deep breath. She hadn't been sure she was going to bring this up tonight. She'd always felt, mostly because Cooper had always felt, that what went on between a husband and wife was sacrosanct, private. "It's not cocktail party chatter," Cooper would say.

Well, although they were drinking cocktails, Juliette thought as she sipped her Southside, a new drink that Lisa had insisted they all order, they weren't at a party, and this wasn't chatter. She was discussing the most important issue in her life with her closest friends, and if he didn't like it . . . She wondered whether she cared anymore what he liked.

"I brought it up, after our dinner last month," Juliette said.

"So how did Cooper respond?" asked Deirdre.

"He said forget it, he doesn't want another child," said Juliette, feeling herself begin to tear up. The room had gotten even more crowded, more loud. She realized she was beginning to shout, which made what she was saying feel surreal. "So now I'm left here, wanting this thing I can't have."

To drive home the fact that she wasn't pregnant, and to give her emotions an extra hormonal kick, her period had started in its usual hemorrhagelike rush this afternoon.

"Not necessarily," Deirdre shouted.

"What do you mean?"

"Women have gotten pregnant before," she said. "By accident."

"You mean trick him into it?" said Juliette, aghast. "I couldn't do that."

"God, no," said Anne. "Imagine how terrible that would be for your marriage."

"But if you really want a baby," said Lisa, "you can't just sit there wanting it. If he won't cooperate, there are other methods. Sperm banks, for instance."

"The UPS guy," said Deirdre.

They all laughed.

"That guy in the hardware store," said Anne.

"Which one?" asked Lisa.

"The young one, with the round face."

"Oh, no, no," said Lisa. "The skinny guy with the beard is much cuter."

"I like the new African guy," said Deirdre. "Have you seen him? He's got amazingly dark skin. He was very patient mixing me the perfect gray-green last week."

There was a sound from the direction of the stage.

"Or him," Juliette said, joining in the laughter, pointing to a very tall man standing onstage, oblivious to the crowd, wrestling with an enormous bass.

They all looked.

"Oh my God," breathed Deirdre, going pale. "That's Nick."

Juliette stared. She hadn't known who he was, hadn't even been able to see his face until now. He squinted out into the audience, but she could tell by the blank look in his eyes that he wasn't focusing anywhere near their table and apparently hadn't recognized Deirdre. Juliette stole a look at her friend, who was gazing raptly at Nick, her mouth slightly open, her eyes gleaming. And then she looked back at Nick, at his hips slim in lean black pants, his arms ropy and muscled in a short-sleeved T-shirt, the top of his head nearly bald but his sideburns long and his chin punctuated with a triangular patch of hair, his neck marked by a jagged blue tattoo. This guy is dangerous, thought Juliette.

Very suddenly, his trio—Nick on bass, a piano player, and a saxophonist—began playing, and Juliette found herself transported by the music, that little girl again transfixed by the wonder of the show. Across the table, she could see Deirdre moving in time to the music, sometimes mouthing the words to a song. Sometimes the piano player sang, and sometimes Nick rested his bass and sang.

After one number, Nick stepped to the front of the stage, out of the glare of the spotlights, and looked out into the crowd. At first, he just seemed to be looking around, and then his gaze seemed to zero straight in on Juliette. She felt her eyes widen as she drew her head back in surprise and looked to the right and then the left, directly at Deirdre, who was still grinning at Nick. And then, when she looked back at the stage, she saw that Nick finally seemed to have spotted Deirdre too, and was smiling back. Then Deirdre gave him a little wave, and he smiled so widely there was no doubt that he recognized her.

He stepped to the microphone and said, "OK, everybody, we'll be back real soon, but right now we're going to take a little break," and then he jumped off the stage and bounded across the room to their table, taking Deirdre into his arms.

Watching them hug, Juliette was pleased for Deirdre, who she knew had waited anxiously for this moment, afraid Nick wouldn't remember her, and wouldn't care even if he did. He was sexy: Juliette could feel that from five feet away—hell, she could feel it from fifty feet away. But that intimation of trouble washed over her again.

Deirdre was introducing them all now. Juliette was last. Nick leaned in close to her as Deirdre said her name, taking her hand. He said, close to her ear, "Chalfont? Are you French?"

"That's my husband's name," said Juliette.

"But she is French," Deirdre informed him. "Juliette's mother is French. She lived in Paris part of the time growing up."

"Oh, really? I lived in Paris for a few years," Nick said. He was still holding her hand and seemed to be resisting her tentative efforts to extract it.

"When did you live there and in what neighborhood?"

"Hmmm, let's see." He laughed, showing a gap between his front teeth. "I lived there from ninety-six to ninety-nine, in the eleventh, near Oberkampf."

"Ah," she said, genuinely pleased. This was a part of the city that tourists usually didn't know, very near the modest apartment where she had moved with her mother, where her mother in fact still lived. "There's a great little café on Oberkampf that's called Le Balto. They have the best café cremes. Do you know it?"

"Yes, I know that café! I love it!"

While Nick seemed to be focused only on her, Juliette looked around at her friends, trying to include them in the conversation. "There's a little black bulldog that spends every day in this café tied to the leg of a table there while his owner, an old man, sits reading the paper," Juliette told them.

"*Il est belle*, Paris," Nick said, still gazing at her, "*mais très belle avec toi.*"

What was this? His French was well accented but ungrammatical. He seemed to be saying that Paris was beautiful, but would be more beautiful with her—though it was unclear whether that meant with her in it, or seeing it with her. Juliette looked around nervously to see whether anyone else had caught this, but it seemed that none of the others—thank God—spoke French.

She said to him, as clearly as possible because she wanted to be certain he got her meaning, *"J'ai aucun interest de voir Paris avec vous et je veux absolument que vous sachiez que je suis ici ce soir pour Deirdre."* I have no interest in seeing Paris with you and I'm here tonight only for Deirdre.

"Do you understand?" she said, snatching her hand away and frowning so he would know she was serious.

He nodded, looking as if she'd slapped him, but Deirdre laughed and said, "The only word I understood was *Deirdre.* What were you saying about me?"

"I was just telling Nick that you told us he'd moved to New York," Juliette said quickly.

Over Deirdre's shoulder, Juliette caught Anne's eye as Anne mouthed the word *Hot.* Juliette looked away.

Nick was saying something about the next set, somewhere they might go afterward, all of them. At this last phrase, he touched Juliette's bare wrist. She jumped as if his fingers had burned her.

"I need to get home," she said.

Deirdre shot her a dark look.

"I'm sorry," said Anne, "but I need to go too. Consuelo's there with Clem."

"The night's just starting," said Deirdre.

"Yes, please stay," said Nick. "All of you." He looked directly at Juliette.

"No," she said definitively, to make sure he knew she was speaking directly to him. And then, "I can't."

"I'm sorry," said Lisa. "But I'm exhausted. I don't know what's wrong with me."

Deirdre looked from one to the next of them, and then at Nick. Juliette kept her eyes turned away because she didn't want to focus on Deirdre's hurt. In the long run, she thought, Deirdre would thank her for getting her out of there. Nick was a guy who could definitely wreak havoc on a suburban mom's life.

"Okay," said Deirdre doubtfully. "I guess I'm overruled here. But maybe we could get together another time."

"Sure," said Nick. "Or you could all come in again. I have a lot of gigs coming up. I'll be glad to get you tickets."

"I'd love to catch up with you," said Deirdre. "Sometime when I don't have to rush off. I have Christmas shopping to do. Could we meet someday at lunchtime? Maybe next week?"

"Sure," said Nick, scribbling his number on a napkin and handing it to Deirdre. "Give me a call. Good-bye everyone. *À bientôt.*"

But Juliette turned and walked away, pretending not to have heard. Why was this guy so clearly focusing his attention on her? And why, in spite of her efforts to push him away, did she find it so unsettling?

CHAPTER 7

Deirdre

Every time she glanced over at him as they strolled down the narrow Greenwich Village street, his bass rolling between them like a chaperone, she felt as if the truth were emblazoned on her forehead: I FANTASIZE ABOUT YOU EVERY TIME I HAVE SEX.

Well, not every time. Sometimes Jude Law slipped in there. Vin Diesel and Jason Kidd made occasional guest appearances.

But mostly, it was still Nick.

It was all she could do, really, to keep from blurting it out. Don't you dare, she told herself, taking him in out of the corner of her eye. This isn't your husband you're walking with.

"I'm sorry I had to rush away the other night," she said, tucking her chin deeper into her coat. "My friends are great but sometimes they're a little . . . suburban."

"What does that mean?" said Nick.

"Oh, you know. A little skittish about staying out too late in the city. Like to be home safe in bed by ten P.M."

"They seemed nice," said Nick. "I don't really know any-body like that. The kind of people I meet don't even start eating until after dark."

Deirdre laughed. "My friend Juliette, one of the women you met the other night, doesn't eat much until night."

He nodded. "That's because she's French," he said. "That's the real secret of why French people are so thin. They don't eat anything all day long and then they eat a lot for dinner."

"But you're not French," Deirdre pointed out. "You're Californian."

"Yes," he said. "But my soul is French."

Deirdre burst out laughing. "That is such bullshit!"

Uh-oh. He looked wounded. He isn't your husband, she reminded herself again. You can't just tease him whenever you feel like it.

"You know, I've changed a lot since you knew me back in Berkeley, Deirdre," he said.

"Oh, really?" She peered at him. True, he hadn't been bald back then. But with his black knit cap pulled down over his head, and his thick black leather jacket with its collar turned up and bound with a woolly charcoal muffler, he looked pretty much the same as he always had. He still had the ear-ring and the creative facial hair, those mournful deep brown eyes and the little gap between his front teeth. "What's differ-ent?"

"All I cared about back then was music and getting wasted

and getting it on. Now I wouldn't mind being home safe in bed by ten P.M. myself."

"There's plenty of time for that when you're old," she told him.

Just then, she caught sight of a shop window that stopped her in her tracks. She'd told Paul, as well as Nick, that she had Christmas shopping to do, which made her feel justified in spending money. From the look of the window, the store was completely filled with French pottery, all artfully displayed on antique farm tables. Now this was the kind of shop that didn't exist in the suburbs.

"Let's go in here," she said.

"Can't with the bass."

She looked at the bass and looked at the store and tried to look at Nick, though he refused to meet her eye.

"Come on," she said. "This stuff is gorgeous."

He snorted. "Overpriced and useless."

Aaaaah! She felt like screaming. Instead, she opened the door of the shop.

"I'll be out in a minute," she said.

He'd always hated shopping, she remembered that now as she wandered among the pottery, lifting a glossy little bowl, olive green with yellow dots, to check the price: $42. In fact, along with getting back in touch with their old sexual charge, she was also remembering the many ways they hadn't gotten along. She loved to troll the Alameda flea market and the Oakland thrift stores; he was an aescetic who bought maybe one well-chosen shirt a year. She was always inviting people over and drumming up parties; he preferred the company of his bass.

Outside the window of the shop, he was walking in a circle around the bass now, as if he and the instrument were doing some kind of slow motion minuet. She was suddenly reminded of the day they'd broken up. They were standing at the door of a record store on Telegraph Avenue in Berkeley when she told him she intended to go on the road with the postpunk band that was called—and she should have taken this as a sign—Road Kill. Nick had asked her how she could take part in producing such trashy music, and she had countered that it was better than playing music that only dead people liked. That time, he was the one who ducked into the store while she ran off, weaving in and out of the crowds around the street vendors selling tie-dyed shirts and silver jewelry, determined to leave him behind.

Not wanting to reprise that ridiculous parting, she grabbed one of the bowls, paid its exorbitant price, and rejoined him on the sidewalk.

"Christmas present for Juliette," she said, holding up the package.

"Let's see," he said.

Pleased that he was interested, she unwrapped the heavy white paper and held out the bowl.

He frowned. "Do you really think Juliette's going to like that?"

"I think she will," Deirdre said. In fact, she wasn't at all sure that Juliette was going to like the bowl, but she felt like she had to buy something, if only to prove to Nick she really did have a good reason for going into the shop. "She's got everything, and everything in her house is expensive, so the only thing I can ever buy her is some exotic thing she might not indulge in for herself."

"I don't know," Nick said. "It doesn't seem like her kind of thing."

"She's my best friend," said Deirdre. "You don't even know her."

"She just seems like the simple type," he said. "Understated."

Deirdre laughed and began moving down the busy street again. "You wouldn't say that if you saw her house."

"Really? What's her house like?"

"Huge. Expensive oversize matching furniture chosen by a decorator. Supersize marble kitchen and bathrooms."

"Wow," said Nick. "I never would have guessed that."

"Yeah, well, it's not really Juliette's fault. Her husband's the one who's into showing off how much money he makes."

"Oh, yeah?" said Nick. "Rich guy, huh?"

"Rich asshole, in my opinion," Deirdre said. "I can't understand why Juliette ever married him."

"Why did she?" asked Nick.

Deirdre stared unseeing at the passing traffic, remembering the last time she saw Cooper Chalfont, at an end-of-summer mojito party at Lisa's house. "Well, well," he'd said, all unctuous charm. "If it isn't our favorite bohemian."

"Beats me," said Deirdre. "Why does anybody marry anybody?"

They had reached the corner of Seventh Avenue and Nick had to stop to maneuver the bass over the curb and keep it away from careening taxis.

"Love," he said. "I guess. Right?"

"That's too easy," Deirdre said, laying a hand on his upper arm, or at least on the bulky leather than encased his upper arm, to help him navigate across the busy street. Even through the stiff material, she could feel how well muscled he was—from playing, she knew, as he would never risk damaging his hands or wrists or forearms by lifting weights. "I didn't get married for love."

"Really?" said Nick, stopping on the sidewalk and leaning into the bass. "What did you get married for?"

She really didn't want to think about Paul in such a concentrated way right now, especially not about his good points. But she was stuck. "Friendship," she said. "Support. Someone I thought I could build a real life with. I'm not always the easiest person to put up with."

He laughed. "Tell me about it."

She slapped his leather. "You're no walk in the park yourself. But sometimes I think . . ."

"What do you think?"

She gazed up at him, so close she could smell the shaving cream on his neck, the cappuccino on his breath. Her lips were tingling, and if he leaned toward her, even a little bit, she was sure she would kiss him.

"I think about what would have happened if we'd ended up together."

He whooped with laughter. "It would have been a fucking disaster!"

She bristled. "I don't think it would have been such a disaster."

"Come on, Deirdre," he said, still laughing, linking his arm

70

through hers and nudging her down the sidewalk. "We were great in bed together, but we've always disagreed about everything, even about whether we've disagreed!"

Deirdre let him pull her along, unwilling to give him the satisfaction of admitting he might be right.

"I married someone based on us being hot in bed," he said.

"You were married?" This she had never imagined.

"She was an actress," he said. "This was in LA, where I was doing movie scores. We worked together on this ridiculous superhero movie, and the next thing I knew, we were in Vegas, getting married at one of those Elvis chapels. I swear to you, I did that. Within a month, we were storming out of the house in the middle of the night. Within a year, we were divorced."

"Because you couldn't take the fighting?" Deirdre asked.

"No," he said. "I wish I could say I had that much self-respect. The fact is, when I finally broached the subject of having kids, it turned out she'd had her tubes tied years before and never told me."

"That's awful," Deirdre said. Looking over at him now, she noticed for the first time that he did look older to her, his boyish face lined, a few gray hairs sprouting in his beard. And he looked something else too: maybe a little bit lonely. "But somehow I don't see you with kids."

"Why not?" he said. "I see me with kids."

"In the suburbs? With a mortgage? Going to Back-to-School Night? I don't think so."

"I could do it," he said, as if he were contemplating life on a distant island, a place where many had tried to find happiness but failed.

They were walking past a pizza place. The aroma of baking cheese wafted out onto the sidewalk, jump-starting her hunger pangs and stopping her in her tracks. Just because he insisted on adhering to some weird vampire diet didn't mean she had to.

"Let me make this clear," she told him. "There are no men like you in the suburbs, at least not in Homewood. I don't think they let men like you across the town line. So if you're going to have a kid, you're going to have to raise it in a New York apartment."

He laughed. "If you can survive the suburban life, I could," he said. "You're not exactly a typical soccer mom."

"You'd be surprised," Deirdre said darkly. Just this past fall, in fact, the twins had started playing in the town soccer league, and Deirdre had found herself on the field every Saturday afternoon, cheering with the other parents. Did it really matter that her earrings were a little bigger, her clothes a little brighter, her hair longer and wilder? She was a doting suburban parent, just like the rest of them. The real question was: could a doting suburban parent also be a self-governing city woman?

"I wanted to talk to you about my singing," she said, feeling herself grow even more nervous than when she'd been thinking about kissing him.

He raised an eyebrow. "I didn't know you still sang."

"I don't," she said. "I mean, I haven't. But I want to. Start again. And I wanted to ask your advice."

"I'm not actually a singer, Deirdre," he said.

"I know, I know, but you're in the music world, in New York. . . ."

"I just moved here."

"You're the only person I know, goddamn it!" she cried.

He reeled back.

"I'm sorry," she said. "But I really want to do this. I don't know who else to ask."

"I'm not sure what I can do."

"Please."

"I'll try," he said, and Deirdre felt more hopeful than she'd imagined possible. And then, as he was walking away, he turned back and called, "Say hello to your friend for me, would you?"

CHAPTER 8

Juliette

School had let out early for teacher conferences, and Deirdre and the twins had walked the two blocks to Juliette's house to bake and decorate cookies with her and Trey. Outside, the first snow of the season was beginning to sift down, and in Juliette's white kitchen, toasty from the oven, the children giggled and chatted amiably as they slathered lurid-colored frosting on the buttery reindeer and Santa cookies.

"So Anne's really going to London?" Deirdre asked.

"Yes. She's so excited. She's leaving Thursday night and she's planning to show up on the set and surprise him."

"God," Deirdre said. "I'm so jealous. Can you imagine having a sexy, romantic marriage like that?"

"No," said Juliette. Things had been polite but tense between her and Cooper since the baby discussion. There had been no sex, no kissing beyond dry pecks on the cheek, and little conversation. All she'd bought Cooper for Christmas was a sweater—the most boring one she could find.

"Three! Three!" It was Trey, looking on in horror as Zoe, her bright red hair practically covering her eyes, sprinkled a miniature mountain of sugar snowflakes on top of her blue-frosted cookie.

"It's okay, Trey," soothed Juliette, trying to catch Trey's eye. "Zoe can use however many snowflakes she wants on her cookie. You can put three on your own cookie."

"No," Trey repeated, trying to brush the snowflakes off Zoe's cookie. "Only three."

"Stop!" Zoe squealed, snatching her cookie out of Trey's reach.

"I don't want to do this anymore anyway," said Zack, hopping down from his kitchen stool and tearing off in the direction of the Christmas tree, which twinkled from a corner of the dining room.

"Come on, kids," said Juliette. The twins, along with Anne's daughter and Lisa's boys, were Trey's only real friends. Because they'd known him virtually all their lives, they were the only kids who didn't see him as "special": a retard, a freak. Juliette wanted to do everything she could to make sure the kids got along.

Zack plopped down beneath the tree and picked up one of the antique train cars that had been Cooper's when he was a child, and that Cooper had passed down to Trey. Trey was so obsessed with the trains, they were probably the only thing that would make him surrender the cookie issue.

"I have an idea," Juliette said to her son. "Trey, while we wait for the next batch of cookies to cool, I bet Zack and Zoe would love to see how your trains work."

Instantly, Trey ran into the dining room after Zack, with Zoe scrambling to catch up. Juliette watched with satisfaction as the three children, snowflake flare-up forgotten, squatted beneath the Christmas tree, their heads bent together over the trains.

"That should be good for ten minutes," Juliette said, sitting back down at the scrubbed pine kitchen table and leaning toward Deirdre. "So tell me. How was your afternoon in the city with Nick?"

"Ooooh," Deirdre said. "That reminds me. I want to give you your present. I bought it when I was with him."

She rushed to retrieve the gift, wrapped in paper Juliette knew Deirdre had stenciled herself in her trademark menorah–Christmas candle print, designed to satisfy her lapsed-Catholic family as well as Paul's Jewish one. Juliette started to peel back the wrapping carefully, knowing the time Deirdre put into making it, but Deirdre cried, "Oh, just rip it!"

And then the bowl was in her hands. "It's beautiful," she said. Never mind that she already had fifty little bowls she didn't like and never used; Deirdre was watching her, eyes shining.

"It's no Pocket Rocket," Deirdre said.

"No, I really love it."

"Ha! Nick said you wouldn't like it."

"He did?"

"Yes, he was so weird. Not just about the present, about everything."

Juliette heard Trey say to the twins, "Hogger to Fireman. We've got the highball. Shake the grate. Need pressure."

He's going to be fine this time, Juliette told herself. The twins are his oldest friends, his best friends. They'll understand how excited he gets about the trains.

Willing herself not to interfere with Trey's game, to keep her focus on Deirdre, she leaned closer to her friend and whispered, "Please tell me you didn't sleep with him."

"Relax," Deirdre said. "You know, the first five minutes I was with him, I thought I was going to jump him right there on Bleecker Street. But then after ten minutes, I remembered all the reasons I left him in the first place."

"Like what?"

"Stoker on. Blower on. Boiler pressure ten-thousand pounds. Drivers spinning. Sand. I want sand. Eighty-four loads, twenty-eight empties. Time Freight, no way. Take up the slack one car at a time. Easy! You'll bust a coupler," Trey was saying.

Juliette saw Zoe stand up and walk over to the window, pressing her nose and hands against the glass. Juliette's heart lurched across the room toward Trey as she heard his voice grow more frantic. It was beyond him to ask Zoe to come back and play with him, or to temper his intensity to involve the girl in the game. Juliette wanted to grab Zoe by the shoulders and yank her back to play with poor Trey.

"He's incredibly opinionated," Deirdre said. "Always has to have his own way. Everything is a battle."

It took a moment for Juliette to remember that Deirdre was talking about Nick, but once she did, she laughed. "Sounds like someone I know."

Deirdre looked at her blankly. "Who?"

"You, of course!"

"I'm not like that at all," said Deirdre. "I'm easy to get along with. Ask Paul!"

Juliette laughed again. "Never mind. So what happened?"

"Well, nothing *happened* happened. And I realized I don't even want it to. My real fantasy now is that he'll help me with my singing."

A few months before, Juliette would have found it very difficult to imagine Deirdre singing on the stage of a Manhattan club. But Deirdre had lost so much weight in the past weeks that she seemed transformed. All the roundness that Juliette had always found attractive in a way she knew the world did not was now replaced by stylish sleekness.

"That would be great," said Juliette.

"I need to shop for some new clothes," Deirdre said. "I've dropped at least three dress sizes."

"How have you been losing all this weight?" Juliette asked. "And why?"

"I've been doing a kind of combo Atkins-anxiety diet. And you know why: I want to look like a fucking sex goddess."

"I thought you'd given up on the fantasy of sleeping with Nick."

"Even if I'm not going to sleep with him," Deirdre said, "I like the idea of him standing there onstage behind me with a big hard-on. I swear to you, Juliette, the man may be a jerk, but in bed he was unbelievable. He used to lift my whole body right up off the sheets with those enormous hands—which are in proportion with the rest of him, I assure you."

Juliette felt herself color, while in the dining room, Zack lurched to his feet, yelling, "I don't get your stupid train game."

"Wrecker. Call the wrecker. It's leaking. Clear the track," cried Trey, jumping up and beginning to advance on his friend. He tended to become so agitated when a game went wrong that words alone wouldn't bring him back to earth.

In a flash, Juliette was across the room, her arms tight around her son. "Trey, honey, it's time to stop playing with the trains now," she said. She could feel his heart hurtling against his chest like a trapped bird.

"Trey," she said, kneeling down, touching his chin to direct his face toward her. "Trey," she said again, holding one finger in front of his eyes to get him to focus. "Listen to me, Trey. The other kids don't want to play trains or talk about trains anymore."

Zoe flicked on the television, and out of the corner of her eye Juliette saw both of Deirdre's children settle down, already riveted, in front of *Yu-Gi-Oh*.

Juliette usually didn't allow Trey to watch TV during the day, but the little boy lifted his head at the sound of Joey's trademark cry: "Believe in the heart of the cards!"

The phone started ringing. Trey was already straining against Juliette's arms toward the twins and the television.

"Okay," she said to her son. "Go."

Back in the kitchen, she saw Deirdre stick her finger in the frosting bowl, bring it to her mouth, and then stop and stare at the blue blob before moving to the sink to rinse it off. Deirdre turning down sugar; would wonders ever cease.

"Hello?" Juliette said, picking up the phone.

"Juliette?" said a deep male voice she didn't recognize, though he sounded as if he knew her.

"Yes?"

"This is Nick. Nick Ruby." And then, when she didn't respond, "Deirdre's friend."

"Of course, Nick," she said, already walking toward the kitchen, trying to sound casual, as if she had not just been listening to a description of his penis. "Deirdre's right here." Though Deirdre seemed to have disappeared.

"Deirdre's there?" he said, sounding surprised. "There with you?"

"Yes, or at least she was, a second ago. We're spending the afternoon here with our kids baking Christmas cookies. Just let me find her."

"No!" Nick cried. "I mean no, I'm not calling for Deirdre. I'm calling for you."

"For me?" said Juliette. "But why?"

From the powder room, she heard a flush, and then Deirdre emerged, drying her hands on a linen towel.

"I know this is crazy," Juliette heard Nick say. "I kept telling myself I shouldn't call you, but I can't stop thinking about you."

Juliette felt the heat rise to her cheeks as Deirdre looked at her and smiled.

"I'm sorry, but we're not interested," Juliette said into the phone. "And please don't call here, ever again."

She pressed the off button on the phone and banged the phone onto the table.

"Oh God, I know," said Deirdre. "Those telemarketers will drive you out of your mind."

"Yeah," Juliette said. She should tell Deirdre. She should tell her right now.

"What was going on in there with the kids?" Deirdre asked.

The kids. Trey and the trains. Now, at least, the only sound from the other room was coming from the TV.

"Trey just gets really excited about his trains," Juliette said. "It's hard for him to tell when other kids aren't as interested as he is."

"How's he doing in school?" Deirdre asked.

How *was* he doing in school? He cried almost every night, because his feelings got so hurt by the other kids, over incidents not unlike what had happened with the trains. Either he became overly enthusiastic and couldn't understand why the other children pulled away from him, or he retreated into his own world.

"It's been hard," Juliette said. She was thinking of the class holiday party, just this morning. It had been mayhem, all the kids running around the room, eating cupcakes and playing games and talking about the upcoming holidays and vacation. Only Trey had stood alone, talking to himself and twirling his hands in a way it would be easy to mistake as playful.

As if on cue, a cry rose up from the other room, so loud and wild that Juliette and Deirdre rushed toward its source. There, in front of the cavorting images on the television, they found Trey with his arms locked around Zoe, shouting over and over, but without expression, "I like you. I like you." For her part, Zoe stood there screaming at the top of her lungs.

"Trey," said Juliette, seizing her son and gently prying him away from Zoe. "Trey, you're scaring Zoe."

"I *like* Zoe," Trey insisted.

"I know you do, sweetheart, but Zoe was screaming because she wanted you to stop."

Zoe was whimpering that she wanted to go home, and in dismay Juliette saw Deirdre bundling the twins into the kitchen, helping them into their jackets and boots.

"You're leaving?"

"I'm sorry," Deirdre said. "I'll call you later."

The phone started ringing again. Juliette stared dumbly after Deirdre and the twins, bustling out into the snowy afternoon. Trey pulled away from her and ran over to his trains, already resuming his monologue. Distantly, Juliette heard the phone stop ringing and the answering machine click into action.

"Oh," she heard Nick Ruby's distinctive voice say. "Um, Juliette . . ."

Scrambling over to the phone, she snatched up the receiver and hurried to switch off the machine.

"I told you not to call me," she said.

"But you picked up."

"I didn't want my son hearing your message and my husband listening to the tape later."

"I thought maybe you were afraid Deirdre would hear."

"Deirdre left."

"I thought she was spending the afternoon there."

"She was," said Juliette. "But the kids had a problem and so she went home."

"What kind of a problem?" asked Nick.

She sighed, fully aware that her disappointment in Deirdre's cluelessness about how to act was the only reason she was letting herself stay on the phone. "You know, I don't know why you'd care, but my son has something called Asperger's syndrome and it causes him—"

"I know what Asperger's is," said Nick.

Juliette hesitated. "I don't believe you," she said finally.

"Why would I lie about that?"

"Why would you call me in the first place?"

"My brother has AS," Nick said, ignoring her challenge. "I mean, when he was a kid nobody knew what AS was—they just thought he was weird."

"So is he?" Juliette asked. "Weird, I mean."

"He's a computer geek, works for Microsoft. Brilliant, great at his job, but a total zero with women. With other people, period."

"That sounds like my son," said Juliette. "He seems to make everybody uncomfortable, even people like Deirdre who've known him forever."

"Not everybody," said Nick. "I, for instance, would not be uncomfortable. Hey, did Deirdre give you her gift yet?"

"You mean the bowl? She told me you thought I wouldn't like it."

"And you don't, do you?"

She hesitated. "No."

Nick laughed. "I told her."

"Deirdre's my best friend," said Juliette. "You better be nice to her."

"I'm nice to her," Nick said.

"You could be nicer."

"What can I do?" said Nick.

"You can help her," Juliette said. "Help Deirdre with her singing."

"Done."

"Really?"

"Really. I'll call her tonight and set something up."

"Really?"

He laughed. "Really."

"She seemed to think you might not be so willing to give her a hand."

"I wasn't so willing," he said. "Until you asked me."

"Why not?" Juliette said. She'd never, after all, actually heard Deirdre sing. "Don't you think she's any good?"

"No, she's good," said Nick, "or at least she used to be. It's been a long time. And she's always been a little . . . mercurial."

"She seems serious about this," said Juliette. "I don't want you to tell her you're doing it because I asked you to."

"I'm not even going to tell her I talked to you," he said. "Are you?"

She hated the idea of keeping secrets from Deirdre, especially about something unimportant. But she hated the idea of upsetting Deirdre more.

"No," she said. But then she grew suspicious again. "This doesn't mean I'm going to do anything for you."

"I'm not asking for anything," Nick said. "All I'm trying to do is reassure you. I want you to know that my motives are pure."

"Pure, ha!" Juliette glanced over at Trey, who was twirling his hands and reciting train model numbers.

"I swear, I have your best interests at heart," Nick said. "Whatever you want, I'll do."

This was the moment, Juliette knew, when she could tell him to go away. Leave her alone. Never call again, for real. But still she sat clutching the phone.

"What I want you can't give me," she said finally.

"Oh yeah?" he laughed. "Try me."

She took a deep breath. "I want another baby," she said. And then, recognizing the opening she'd left for him, added quickly, "With my husband."

"And so why aren't you?" he asked. "No, wait. Let me guess. Your husband is stonewalling."

"You don't know anything about my husband."

"I know he's luckier than he thinks," said Nick, bringing a flush to Juliette's cheeks, even though she was alone in the room. Alone except for Trey, who continued to stare into the distance and chant his numbers as if she didn't exist.

"He's probably jealous of your son," Nick continued. "Wants you all to himself."

"No! No! It's going over. Chlorine. Ammonia. Hazmat Alert!" cried Trey, suddenly spotting the cookies and grabbing one from the plate.

Juliette turned away from her son and curled into herself. "How did you know that?" she whispered.

"We men are all alike," Nick said. "Haven't you heard?"

In spite of herself, Juliette laughed.

"I know I'm shooting myself in the foot by giving you advice here, but you've got to meet the guy halfway," Nick said.

"What do you mean?" said Juliette.

"You know, show him that you can be there for him even if you do have another kid."

"I already told him that."

"Not tell him, *show* him. You know the guy. What does he want?"

"He wants me to be a babe," Juliette said.

Nick laughed. "I didn't realize he was blind."

"I hated being a babe," Juliette said with vehemence, the memory still vivid of how uncomfortable she'd felt, before she realized she could deal with the attention and the pressure that came with beauty by choosing to obscure her looks. "I don't want to do that again."

"Do you not want to do that more than you do want to have a baby?" Nick asked.

That was it, the question that reduced the whole issue to a simple mathematical equation. Trey, his mouth ringed with blue frosting, began swaying as if in a dream waltz, and Juliette felt equally entranced. The way ahead was suddenly clear, from this most unlikely of sources.

"You're right, you're right," she mumbled to Nick, and then set down the phone, without saying good-bye, without actually hanging it up, moving across the room to put her arms around her child and hold close the dream of how she would have another.

CHAPTER 9

Anne

By the time she took the train from Heathrow Airport to Victoria Station and then a big black cab to the place where Cloth Fair met Smithfield Circle near St. Bartholomew's ancient church—a challenging place to find even for London's famously savvy taxi drivers—Anne felt as if she would pass out. She used to fly overnight across the Atlantic every few weeks, springing from her cramped airplane seat to work through the day. But she was no longer used to the long flight or the jet lag, and after an endless frantic day at her office, followed by a race back to New Jersey to squeeze in a good-bye hug with Clementine when she dropped her off at Juliette's, and then a heart-stopping battle with traffic to the airport, she thought at least she'd sleep on the plane. But the prospect of surprising Damian on the set, of having five days completely alone with him in London, was too exciting. She'd been awake all night, nervous about how he'd react to her appearance.

Once the cab finally found the right place, Anne set off down Cloth Fair, a narrow lane lined with restaurants and pubs and low medieval houses. She pulled her red wheeled suitcase behind her and was sweating inside her winter coat, too warm for this British December, which was more damp than frigid. Finally, the black iron gate and the park surrounding St. Bartholomew's appeared on her right. She could see the blocky towers of the church, but she couldn't get into the courtyard.

She'd forgotten this. She'd been here years before with Damian; they'd even fantasized about getting married in the gorgeous old church. But without a father to give her away or a mother to sit in the front pew dabbing at tears, Anne said they might as well go to the registrar's office. Spend their money on a grand honeymoon trip to Asia, invest it in his films, save it for her restaurant. And so that's what they did.

This was part of the reason she was so disappointed that he'd decided not to have his characters in the movie actually get married. It was as if she'd been cheated out of yet another wedding in this wonderful church. But his new climax sounded exciting, she told herself. Less expected than the wedding, even more fun to watch being filmed. Turning around, she headed back to the passageway she remembered would give her entrée to the church.

The cool moist air misted her face, reviving her, so that by the time she found the correct path and made her way down it, she felt almost like herself. She knew she was in the right place now because the narrow walkway was clogged with equipment.

The kind of thin and scruffily good-looking young women and men who always seemed to be hanging around movie sets were there in droves on this one too, but no one paid any attention to her as she wove her way around the oversize trunks and piles of scaffolding pipe toward the door of the church. Finally, though, she reached the first bank of chairs and the more serious equipment that signaled that she had reached the front ranks of the set.

"Sorry, ma'am, but the church is shut," said a British girl with a clipboard.

Ma'am, indeed.

Up ahead, Anne spied Rodney, the sound man on most of Damian's films. She managed to catch his eye, giving him a little wave. He looked stunned to see her, raising his eyebrows and cocking his head toward where she could just make out Damian in the gloom of the church, standing near the altar giving direction to the blonde actress who could only be the hooker bride. To Rodney, Anne shook her head no, to indicate he shouldn't disturb Damian. She'd watch the filming for a while, surprise Damian during a break, then retreat to his hotel room to sleep off the jet lag. There'd be time enough for them to connect tonight.

Anne inched forward, to get a better look at what was happening inside the church. She now found herself filled with awe at the sight of the vaulted wooden ceilings sailing so high above her and the windows, which seemed to beam the light in directly from the sky. The floor was like a riverbed, made up of smooth slabs of centuries-old stone, carved like gravestones, now snaked with electrical cables. The wooden pews, set up in three long rows on each side of the church, facing one another rather than the golden altar, were filled with the actors playing the wedding guests: the bride's friends in their hooker-style gear on the left, and a couple dozen extremely tall young men—the basketball-playing groom's cohorts, evidently—on the right.

Anne had a better view of Damian from here. It had been years, literally, since she'd visited him on a set, and it gave her an almost-sexual thrill to see him in charge of this enormous production. To her, too often, he was the dad who picked up all the loose ends at home, the entrepreneur struggling for money or corporate support, the artist plagued by insecurity. She tended to think of herself as the one in their relationship with the power and the worldliness, but here, on his turf, she saw he was in command.

Now two of the assistants were herding the actors into their places in the pews. The big lights clanged on. Near the altar, Anne could see Rodney positioning the booms over where Damian still stood with the bride.

"Okay!" Damian called then. "Let's try this."

He stepped back into the shadows, and after several calls for quiet, the curvy bride and the groom, who seemed freakishly tall beside her, joined hands and began to say their lines.

They hadn't gotten very far, though, when Damian yelled, "Cut!"

He rushed forward, leaning in close and speaking to the bride again. Then they repeated the whole thing. And repeated it again. The more they tried to get the lines right, the more agitated the bride became. The groom was now visibly rolling his eyes. The wedding guests were talking and laughing and eyeing one another.

Then suddenly the bride put her face in her hands and began crying. Damian rushed once more to her side, gripping her elbow and calling out to the crowd, "Quiet! I need absolute quiet here!"

Anne, along with everyone else in the church, leaned in, trying to hear what they were saying. What could he say to her now, when she was totally upset, that could coax the performance out of her she wasn't able to deliver when she was calm?

And then she saw it. Damian, his head bent toward the bride in concern, ran one hand up the back of her neck, lifting the stray wisps of blonde hair, while with the other he stroked the length of her back. It was such a distinctive move, and one that held such special meaning for Anne, that there was no question she could misinterpret it.

She pushed through the crowd of technicians and strode up the broad center aisle of the church toward the altar without even thinking. Someone may have tried to stop her; she didn't care. When she got to where Damian was standing with the actress, she grabbed his shoulder, feeling as if she could dig her fingers clear through his flesh.

He looked frightened even before he recognized her, frightened because of the pressure with which she was gripping his shoulder. Then there was a moment of incomprehension—he knew it was her, but what was she doing here?—and then she saw his eyes fill with total understanding. Even in this, Anne thought, we communicate perfectly.

"You're fucking her," Anne said, seeing the small smile of satisfaction on the actress's tear-streaked face. She wasn't expecting a response from Damian, and she didn't wait for one.

"Do you love her?" Anne asked.

"Anne," he said. "Darling."

"Don't."

"Anne, you know this has nothing to do with us."

Anne was aware that the entire church, the dozens of people, had gone absolutely silent.

"There is no us anymore," she said, not bothering to lower her voice. Let them hear. Let everyone know that everything that was happening here wasn't make-believe.

"Anne, God," he said. "This is nothing. It's you that I love."

At that, the blonde actress burst into loud tears and stomped loudly down the aisle of the church, her hurled, "Fuck!" echoing through the hallowed space.

When the heavy wooden door finally slammed and the church was silent again, Anne spoke once more.

"I love you too, Damian," she told him, though she was sure he knew that as well as she knew it herself. "But it's over. You've wrecked it, it's over, and there's no going back from here."

CHAPTER 10

Lisa

It was her favorite moment of a party, the moment that made all the rest of it—the writing of the invitations, the hours pushing the enormous cart at Costco with all four kids perched atop the mounds of supplies, the days spent whipping the eggnog and baking the *bûche de Noël* and concocting the homemade truffles—worth it. It was, in fact, an orgasmic moment, when the door started opening and closing so quickly she couldn't keep up and the faces of the people kissing her cheek turned into a blur and the party crossed that divide from anticipation to event and spun breathlessly out of her control. Exactly like an orgasm, and even more thrilling.

Lisa stood at the mammoth sterling punch bowl set on the starched linen cloth on the table near the door, ladling her killer eggnog into red and green plastic cups. This was the first time she had ever stooped to plastic, but earlier this week she'd been in the middle of washing the three hundred crystal glasses she'd collected just for this purpose when the doctor had called, telling her she needed to come in for yet another test, yet another useless examination, and that had eaten up so much time she'd had to go with plastic. But no one else seemed to notice or mind: the tree twinkled gorgeously at center stage in the living room, the conversation had risen to a lively and convivial buzz, and she could hear the feet of dozens of children racing through the bedrooms overhead. Then suddenly a pack of them thundered down the stairs, heading for the front door. She was about to stop them but then she remembered it was warm outside, still more like fall than winter, too warm to even light the fireplaces. Let them go, she thought, smiling and passing a cup of the eggnog to Betsy Foss from down the street. Let them do whatever they want, as long as I don't have to deal with it.

From the far end of the living room, Tommy caught her eye and raised his glass to her. He was smiling, happy, playing his host role as he saw it: supervising the music and being friendly to all the guests. Life was one big Reed Jeep-Honda to him, offering an endless supply of stability and pleasure while requiring very little in return. Lisa usually enjoyed making eye contact with her husband across the crowded room at one of their parties and usually basked in his literal and figurative nod to her entertaining acumen while she admired his broad-shouldered, thick-haired hearty good looks. But today his confidence in the rightness of his world irritated her. Why should he get to believe that all this happened as if by magic, without ever stopping to look behind the curtain to where she operated all the levers?

Smile, she reminded herself. The most important factor in a successful party was a relaxed, friendly hostess. This would be a perfect detail for her book, the kind of humanizing advice that would give people their confidence back after they'd been daunted by the thirty-seven steps necessary to concoct her killer eggnog. She should call it Killer Eggnog, she realized: that kind of exaggerated term leant her formula an air of freshness, even edginess, that would be the key to its success.

"Great party."

It was Juliette, leaning in over her right shoulder to kiss her beneath the ear, smelling of Chanel No. 5, her shimmering chestnut hair gathered at the nape of her neck, lying smooth and lovely against her faultless black velvet blouse.

"Thanks," Lisa said, wishing suddenly that she could put down her plastic cup and ladle and walk out of here with Juliette, go somewhere, just the two of them, and have a drink.

At the moment this thought crossed her mind, Deirdre and Paul bustled in the door with their kids. Zoe and Zack, both moving so quickly they registered as simply matching mops of flaming red hair, tore away from their parents, Zack pounding up the stairs and Zoe scampering back outside. Deirdre pulled off her flowing maroon coat, revealing her body-hugging red and green flowered dress.

"God, it's another fabulous Lisa Reed production," Deirdre said.

"Talk about fabulous," Lisa said. "Look at you."

"Yeah, I swear, I feel like I could fly," Deirdre said.

"Eggnog?" Lisa asked.

Deirdre narrowed her eyes at her. "I'm not going to let you fatten me up. That stuff is probably a thousand calories a glass."

Two thousand, Lisa calculated, with each batch consisting of a dozen egg yolks beaten with a pound of powdered sugar, a dozen egg whites whipped into a meringue, a gallon of cream, an entire bottle of brandy, and another one of bourbon.

"I don't care if it has ten thousand calories," Paul said, reaching for a glass. "God, I look forward to this stuff all year."

Lisa liked Paul—everyone in the world seemed to like Paul—but she wished she could give him more backbone when it came to dealing with Deirdre.

"You shouldn't be drinking that," Deirdre snapped, grabbing the glass from his hand. She shook her head at Lisa. "You'd think as a doctor he'd know enough to watch his cholesterol."

And Paul, the patsy, just stood there smiling.

"So who's here?" Deirdre said, surveying the now-crowded room.

"Juliette's somewhere," Lisa said. There were probably more than a hundred people in the house now; all the faces swirled.

"I think Juliette's annoyed at me," said Deirdre.

"Why's that?"

"I don't know. Maybe she disapproves of my music thing."

"What's happening with that?"

"Well, it's amazing. Nick called and said he's going to try and fix it for me to sing with his band."

"Deirdre, that's fantastic," said Lisa, feeling a little burst of competitiveness. Once the holidays were over, she really had to get busy on her book.

"I know. I wanted to tell Anne too. Is she here?"

Lisa frowned. "She said she was going to come, but I haven't seen her."

"She's really devastated," said Deirdre. "She's starting to think maybe she made a mistake in London, maybe she was too hasty, maybe she should give him another chance."

Lisa shook her head. Anne and Clementine had been there for Christmas dinner, and Anne had been withdrawn, even paler and thinner than usual, seemingly in shock. Lisa was certain it was difficult, but in Lisa's experience—and surely losing your mother unexpectedly at sixteen counted for a lot—lying around letting yourself feel terrible only made things worse. Lisa had invited three unattached men here today expressly with Anne in mind.

"She should just move on," Lisa said. "She's so much better off without him."

"I don't know," said Deirdre. "I always liked Damian. I would have voted him the husband I most wanted to sleep with."

Deirdre acted unconcerned about Paul's whereabouts—whether he was close enough to overhear—but Lisa only relaxed when she spotted Paul a few feet away, seemingly absorbed in another conversation.

Lisa laughed. "Not me."

"So who's yours?" Deirdre said.

Lisa darted another glance at Paul, who, she was pleased to see, had helped himself to a fresh glass of eggnog, which he seemed to be drinking with gusto. Taller by a head than everyone in the room, lean and round-shouldered from perpetually bending down in conversation, he was kind and thoughtful, attractive qualities. But kind and thoughtful were a step away from sensitive, and Lisa didn't find sensitive all that appealing, even in a girlfriend. No, definitely not Paul.

Farther across the room stood Cooper Chalfont, deep in conversation with the mayor of Homewood, who always came to their holiday parties because Tommy got him his cars wholesale. Cooper Chalfont was the kind of guy Lisa dated when she worked as a bond trader and thought she never wanted to have kids, after all the work she'd put into raising her three younger siblings. She'd found his type sexy enough then; she'd liked the confidence, the sophistication, even the selfish edge—it was a permission slip for her to be selfish too. But once she'd decided she wanted a family after all, this kind of man lost his appeal for her. She knew enough about raising children to look for a partner who was more physical and down-to-earth, someone who wasn't afraid of getting his hands and knees dirty.

Where was Tommy, anyway? There, across the room, laughing uproariously and fiddling with the stereo. They'd married a year after they met, had Matty a year after that, with Tommy as enthusiastic as she was about living in a big house in the suburbs filled with a dog and kids. They agreed absolutely that labor would be divided the old-fashioned way, with Tommy joining his family's auto dealership and Lisa in charge of home and kids. Not that Tommy had any kind of Stepford Wife idea of how she should be spending her time: she was the one who liked to keep the house spotless, who insisted on the cooked breakfasts and dinners with candlelight, every single night, who instituted the TV limits with the kids. Tommy was proud of Lisa's tennis game and her volunteer work, and he'd be delighted when he found out about her book, which she planned to present to him as a finished product, already published.

"I'll take the husband I have," Lisa said.

"Oh, come on, Lisa, tell the truth," said Deirdre. "Anybody in this room."

She looked around. But, even to her own surprise, she told Deirdre that Tommy was still the one.

Deirdre laughed. "You're hopeless," she said. "I'm going to go find someone more interesting to talk to."

The front door opened and another wave of guests swept into the hallway, and just when Lisa had summoned Tommy over to take their coats and ladled their eggnog, the early comers began to leave. She felt she'd been standing in the same spot, saying hello and good-bye for hours, when Deirdre appeared back at her side.

"Lisa," Deirdre said. "The phone."

Lisa hadn't even heard the phone ring. "I can't take it now," she said. "Could you find out what they want and if it's directions, help them?"

"It's your doctor," Deirdre said in a low voice. "She says it's important."

Lisa sighed. Doctor Kaufman had no compunction about calling at seven in the morning, eleven at night, on the weekend, whenever she had the tiniest piece of information she thought Lisa should know. But Lisa forgave her every interruption because she loved Dr. K's attitude: thorough and efficient, yet always positive and upbeat. I'm certain this test is going to come back negative, she'd tell Lisa, but let's go ahead with it just so we can rule this out. And then, when that test did not come back negative, she always had an explanation for why, and confidence that the next test would prove there was no reason for alarm.

Lisa pressed the phone to her ear, looking down to wipe a tiny speck of eggnog from the cream satin of her blouse, unprepared for what Dr. Kaufman was saying.

"I'm sorry, Lisa, but the news is not good."

Lisa looked out the window to see a line of children, Daisy in the lead, racing down the driveway, coatless and laughing.

"What?" Lisa said.

"We didn't get the results we'd hoped for. I want to schedule you for surgery right away."

Surgery? That couldn't be right. They didn't tell you these things over the phone.

"I'm having a party right now," Lisa said. "Can I call you back later? Or tomorrow?"

"We've already spent a lot of time on all these tests, because I was so sure they were going to be negative," the doctor said. "It's important that we move as quickly as possible, and I want to schedule you into the hospital before New Year's. Tomorrow morning, if possible."

"But that's only hours from now," Lisa said. Someone tapped her on the shoulder, but she did not turn around. "It would be so much better for me if we could wait—"

"We've waited long enough. Things are quiet at the hospital because of the holidays, and I want to get you in as soon as possible. If we put this off until after New Year's we're going to have a harder time scheduling the OR, even getting a room for you."

"What are you saying?" she asked, the noise from the party

and the sense of a crowd around her suddenly ceasing, as if they'd all disappeared. "Are you saying I have cancer?"

"Lisa, the results haven't been good so far. Given your age and your excellent health, I'm more surprised than anybody. Chances are, we're going to find that any cellular irregularity is strictly localized at your cervix, we're not going to have to do anything major. But I want to go in there as quickly as possible and find out exactly what it is we're dealing with."

Cancer, Lisa thought. The doctor wasn't willing to come out and say it, but it was time now to face the word, to take it in and be done with it. She had cancer, just like her mother. But she was not anything like her mother, she'd made sure of that. She'd never smoked, as her mother had, and she'd always been thin, while her mother was plump and out of shape, and she got regular checkups.

"What time do you want me?" Lisa said, already starting to plan—who would stay with the kids, what Tommy could handle, what she'd have to farm out, how long she'd be out of commission.

"Early," said the doctor. "Eight."

"Okay," Lisa said. "I'll be there."

She set down the phone and headed for the door, staring straight ahead. She felt hands on her arms, heard people calling her name, but she didn't pay any attention. From far across the living room, Tommy smiled at her and she smiled back automatically, not meaning it. She could not stand the heat of the room, the crush of bodies, the noise that surged all around her.

Outside, Lisa looked up their quiet street and had the sudden urge to run, to take off on a jog away from the party and keep going until she fell sweaty and exhausted onto the street. But she was wearing heels and was so unaccustomed to moving in them that she could barely maneuver the stairs.

The children were three backyards down, playing what looked like a wild game of tag, and the sound of them, the distant bright blur, lightened her heart a bit. How could anything serious be wrong with her, if she had four small children depending on her? It *couldn't*, that was all. She wouldn't allow it.

She tripped in her heels toward the backyard, thinking of the cedar bench, one of her favorite pieces of furniture, silver from the years it had spent first in her parents' backyard and now in hers, set under the pear tree. She'd left it out late this year because the weather had been so warm and she thought she'd sit there for a minute, out of sight of the revelers inside.

But three feet from the bench she was brought up short by the sight of Deirdre's husband Paul, sitting there on her bench. Paul had evidently already seen her and was looking startled himself, his face red and his pale eyes watery. In the next instant, Lisa smelled pot, unmistakable though she hadn't had so much as a whiff of it since college.

"I had to get away," Paul said.

Lisa had the impulse to pretend she'd just been checking up on the children, to look in their direction and, acting satisfied, twirl around and head right back inside.

But then Paul held out the joint to her.

"Oh, no thanks," Lisa said quickly, casting a glance toward the kids, who were hurtling in the other direction.

"You sure?" Paul said, shrugging, then taking a drag himself. "It's amazing stuff."

"I didn't know anybody smoked pot anymore," Lisa said.

"Nobody does," Paul said. "I just rediscovered it myself. It makes me realize why my teens and twenties were so great."

He took another hit, then held in his breath.

"Well," Lisa said. "I was just looking for the kids."

"They're fine," Paul said. "But you don't look so good."

"No, I'm okay," Lisa said, wrapping her arms around herself. "Just a little, you know, exhausted."

"Sit down," said Paul, patting the cold wood.

She crossed the lawn and sat, at the other end of the bench from him.

"What's going on in your life?" Paul asked.

She was about to say nothing, assuming it was one of those polite questions that doesn't really require an answer, but then she looked up and saw that Paul was staring intently at her, looking directly into her eyes.

"You seem sad," Paul said matter-of-factly. "Distracted."

"Really?" She hadn't realized it showed.

He nodded. "You look like you're about to cry."

She looked at him with her mouth open, but then instead of words a sob escaped from her throat, and she found tears rolling down her cheeks. She wanted to say something to dismiss or explain her tears, but every time she opened her mouth, all that came out was the word "oh," weighted with feeling.

Paul reached over and squeezed her shoulder and held out the joint to her again. This time she took it, sucking in a great lungful of searing smoke.

"Oh God." She choked, doubling over, coughing and crying at the same time.

Paul patted her back, his long fingers feeling warm and reassuring against the thin satin of her shirt. She had always seen him as flimsy before, an inconsequential person, but suddenly he felt as substantial as a mountain, and she wished she could crawl onto his lap and have him cradle her in his arms.

"I'm just . . . ," she began, then reconsidered. "Don't tell Deirdre," she said.

He laughed a little, drew on the joint, passed it back to her. "I wouldn't tell Deirdre," he said when he finally let out the stream of smoke. "I don't even know what I'm not supposed to tell Deirdre."

In her increasingly high state, Paul's statement made sense. The reality of the party inside the house and the children in the distance had faded nearly to nothingness, while the cold hard bench and Paul's hand on her back and the bare branches of the pear tree above them seemed to be the only things that were vivid and real.

"Don't tell her I'm . . ." She searched for the right word. "Weak," she said.

He burst out laughing. "You, weak? I can't imagine you weak."

He was wearing a black turtleneck, smeared with eggnog, and black jeans faded to gray. His legs were crossed at the ankle, and his feet, encased in brown suede desert boots, were flopped outward on their sides, as if they were broken.

There was something about him, sitting there so sympathetic and available, that made Lisa want to tell him everything she couldn't tell anyone else, not even Tommy. God, especially not Tommy, who turned queasy if she happened to mention she was having her period. Slowly, tentatively, she lowered her head until it was resting on his substantial shoulder. For what felt like a very long time, she sat there looking at the world tilted on its side.

Finally she said to Paul, "Tell me this. What would you do if you found out you were sick?"

She knew that, whatever he said, it would be something completely different from anything she could think of on her own. Very gently, he pulled away from her and turned so that he was looking directly in her eyes, and she was forced to look at him.

"Are you sick?" he asked her.

"No," she said immediately, feeling at first as if she were lying but then realizing it was true, she wasn't sick, they didn't know what was growing inside her, it could be anything, and she was taking care of it.

"What's going on?" he asked. "Is there something—"

"No!" Lisa cried, springing to her feet. She never should have gone this far. Now Paul would tell Deirdre she'd been acting strangely, and Deirdre would tell Juliette and Anne, and everyone would be fluttering around her, trying to turn this nothing into something. Facing this, she knew exactly how to be herself, which was to take the medical steps she needed to take and otherwise go on with her life exactly as before. This would be an excellent opportunity, in fact, to work on another chapter of her book. How to Handle a Crisis.

Step one: pretend everything is all right, and you will have the power to change reality.

CHAPTER 11

The January Dinner

Lisa was wiggling into her skinniest jeans, the ones that dated from before even her first pregnancy, when she heard the ding of the hospital elevator down the hall followed by her friends' voices coming toward her. God, this was great—she thought she'd never wear this size again. A quick look in the mirror, an adjustment of the cuff of her cashmere sweater to hide that tacky hospital bracelet, and then her friends swooped into the room, Lisa moving to the door to kiss them one by one.

"God, you look fantastic," Juliette said. "But I'm confused. When are they going to do the surgery?"

"They already did it," Lisa said. "Three days ago."

This was it, the payoff she was looking for, as her friends surveyed her sleek figure and perfect hair and makeup, as they took in the antique white linen and lace coverlet she had com-manded Tommy to bring from home to disguise the hospital bed. He had also, reluctantly, brought a silver platter and her favorite blue and green dishes and the cocktail shaker and glasses, as well as all the groceries for tonight.

"Couldn't you all just eat in the hospital cafeteria?" he'd asked.

"This will be more fun," Lisa had assured him. "Just, please, if anyone asks you what was wrong with me or what I had done, say something vague about female trouble and leave it at that."

"Even Deirdre and Anne and Lisa?" he'd asked doubtfully, though he was relieved, she could tell, not to have to say words like *cervix* and *uterus* and *hysterectomy*.

"They're my best girlfriends, Tommy. I'll explain everything myself."

Which, of course, she had no intention of doing. Tommy, as her husband, had to know about the hysterectomy, though she'd avoided using the word *cancer* and had instead reassured him that while they'd found some cellular abnormalities down there, they'd gotten everything and now she was fine. There was no reason for him to call her family in Michigan, she told him. They saw Lisa as the big sister who'd made good, the one who sent them money and clothes for the kids and got them cars at wholesale, not the person who needed their help. And that's the way Lisa wanted to keep it.

"Ooops," Lisa said, sniffing the air. "I almost forgot."

The cheese straws needed to be turned in the toaster oven. She had disarmed the timer for fear it would alert the nurses to the illegal cooking she was doing in her room. It was hard enough to cobble together enough uninterrupted moments, what with all the blood-taking and bandage-checking, to make the items that didn't require cooking, her special guacamole and sundried tomato dip and now, most illicit of all, her brandy sidecars, the perfect drink for a chilly night.

Anne, her face so chalky anyone would guess she was the patient, sank into one of the plastic visitors' chairs. "Oh, good," she said. "I really need a drink."

"Are you nuts?" Deirdre said. "We can't sit around and let Lisa serve us. Aren't you supposed to be in bed, Lisa?"

"I'm perfectly fine," Lisa said, trying to keep her voice calm to deflect what Deirdre was saying. "Really, I haven't had so much time to pull together a cocktail party in years." She ran a wedge of lemon around the edge of one of the cocktail glasses, then held it above a little blue willow plate she'd coated with sugar. "Everybody want sugared rims?"

"What are you talking about, sugared rims!" Deirdre cried. "You've just had cancer surgery, for God's sake!"

Lisa stiffened.

"Who told you that?"

"Isn't that why you're here?" Deirdre said. "You're on the women's cancer ward, Lisa. I know Dr. Kaufman performed the surgery, and she's an OB-GYN. We just assumed—"

"Well, you assumed wrong," Lisa said.

That would have been such a perfect moment to tell them, if she'd wanted to. She'd considered it too. But she'd seen what could happen when people knew you'd had cancer. She saw it happen with her mother, who for years was Lisa's nice mom and the lady who baked the best cakes for every bake sale and was the voice for literature on the library board, and then overnight she turned into that tragic woman with cancer. Which she remained, even to her friends, who claimed they wanted to help, who tried to help, briefly, before retreating into the busyness of their own lives.

Why condemn herself in the same way? Dr. Kaufman had said they thought they'd gotten everything, she didn't need to have chemo, just a little radiation while she was in the hospital.

"What I had was very minor, and I'm completely fine now," she assured them. "I can't believe how long the days are in here, with no kids, no housework, no obligations. I'm so relaxed. This may be the best thing that ever happened to me."

And really, she thought, it might be. There was the eight-pound instant weight loss. The break from all the hubbub of home. If she could not now have any more children—and really, as Tommy once put it, they had not been completely ready to close up shop—then she could just feel more delighted that she already had four. And there was the perfect excuse to take the time to plan her book, plus a new focus and determination to do what she wanted with her life.

The only discernible bump on her highway to success was Henry, who was so distraught at his mom's absence that even though Lisa had not wanted the children to see her in the hospital, Tommy had finally insisted that she make an exception for Henry alone. Sitting in the hospital bed with the little boy curled in her lap, the kind of one-on-one event she rarely had time for with four small children, the full terror of the illness seemed to grip her around the throat, and she felt as if she might dissolve as thoroughly as her son had.

But indulging those emotions wasn't what she really needed,

she told herself, and it wasn't what Henry needed either. She had to be strong and build for the future, so he could grow up in a stable home and go to college and have a family of his own, whatever happened to her.

"Sit down," she told Anne, handing her the first drink. "You guys are the ones with all the crazy stuff going on. Tell me what's happening."

"I miss him so much," Anne said, tearing up as she sipped her drink. "I know I shouldn't, but I do."

"You two had an incredibly sexy, romantic relationship," said Deirdre, finally taking a cocktail from Lisa. "I know I'd find that hard to walk away from."

"I don't know," said Juliette. "I know what he did was terrible. But maybe you ought to give him another chance. See if he can change."

Lisa lifted the brandy bottle to refill the cocktail shaker and felt a twinge in her side. Go away, she told it, breathing deeply and focusing on a vision of herself, a year from now, accepting the Pulitzer Prize for her brilliant book. Repression was so underrated, she thought as she poured out the drink and the pain subsided.

"I have a new tactic with Cooper, about the baby thing," Juliette told Lisa. "I've decided I've got to meet him halfway, be the wife he wants, if I want him to be the husband and dad I want. Does everybody in the world but me know about Cosabella underwear?"

"That's what Damian sent me for Christmas," Anne said glumly. "He felt so guilty I think he bought every piece in the line."

"And who paid for that?" Lisa said.

They all looked at her. Did I really say that? she wondered.

"I mean Cosabella underwear, it's beautiful stuff, but the panties cost forty dollars," she said, attempting to explain her outburst. "We all know you're the one who makes the money, so I just wondered how Damian was able to buy you this lavish gift, especially when you'd already broken up."

"It's the thought that matters," Deirdre said. "Paul and I have all our money together. When I buy him a gift, he's actually paying for it."

"But you're married," Lisa pointed out. "Anne's separated. It isn't like she asked for this expensive stuff. She's trying to get away from this guy who did something really shitty to her."

Lisa knew she was being negative, and blunt, but not as negative and blunt as she wanted to be. The fact was, Deirdre might be dazzled by the sexiness of Anne and Damian's marriage, and Juliette might believe right now in the possibility and power of change, and Anne might be feeling bereft, but what Lisa really thought was that Anne should put her emotions on ice, hire a shark lawyer, and get Damian out of her life forever.

"You know, Anne," she said, trying to soften her tone. "It's normal to miss Damian—but missing him doesn't mean you should take him back."

"I know," said Anne. "But it isn't like he was only my husband and my lover. He was also my entire adult family, you know? And Clementine is devastated, even if she tries to act as if everything is all right. Oh God. Can I have another drink?"

Anne held out her glass, and Lisa moved quickly to refill it, hoping to stem a fresh round of tears. After a week in this place, it was difficult to view a breakup with a cheating husband as something worth crying over.

"What's going on with you, Deirdre?" Lisa asked, hoping to change the subject. "Anything new with the singing career?"

"Yes!" Deirdre cried. "My first official gig, with Nick's band, has finally been scheduled, so I hope all of you can be there. It's next Tuesday night."

"Oh," said Anne, taking out her Palm Pilot. "Tuesday the fourteenth? I've got to be in Cleveland on the fourteenth."

"God," said Juliette. "I think Cooper's going to be out of town on the fourteenth, too. I'm sorry, Deirdre."

"You're kidding, right?" said Deirdre. "You have a live-in nanny. It's not like Cooper watches Trey at night even when he is in town."

"Heather has a class on Tuesday nights," Juliette said. "Plus I know I have an appointment on the fourteenth to get a bikini wax. I've heard those hurt like hell."

"It's not a root canal!" Deirdre said. "Jesus! What's wrong with you all? Are you afraid I'm going to suck and you won't know what to say? Is that it?"

"No, no," Juliette said, reaching out to grip Deirdre's arm.

"Then I want you to be there!" Deirdre said. "Really, Juliette. I don't expect you to show up at every little gig I might do, but this is my first one, and it's really important."

Lisa had been sitting there silently, assuming Deirdre's expectations didn't extend to her. She should be out of the hospital by the fourteenth, but she wasn't supposed to leave the house for anything more taxing than, say, a teacher conference. She certainly couldn't go into the city and sit in a club for several hours into the night. But since she hadn't told her friends she'd had a hysterectomy, she couldn't very well now use it as an excuse.

"What about you, Lisa?" Deirdre said.

Oh, no. "I won't be able to make it," she said, "because of this." She gestured vaguely around the room.

"You mean you'll still be in the hospital."

"No, no," she said. God, if they thought she had to be in the hospital for another week, they'd really think she was sick. "I'll be home but I'm supposed to take it easy."

"Why are you supposed to take it easy?" Deirdre said. "I thought what you had was very minor."

"It was," said Lisa, trying for a reassuring tone. A tone that warded off further questions.

"You know, you haven't told us exactly what was wrong with you," Deirdre persisted, "or what kind of something you had done."

"It's complicated," Lisa said, trying to laugh it off. "Even Tommy doesn't know."

"But *you* know," Deirdre said, looking hard at her. "Why won't you tell us?"

"There's nothing to tell," Lisa said. "Listen, I'm sorry I'm not going to your singing thing, but the truth is that after a week in here, I just want to go home and be with my family. I have to do what's most important."

"And I'm not important," Deirdre said flatly.

"It's hard for me to take your wanting me to see you sing in New York too seriously!" Lisa cried, feeling herself explode. "I mean, after the things I've seen in here—mothers of infants who didn't get chemo because they didn't want to have abortions, and now they're going to die, and twenty-two-year-old girls who are never even going to get to have children—"

She stopped, lost in the vision of all the other women she'd seen walking the halls, trailing their IVs, or sitting hollow-eyed in the sunroom. The women she now wanted so badly to avoid that she refused to leave her room. She was not like those women. But she could no longer forget that they existed, or believe that she would never become one of them simply because she didn't want to.

She looked up. Her three friends were staring at her, shocked. Over the loudspeaker came the announcement: "Visiting hours are over in ten minutes. All visitors must leave the building."

"See, they never do that in a restaurant," Deirdre said.

No one spoke.

"We're in a hospital, Lisa," Deirdre said. "We're concerned about you, about you and Tommy and the kids. Why won't you tell us what's going on?"

"I have told you," said Lisa, thinking it all might have been easier if she'd just told them the truth from the beginning. Now she had given them a view of the abyss she'd been peering into, and they didn't even understand what they were looking at, or why.

But it was too late now. Telling at this point would be self-indulgent. If she had had cancer, if she had had a hysterectomy, it was all over now, and there was nothing anyone could do. Better to make excuses and stick to the original plan.

"I'm sorry, Deirdre," she said. "I'm just tired. I wish I could go to the city to hear you sing. Really."

That part, she realized, was true.

"We'd like to help you," said Juliette as Anne nodded beside her.

"That would be great," said Lisa, finally seeing her escape route. There was a patients' lounge at the end of the hallway she had stopped visiting because she didn't want to hear any more sad stories. But now, right now, even that place seemed preferable to being here.

"I just remembered I've got to go get my meds from the nurses, because I didn't want to let them in the room before," Lisa continued, refusing to meet her friends' eyes. "I'd love it if you could get rid of all this evidence, take all this food and everything with you." And by the time I get back, she thought, they'll all be gone.

CHAPTER 12

Deirdre

The owner was closing up for the night. Nick was slumped in a chair, drinking ice water, and Juliette was resting her head on her arms on top of the table. But to Deirdre, it might as well have been the brightest hour of the morning. Still buzzing with the excitement of the evening, she felt as if she might never sleep again.

"God, that was so fucking fabulous," Deirdre said.

"You were great," said Juliette, raising her head. It had been so steadying to have Juliette's face smiling up at her from the front row. Earlier in the night, she'd had on bright makeup and big gold earrings, but the makeup had faded and she'd pulled the earrings off.

"The audience loved you," Nick said, taking a long swallow of his water. "You saw them."

Yes, she had seen them, all those faces turned in her direction, and felt them, all that attention trained on her. She felt them feeling what she was feeling when she sang, felt transported by the explosion of their applause.

And then there was more: the attention from one person in the audience who actually had the power to do something for her career. The little balding man who had pushed his way to the front of the room at the end of the first set and thrust his card at her. She slipped her hand into the satin-lined pocket of her beaded pants and fingered the card now, its edges already curled from all the times she'd touched it.

"Call me," the little man had said to her. "I can make you a star."

Drawing the card out, she peered at it in the dim light and read the words again: ELLIOT LESSER, LESSER MANAGEMENT, with an address in the West Forties, a telephone number, no e-mail address.

"There was this guy," she said, still focusing on the card. Now that the card was out, in her hand, now that she had decided to ask Nick about it, she felt herself grow nervous for the first time all evening. There had barely been a moment to mention it to Nick before, and then she'd also been reluctant, in case Nick had been dismissive or negative about Elliot Lesser, to shine the light on her hopes about what this manager could do for her. Better to keep the card in her pocket and her hopes to herself, where they could be as grand as she wanted them to be.

Nick reached for the card. Even Juliette looked interested.

"Hmmm," Nick said. "I've never heard of Elliot Lesser."

See, that's why it was better keeping it in my pocket, she thought, feeling her energy drain away. "I guess he's probably just some creep," she said.

"No, no," said Nick. "I didn't say that. I don't really know many people in the business here. He's probably legit. I'll ask around."

"Really?"

"Sure," Nick said, smiling. "Hey, if a manager comes up to you, just like that, that means he's seriously interested."

"Really?" Deirdre said again.

Nick laughed. "Of course. You're on your way, baby."

Deirdre shook her head fast to clear it of the sound of that "baby." Too distracting. All she wanted to think about now was Elliot Lesser and what might happen next.

"Oh my God," Deirdre said, her heart beginning to beat faster. "This is unbelievable. I'll call him tomorrow. So if you get a manager, what happens then?"

"If he's any good, he'll help you get your head shots, put together a résumé, send you out on auditions, that kind of thing."

"Auditions," said Deirdre, picturing herself on a Broadway stage, belting out a song, the producer out somewhere in the darkened house, asking her to stay. It had happened like that, on one of the few real auditions she'd been on, when she was offered the role in *Cats*. That had made her think, back then, that the whole thing was easy. So easy she could do it anytime she wanted.

"I could pick up the kids from school if you had to be in the city," said Juliette.

"That could be an issue," Nick said. "The hours are going to be highly irregular. Lots of last-minute calls. It's going to be hard to plan."

"I don't know if I can justify to myself spending money on a sitter," said Deirdre, "unless I had an actual job."

"I'd try to help you out, and get Heather to fill in," said Juliette. "If this is what you really want."

"You'll probably have to come into the city a lot too," Nick said to Juliette, "to be supportive, that kind of thing."

"Why would I have to come into the city?" asked Juliette.

"I don't know—go to gigs, just be there."

Juliette made a face. "That's ridiculous."

"With all the late nights and unpredictable hours," Nick said to Deirdre, "it's really easier if you live in Manhattan."

"I know, I know, but there's no way we're going to move into the city with twins who are just starting school."

"If you had a lot going on here and it was going to be hard going back and forth, you could always crash at my place," said Nick.

"Really?" said Deirdre.

Her heart catapulted into new more dangerous territory now, though not at the prospect of spending nights alone in his apartment with Nick; in fact, Nick was already saying that he was planning to be on the road a lot. She registered his statement, but she was focused on the idea of leaving her twins at home for who knew how many nights, or for days on end, with a sitter or even with Paul. Leaving home and navigating the world by herself while her children learned to make do without her. It was as if their hearts, hers and the children's, were joined together and now she was ripping them apart.

Since having the twins, she had always worked, or at least had wanted to, even when she couldn't think of what kind of work she wanted to do. But that had been mostly at home, around the twins' naptimes, and then during school hours, at low-level jobs where she controlled the schedule and the pace.

Not anything a hundredth as demanding as trying to launch a singing career. Not anything she cared about a hundredth as much.

"What's Paul going to think about that?" Juliette was asking in a worried voice.

Paul? What did Paul have to do with any of this?

"Paul's already encouraged me to do whatever I need to do," she told Juliette. "He even said he'd go to work for that family practice in Homewood if that made more sense. I'm more worried about making sure the kids are all right."

"It's good for kids when their parents are happy," Nick said.

"Spoken like a true childless person," Juliette snapped, her eyes flashing. "I'd say it's the other way around."

"I'd say both parents and kids should be happy," Deirdre said. "The real question is, is it possible? Can the kids handle it? Can *I* handle it?"

"You'll never know unless you try," said Nick.

"But what if it doesn't work out?" Juliette said. "What if you do try to get what you want, and you end up screwing up your children?"

"Or what if you go through all this pain and effort and it doesn't even work out?" Deirdre said, leaning toward Nick with all the intensity that was still coursing through her body. "I mean, do you even think I can make it professionally as a singer?"

"That depends," he said.

"On whether anyone will hire me?"

He smiled. "That," he said, "but more to the point is whether you're willing to put yourself out there. Can you tolerate all the rejection you're going to have to face? The rooms where everybody isn't clapping, where they don't even give a shit about hearing you? Can you put up with the endless years of no money, no glory, just because you love it so much you're incapable of doing anything else?"

Deirdre slumped back in her chair. "You make it sound so hard."

"It is hard!" he cried. "It isn't easy for anybody—that's the illusion. The people who make it, it's not because it all works out for them, but because when things go wrong, they get up and try again."

"I don't think I could do it," Juliette said, shuddering.

"Sure you could," said Deirdre. "I see the energy you put into Trey."

"That's for my kid," said Juliette. "For my kid, I could do anything. For myself, it's a different story."

"But what's the alternative?" Deirdre said, feeling the energy begin to fill her again. "Forget that tonight ever happened? That I never began to want this again? I think I'd rather deal with a little rejection."

"Maybe more than a little," said Nick.

Juliette stretched and yawned widely. Even at this hour, she looked amazing, with her hair full and loose again, the way it had been when Deirdre first met her.

As if he were reading Deirdre's thoughts, Nick said to Juliette, "You look really different. What did you do?"

"I'm making an effort to please my husband," Juliette said,

raising her newly shaped eyebrows at both of them. "Don't you approve?"

"I think my approval is beside the point," said Nick.

"My husband is thrilled," said Juliette, tilting up her chin.

"I'm happy for you," said Nick. "I'm happy for both of you."

Juliette stood up and stretched. "We should go, Deirdre. I have a big night out in the city tomorrow, with Cooper." She looked at Nick. "That's my husband. We're having dinner at this fabulous restaurant and we're even going to a hotel. Not for the whole night, of course, since I don't subscribe to your theory that what's good for the parents is good for the children."

Why was Juliette being so combative? Deirdre wondered. Deirdre knew Juliette felt protective of her, but she seemed to be carrying it to an extreme. Plus, Deirdre had dragged her out tonight in the first place; now it was evidently time to take her home.

Kissing Nick good night, casting one last look at the stage, linking her arm through Juliette's, Deirdre thought she hadn't felt this alive since the day the twins were born, when those two tiny bodies, their heads already sprouting her Wylie grandmother's red hair, were laid upon her chest.

As they walked out into the night, so cold the air seemed made of ice, Deirdre looked toward the black sky. It was so late, so dark, that even here in Manhattan the stars were visible. It's a sign, she told herself, breathing in deeply and loving the bite of the cold night in her nostrils. I'm going to be a star.

CHAPTER 13

Juliette

She was ovulating. Again. Walking down Spring Street after her day at the Bliss Spa in Soho, going to meet Cooper for the big night out she'd engineered, Juliette passed a shop window and didn't even recognize her own reflection. She'd had a facial followed by a full makeup application, a hot stone massage for relaxation, and her first-ever bikini wax, though she'd realized too late that maybe she should have done that a few days ago.

She'd booked a table at a romantic restaurant, a short cab ride from Cooper's downtown office, and a room at a nearby luxury hotel. They wouldn't stay the night, she'd never spent a night away from Trey, but an hour or two was all she needed. The price of everything had made her nervous—including the day at the spa and extra babysitting pay for Heather, more than $1,000—but she rationalized that that was far less than the cost of marriage counseling or, for that matter, divorce. Plus, it was she alone who valued frugality. Cooper didn't mind spending lavishly, and it was, as he had so insensitively pointed out, his money.

As she turned onto West Broadway, she suddenly thought she spotted Nick on the crowded sidewalk, and her heart leapt, but then almost instantly she realized it wasn't him. She'd been rude to him last night, she knew, but she was so uncomfortable being with him and Deirdre at the same time. It wasn't that anything was going on between her and Nick, or between Deirdre and Nick, but she still didn't want Deirdre, Cooper, or anyone to know about their phone conversations.

He called her nearly every day. They kept their topics safe, sanitary: Living in Europe versus the United States, raising children, and books and art. Nick tried to educate Juliette about music (her father had helped her memorize long passages of Shakespeare, but they'd never had a radio at home, not even one in the car) and Juliette talked to him about the graduate program she hoped to pursue one day. She knew, hurrying along the wide sidewalk, toes pinched by the unaccustomed high heels, that what was going on with Nick was not completely innocent. She found herself thinking about Nick as she lay beside Cooper in bed at night, falling asleep; she found herself, whenever any little thing happened in her life, looking forward to telling him. Only him.

But it was for Cooper she'd worn makeup, she reminded herself. It was for Cooper she'd let her hair down, literally. It was for Cooper she'd strapped herself into the expensive Italian white lace bra and thong; for Cooper she'd arranged the lavish dinner and the hotel sex and the long evening away from her child. *Their* child.

Cooper was already at the restaurant, waiting for her, and he nearly knocked his chair over standing up to greet her. He's nervous, she realized with surprise. Nervousness was not one of Cooper's customary traits, but then again setting up dinners for just the two of them in the city—she hadn't even sprung the hotel room on him yet—wasn't something Juliette usually did either. Suddenly it occurred to her: he thinks I'm going to ask him for a divorce.

Juliette leaned toward him and, taking care to invest the gesture with feeling, kissed Cooper on the lips. It took him a moment to respond. She took his hand and kept holding it when they sat down.

"I decided you were right," she told him.

"What?"

"That I need to start paying more attention to you. To our marriage."

It couldn't be fake, Nick had cautioned her. She had to genuinely intend to meet Cooper halfway. Did she really mean it? Nick had asked her. Did she really want, not only to have another baby, but to make her marriage work?

Yes, she'd said. When she'd married Cooper, it had been forever, and she was committed to giving the relationship her all.

"Well," Cooper said, nodding in a considered way. "I'm happy to hear you say that."

"What do you think?" she asked, brushing her hair back from her face. Cooper had long campaigned to get her to color the gray in her hair, to dress to show off her figure, to play up her beauty. And why not? she thought now. When he met her, when he married her, she hadn't been shy about making the most of her looks, wearing fitted clothes the designer she worked for made especially for her slim figure, coloring her lips a trademark bright red, and wearing her hair even longer than she did now. Snow White, her friends used to teasingly call her.

"You look amazing," Cooper said. "What have you done?"

She smiled to herself. "A lot of things. Let's have a drink and order our food."

Juliette had decided beforehand not to talk about Trey, at least for tonight, or about having a baby—at least not yet. Of course the topic of school was also off-limits, and she was well aware that Cooper was completely uninterested in other subjects—an art show, her friends—she might ordinarily discuss. And she had always been hopeless at finance or markets, Cooper's work interests, or tennis or golf.

What had they ever found to talk about? Oh right. Cooper himself.

It all came back to Juliette as she sat there through dinner, listening to Cooper go on about how he'd handled himself at yesterday's meeting and what he'd said to the head of the London office and what he'd read in this morning's *Journal*. Cooper certainly had an easy enough time slipping back into practice; she nearly winced at the eagerness in his voice to tell her everything he'd been saving up for so long, since the verbal freeze that started when they had their first disastrous baby conversation. It wasn't that he'd become more boring over the years, just that she'd become more bored.

But that wasn't fair, was it? She was the one who'd changed since they'd gotten married, not him. The right thing to do, the thing she was at this moment endeavoring to do, was for her to change back.

And so she listened, working hard to keep her eyes wide and

fascinated-looking, even though only about a quarter of what he said penetrated her brain. Cooper didn't really care whether she digested what he said anyway, she told herself. He wasn't looking for her to voice any opinion in return or for any response at all other than attention. Or at least the appearance of attention.

The only problem was that when her mind drifted off to some other subject, Trey's new classroom aide or Deirdre's fledgling singing career or Nick himself, she felt herself getting into trouble. So far she'd managed to bring herself back to the table before Cooper noticed she was gone, but she was afraid she'd forget and blow everything.

"I rented a hotel room," she blurted out, instantly feeling more alert.

Cooper's eyes widened.

"For us," she said.

That was brilliant. For who else?

"At that place right down the street. Not for the whole night, of course, because of Trey. I mean, I rented it for the whole night, but I thought we'd just stay a few hours."

"Wow," he said, reaching for her hand while also signaling for the check. "This is amazing."

And that's when she felt it: the doubt. Maybe she'd been fooling herself about this whole thing, even more than she'd been fooling Cooper. *Was* she trying to trick him into getting her pregnant, as surely as Lisa had advised? Cooper might be right: if she got pregnant, she'd go back to not caring about how she looked, to not caring about him. Maybe she wanted him to be a sperm donor and a paycheck, that was all. Maybe she didn't really want *him*.

"Cooper," she said. "I have to tell you something."

He was already on his feet and was pulling her to stand up too.

"God," he said. "I am more turned on tonight than I have ever been with you."

"Cooper, please." He was standing very close to her, and she laid a freshly manicured hand on the silky smooth lapel of his charcoal Prada suit jacket. "I feel as if I've been less than honest."

"Mmmmm," he said, putting an arm around her and letting his hand slide down her hip. He was drunk, she realized. "I like you less than honest."

"Cooper, really," she said. There was no soft-pedaling the issue; she had to plunge ahead now and say it straight out, even at the risk of making him hate her. There was no point in going ahead with their marriage, with any marriage, on such dishonest grounds.

"Cooper," she said again. "I planned this whole evening to persuade you to go ahead with the baby thing."

He reared back, his gray eyes wide with surprise.

"You did all this so I'd agree to get you pregnant?" he said.

"I'm afraid so."

"And what else are you prepared to do?"

"Cooper," she said in a warning tone, conscious that they were having this conversation in the middle of the crowded restaurant.

"Really, I want to know," he said, taking her arm and steering her toward the coatroom. It wasn't until they were outside, all buttoned up, that she answered him.

"I was prepared to, you know, get really sexy," she said.

"Really?" His hand was gripping her elbow. "Like how?"

"I'm wearing this special lingerie, and I thought I'd really do it up, you know, soft music, little striptease." She laughed self-consciously. "I even have scented candles in my bag."

"Let's go do it," he said.

"It's wrong," she insisted. "It was like I was tricking you. Getting you all hot and excited, and then, when you could hardly say no, asking again if we could try for another baby."

He stopped in the middle of the street and looked down at her.

"You were going to ask me," he said.

"Ask you?"

"You weren't just going to have your way with me, thinking you'd 'accidentally' turn up pregnant. You were going to ask me again whether I wanted to."

"Of course," said Juliette, stung that, even after her confession, he'd imagine she would do it any other way.

"Then the answer is yes," Cooper said.

"What do you mean?" She held her breath, unable to let herself believe he was saying what it sounded like he was saying.

"The answer is yes," he said, taking her arm again, leading her again down the wintry street toward where the lights of the hotel shone like a beacon that signaled the beginning of a brand-new life. She filled her lungs with air and then let herself relax against him as her breath rushed out in a lovely cloud.

"Yes," he said, gripping her elbow so tightly she could no longer feel anything but certain. "We can have another baby."

CHAPTER 14

Anne

Why exactly was she baking him a cake? It wasn't for him, she told herself: She needed to try out recipes she might want to use in her theoretical restaurant. And a Red Velvet cake was the perfect antidote to the cold of that wintry Sunday afternoon, with icicles twinkling outside the kitchen windows. It was a treat for Clementine after the weekend at Damian's Manhattan hotel apartment, during which they inevitably ate nothing but Big Macs and tekka maki. Although Clementine would undoubtedly prefer white cake with chocolate frosting, and Red Velvet cake just happened to be Damian's favorite.

She didn't care about making Damian happy. She'd held out through Christmas, over New Year's, for an entire month of late-night telephone calls from him and weekend visitations with Clementine that he'd try to turn into visitations with her.

She'd resisted through hours of her daughter's tears and even more hours of her own longing for him. It should be getting easier now.

So why was she baking a cake?

Well, they should talk, she told herself as she swirled on the frosting—cream cheese frosting, colored red, of course. Talk in a relaxed, unemotional way. She'd been too angry to let him in the house before, had left two suitcases of his clothes on the front porch, had sent him by FedEx his tapes and scripts, had boxed up everything else of his that might make her burst into tears. Now that the hurt of those early days was past, they really needed to talk about Clementine and their finances and their future. Their *futures:* plural, separate.

And that kind of difficult conversation might go more smoothly over cake.

She rummaged around in the bottom of an overstuffed crumb-filled kitchen cupboard—who managed to organize and clean the cupboards when there was barely time to wipe the countertops?—for the cake plate, remembering too late that this one had been given to them by Damian's mother. Another piece of evidence for how completely intertwined their lives were.

Anne had done more serious cooking in this kitchen in the past month than she'd done in the entire seven years that they'd owned the house. It was a distraction, a way of relaxing and finding satisfaction, something she could do with Clementine or by herself. Trotting around to her friends' houses over the holidays had at least provided a focus for her kitchen activities: she baked stollen and challah, sweet potato pie and *fois gras en papillote*. And then when Lisa landed in the hospital, Anne cooked dinners for Tommy and the kids, as well as treats for Lisa, who thanked her and then set the walnut fudge and the tangerine jam aside, saving it, Anne suspected, for the garbage can.

The kitchen needed help, that was for sure. They'd known it was due for a total renovation when they first bought the house—a bare-bones three-bedroom 1920s Sears Colonial, definitely one of the most modest places in Homewood—but Anne had stopped seeing the chipped cupboards and scarred counters over time. She'd stopped seeing a lot, she thought. She wasn't blaming herself for what happened in London, but her marriage was obviously very different from the idyll she'd believed it to be. Of course, she'd had twinges, intimations that all was not right, but she'd shuttered these away, choosing to believe that all wives had misgivings and the wise ones ignored them.

But maybe, she thought as she set the cake on the dining room table and slicked on the red lipstick she'd stopped wearing and checked the dusky street for Damian and Clementine's arrival, she should have challenged him more. Voiced her own needs and pushed for the changes she wanted, the way Deirdre did. Taken more control, as Lisa would have. Even Juliette was now lobbying Cooper for another baby. While Anne had been so in thrall to the sexual power of her relationship with Damian that she hadn't wanted to look too closely at anything else.

Maybe it had been precipitous for her to have said in London she didn't want to be with him anymore. Maybe, with work, there was still a chance for them. The mere idea of this was so thrilling that it scared her. Hearing their footsteps pound up the wooden stairs to the front porch, Anne rushed to the front door and opened it, letting in a rush of frigid air along with her daughter. Damian continued to stand on the porch.

"You can come in too," she said, standing to the side and smiling to let him know she'd decided to be friendly.

He looked shocked. "Really?"

"Really."

He stepped into the house and looked around, as if he'd never been there before. Then he turned to her. "It smells fantastic in here."

"Cake," she said, nodding toward the dining room, where the cake sat like something from *Alice in Wonderland:* eat me and be transformed. That's what she'd been doing when she baked the cake, she realized, attempting to create some magic substance that would lure him back. Lure her back too.

"Want a piece?" she asked.

"Really?"

"Yes." She laughed, touching his arm lightly. "Really."

She took her time gathering the plates and the forks, unearthing the cake server that had also come from Damian's mother. If they were really going to split up, would he take these things back? What would she have left? What was purely hers? Because she'd been a student when her parents were killed, she'd sold their house and everything in it, thinking she'd never want the fussy flowered china and the silver packed 364½ days a year into its brown felt holder. Living in London right after college, she'd collected nothing, and it was only on moving back here with Damian that she'd bought dishes and furniture, clean and modern as Damian preferred but nothing fancy. Everything, it seemed, belonged to both of them.

"Here," she said, finally reappearing in the dining room

where he was already sitting at the table. "Where's Clem?"

"Upstairs kissing her toys hello, I think," he said.

The word *kissing* flustered her, and she felt her cheeks flame as she inclined her head over the cake and cut into the lurid red frosting.

"How big?" she said.

"As big as you'll give me."

She smiled but could not look at him as she handed him the cake.

"Do you have any tea?" he said. "I'm still thoroughly chilled."

She had, in fact, gotten rid of all the tea as a reminder of him, but she didn't want to admit that.

"How about coffee?" she said quickly. "I'll make a fresh pot."

"All right, then. God, this cake is brilliant."

She found herself humming as she moved about the crowded kitchen, grinding the beans, filling the pot with water from the filtered jug instead of the tap.

"Anne?"

He was there suddenly, in the kitchen.

"The coffee will be ready in a sec," she said. "I'll bring it into the dining room."

But he kept standing there, right behind her, and when at last she turned around to see whether he was waiting for her to move so he could retrieve something from the cupboard, she found that his face was just inches from hers.

"Anne," he said.

"What is it?"

And then he was there, his lips on hers. She hesitated for only a moment before giving herself over to him. I don't care, she thought. I want him too much. Kissing him was like drinking water when you'd been thirsty for a month. Sweet Jesus, she thought. I love him.

They hadn't kissed like this in years, just kissed, and that plus the month without sex made her crazy almost instantly. He was crazed too, it seemed, pushing against her as she pushed back, moving his hand to grip her breast as she slid hers between his legs. She bit his lower lip—there was anger in that, and satisfaction—and in response he lifted her onto the kitchen counter so that he was standing between her legs.

"Clem," she whispered.

"She won't hear."

"No," she said, shaking her head and placing her fingers on his lips.

She wiggled away from him and hopped down from the counter, taking his hand, leading him out of the kitchen, trying to think. She could hear Clementine in the small TV room upstairs, talking to her stuffed animals as *Rugrats* played in the background. Satisfied that her daughter was occupied and safe, Anne led Damian away from the stairs. The hall closet? Not enough room. The powder room? Yuk. Anywhere else downstairs was too exposed.

"I know," she said.

Looking back at him for approval, she led him back through the hallway, stopping short of the kitchen and opening the door to the basement, where they'd set up a makeshift office for Damian. He raised his eyebrows as if to say, This is really okay with you? She nodded.

They had barely shut the door when they started, right

there on the stairs. She tore off her jeans and he unzipped his. She gripped the splintered wooden banister, half afraid they would fall. He was below her on the stairs, kissing her neck, her shoulder, her breasts, slipping his finger inside her. How were they going to manage? He nudged her back and first she sat down and then lay back on the stairs, spreading her legs, making way for him to lower himself on top of her. Oh, this was good, this was good, this was good. All of her skin was alight, her mouth was open as she gulped for air and tried to open even wider for him. He wrapped his arms so tightly around her and moved so compellingly she felt weightless. She couldn't have stopped if she'd wanted to. And then, as quickly as their lovemaking ignited, he pushed into her and came, collapsing on top of her, his heart beating so hard she thought he would die.

"Damian," she whispered finally, her mind suddenly riveted on her daughter, upstairs alone, so far away.

"Hmmmm?"

"Damian, get up. Clementine."

He raised his head and looked around in bafflement, as if he'd just now fallen from the sky. She felt the bite of the gritty wooden stair against her back.

"Damian," she said, nudging him with her hip. "Now."

"Mmmmm," he said, lifting himself from her with difficulty.

She bounced to her feet and grabbed her jeans from where they lay tangled at the top of the stairs, struggling into them and pushing the door open at the same time, attuned now only to Clementine. From upstairs, the TV still blared.

"Clem?"

Nothing. This was it. She'd be punished. Clem was all she had, and now, because she was so selfish, something terrible had happened to her daughter. Don't be silly, she told herself. Clementine is fine. And you have your friends too, and your business smarts. And Damian, she reminded herself.

She climbed halfway up the stairs.

"Clementine?"

Nothing.

Her heart somersaulting, she bounded up the stairs to the tiny television room and was stunned to find her daughter sitting placidly in her pink bean bag chair, her thumb in her mouth, staring at the TV.

"Clementine!" Anne said.

Clementine turned to her slowly, with sleepy eyes.

"I was calling you," Anne said in a gentler voice.

The little girl shrugged. She had Damian's pale skin and chocolate eyes, and Anne's thin stick-straight hair, which she insisted on wearing long. She always came home from her dad's exhausted, Anne realized, though she wasn't sure whether that was from trooping around the city or sleeping on the apartment's pull-out sofa or from being upset by the separation.

"Here, sweetie," Anne said, opening her arms. "Do you want me to put you to bed?"

The little girl nodded, although it wasn't even time for her favorite shows yet. Anne decided to forgo a bath or a discussion of dinner and lifted her soft, warm child up and into her arms, humming softly as she moved to the bedroom. She'd become accustomed to doing all this alone and, strangely, despite what had just happened on the basement stairs, lost track of the fact that Damian was even in the house until she was smoothing the now-sleeping-and-in-bed Clementine's hair back from her forehead and heard a thump downstairs.

She found him in the living room, sprawled on the sofa, his bare feet propped on the old black wooden trunk that served as a coffee table. A plate bearing only cake crumbs lay beside his feet. He sat in a pool of light, reading what looked to be a script.

"Clemmie's okay?" he asked, smiling up at her.

"She was zonked. I put her to bed."

"These weekends are a lot," he said carefully.

She nodded and sunk onto the couch beside him. Here was her opening, she thought. They could start talking about it right now, what had happened in London, what had happened since, whether they could move beyond it. Or they could even, she thought, not talk about it. She could rest her head on his shoulder and they could order in some Thai food and when it was time for bed, she could simply lead him upstairs. She would get up early in the morning and leave for work unencumbered the way she used to, letting him take care of getting Clemmie to school. It would be so easy. But something stopped her from letting herself fall off this particular log.

"Is that a script?" she asked.

He nodded. "The new one."

"Oh," she said happily, remembering. "The guy who switches bodies with his ex."

"Well," he said. "I changed that."

"You did?" she said, feeling strangely insulted. Didn't he find the ex's body appealing anymore?

"Right. Check this out. Now the guy is a woman. Not only

a woman, but a black woman. And she now changes bodies with the president."

"You mean the president of the United States?"

"The very one," Damian said, nodding excitedly.

Anne could see it now. "Featuring Whoopi Goldberg," she said.

Damian shot her a nasty look.

"Or maybe Oprah would option it as a star vehicle for herself."

Damian did not look amused, though Anne was feeling inspired.

"I know, I know!" she cried. "Arnold Schwarzenegger could play the president who gets demoted to black woman!"

"You know, Anne," he said, "you're not being very supportive."

"I'm sorry," she said, trying to stifle her giggles. "Really, I'm sorry."

"You're the one who wants me to sell out."

Ah, so she wasn't the only one who was playing with knives. "I thought you wanted to do more commercial things," she said.

"I do," he said. "Of course I do. In fact, you'll be happy to hear that at the test screening for the other film, the rumble tanked, so now they want me to reshoot it as a wedding."

She straightened up. Held herself very still. "You're kidding."

"Unfortunately, no."

"You're going back to London, to St. Bart's, to reshoot." The idea of that scene, even the fictional side of it, being reenacted seemed beyond nightmarish— *Groundhog Day* meets the worst moment of her life.

"No, actually we're reshooting in New York. They won't spring for everyone to return to London. Shame to lose the church, though."

"But you're reshooting with the same cast."

"Of course."

"In New York."

"Yes."

There was a silence, and then he seemed to apprehend what she was driving at.

"Doll, you have nothing to worry about with me and Gwendolyn," he said. "That ended that day in the church."

The funny thing was, she'd even, over the past month, begun to have doubts about what she'd seen. Maybe she'd misinterpreted. He'd never come straight out and admitted it, after all. Until now.

"Gwendolyn," she said, the girl's face appearing in her mind's eye. "I wanted to keep thinking she didn't have a name."

"Baby," he said, trying to take her hand. "That was nothing. It's you that I love."

Almost exactly what he'd said in the church. In fact, she was beginning to see that everything was really exactly as it always had been. The slick words and the career that never quite took off. The fantastic sex and the assumption, on his part, that she would always be his. Her enormous need, and his failure to satisfy it.

"I'm beat," she said. "Monday tomorrow."

He looked shocked. "What are you saying?"

"I'm going to bed, Damian. I think it's time you went home."

"I can't believe this. You're kicking me out?"

The outrage that she would do the utterly reasonable thing—that was familiar.

"I'm afraid so."

"I could sleep on the couch," he said. "Be here for Clem in the morning."

"We'll manage," she said, beginning to move toward the door. She opened it and held it open despite the frigid air.

"But Anne," he said, fumbling with his bag, his papers, looking befuddled as he searched for his coat. "I thought—the stairs—the cake."

"Would you like to take the cake?"

"No, I didn't mean—"

"I insist!" she said, glad to have something to do besides holding the door waiting for him to leave. She marched over to the dining room table, carried the red cake on its ceremonial stand into the kitchen, covered it with plastic wrap, then set the whole thing, plate and all, into a paper shopping bag.

When she returned to the front hall, Damian was wearing his coat, standing by the door, looking completely miserable.

"I'm confused," he said.

"I'm confused too."

"Anne, I want to come back."

"I know."

"What do I have to do? Just tell me, Anne. Anything, and I'll do it."

"You have to be someone else, Damian. Do you think you're up to that? You have to be the person I used to believe you were."

CHAPTER 15

Lisa

"Mommy! Mommy!"

Lisa could hear their squeals of greeting from inside the house as soon as Tommy opened the door of the minivan. They must have been waiting at the window for her, and the house seemed to vibrate with the pounding of their feet. At least the ice on the front path gave her an excuse to cling to Tommy's muscled arm. Even through the hospital-strength Motrin, the pain was asserting itself, but she wasn't about to admit that to anyone. Thank God it's over, she thought. Thank God I'm back to my real life.

The red-painted door flew open and there they were, their four happy and eager faces beaming at her. Even Laddie, tail wagging furiously, was trying to nose into the front row. Before she had a chance to cross the threshold they crowded around her. Henry's head butted right against her stitches and Daisy's finger seemed to jab right into the hollow space inside her.

She started to hug them, to gather them to her, but then, over their heads, she saw the house: the plastic-bright litter of toys strewn across the Oriental carpets, the dark jumble of coats and hats and scarves heaped on the sofa and on every chair, the mountains of newspapers and school papers and mail teetering on all the tabletops, the lamp shades askew and the picture frames crooked. There were empty glasses and half-full glasses; bowls that had once held breakfast cereal now stood with spoons embedded in thick yellow crusts of milk. There was the smell of sour milk too, and of scorched pasta and of fried hot dogs, even though it was only ten o'clock in the morning. This was the state of things, after Lisa had been away for nine days.

The thirteen-year-old babysitter Sonia from around the corner stood sullen and oblivious to one side, her coat already in her arms.

"Can I go?" she asked.

"Just a minute," said Tommy, easing Lisa into the house and letting the storm door close.

"Take what I owe you," he said, pulling a wad of bills from his pocket and holding them out to the girl, who grabbed them all without looking.

"What are you giving her, Tommy?" Lisa said.

He looked confused. "What?"

"How much are you giving her? Because I don't think you should give her anything. It's a nightmare in here."

The girl looked frightened and put on her coat.

"Didn't you know I was coming home from the hospital?" Lisa said. "You could have made a little bit of an effort to pick up."

Sonia dropped the money on the hall table. "You can keep this," she said stonily.

Tommy picked up the bills and held them out to her, trying to tuck them into her folded arms. "No, Sonia," he said, sounding frightened. "Please."

"It's okay," Sonia said, but with a warning edge to her voice. Not: it's okay, I understand. More: it's okay, just let me go and I won't press charges. The girl turned away and slipped out the door.

"Thanks a lot," Tommy said, anger clouding his big handsome face. "Now we'll never get her back."

"Good," Lisa muttered.

"No, *not* good!" Tommy cried. "Do you have any idea what it's been like around here without you? How much attention the kids have needed? How hard it is just to get the basics done?"

"Do I have any idea?" Lisa said. "How do you think I've been spending the past six and a half years of my life?"

"Yes, but that was your full-time job! I have a full-time job, and now I have this too!"

"Well, I'm sorry I had fucking cancer!"

Henry burst into tears. He'd been standing there, stunned and brave, but now he broke down and sobbed, hanging his head, the tears dropping straight down from his cheeks onto the golden oak floor.

Lisa moved to her son's side and drew him to her. "It's okay, sweetheart," she said, wishing with all her might that she could take the word back. Cancer was one of those words, like *love*, like *divorce*, that could sometimes be more powerful even than the feelings behind it, assuming the ability to influence events.

And Lisa did not intend to let that happen. "Mommy didn't mean that."

Henry gazed up at her in wonder and terror. "What's *fucking?*" he asked. "What's *cancer?*"

Matty reached out and swatted his little brother, which made him start crying again.

And then Daisy let out a screech like something that might emanate from a wild animal. She flung up her little hands and tore off around the living room, leaping over the scattered toys and magazines and mittens, screaming and waving her arms and running in circles, the dog running and barking behind her.

"Daisy," Tommy called. "Daisy, calm down right this instant."

Yet Daisy kept running, kept squealing, even faster and louder than before.

"You see?" Tommy said. "This is the kind of thing that's been going on."

"It's all right," said Lisa, taking off her coat. "I'll take care of it."

Tommy hesitated. He was torn, she could tell. He didn't really expect her to take care of it. But he wanted to believe, more than anything, that she could.

Which was what she wanted too.

"Come on, Lisa," he said. "I want to be here for you."

Then you should have made sure everything was together when I came home, she thought, but then immediately chastised herself for being mean. This isn't his domain, she thought. He'll never get it right and then I'll just be more annoyed. I don't want him lurking around, asking me how I feel every two minutes. I'd rather have him clear out and leave me to get this place back the way I want it.

"You've already taken enough time off," she said. "The kids will help me clean up the house, won't you, guys?"

Matty and Henry straightened to attention, Will slumped in some facsimile of good behavior by their side, but Daisy was still running in circles. At least she'd stopped squealing. Lisa noticed for the first time that her color coding had completely fallen by the wayside. Matty was wearing blue, but Will had one red and one blue sock on, and Henry was wearing Willy's old green sweatpants with his red turtleneck.

"I'm serious," Lisa said to Tommy, pointing toward the door. "Go."

She waited until she heard the door click tight behind him. Then she clapped her hands.

"Children," she said. "You know your jobs. Matty, you're in charge of bringing all plates and glasses into the kitchen, filling the sink with soapy water, and clearing all table and countertops."

Matty, who at nearly seven had been at this the longest, sprang into action, Lisa saw with satisfaction.

"Will," said Lisa. Will was sitting on the floor, staring into space. He was her questioner, a natural second-born, and while he'd never actually rebelled before, he had evidently gotten away with a lot during her absence. "Stand up."

Willy stood up but still wouldn't meet her eye.

"Your job is to pick up the toys," Lisa said.

Will smirked. "I want to play video games."

"Video games? Since when do we have video games in this house?"

"Dad bought them for us," said Matty, heading toward the kitchen with a stack of dirty paper plates in his hands.

"Well, there will be no more video games," said Lisa.

The pain in her abdomen that had felt so sharp when she was navigating the icy walk had now settled into a dull throb. She felt a headache coming on too. Shutting her eyes, she took a deep breath and summoned the image that kept her going through almost any crisis: Madonna crying on her cell phone while running on a treadmill. She'd read about that in a celebrity magazine once, while running on a treadmill herself, and though she'd never been a huge fan of Madonna's, she had to admit she admired this kind of determination.

"I'm going," said Willy, walking out of the room.

"Young man, get back here this instant!" she screamed.

With that, Henry began crying again. He was still standing at attention, but his little shoulders began to heave and his chin dropped to his chest.

"Oh, Henry, for goodness sake, buck up," she said.

Which of course made him cry all the harder.

Daisy, meanwhile, continued on her circle around the room, only now, each time she passed something that was not stationary—a cushion, a magazine, a dirty napkin—she picked it up and, giggling, tossed it into the center of the floor.

"Stop!" Lisa shouted as loudly as she could, more loudly than she'd ever needed to shout before. "You will all come into line! I am back and you will come into line right this instant!"

But it didn't seem to matter that she was back and that she was screaming. They all kept doing exactly as they pleased.

CHAPTER 16

The February Dinner

Anne thought that having their monthly dinner on Valentine's Day would be a good thing, taking her mind off Damian. She was surprised to discover, in fact, that of the four of them, she was the only one who still, until now at least, celebrated Valentine's Day. Impossible to get a babysitter, the other moms said. Even more impossible to get a restaurant reservation. Difficult enough to buy him gifts for birthday and anniversary and Father's Day and Christmas (and Hanukkah! Deirdre chimed in) without finding some ridiculous Valentine's gift as well. No, they were all free on Valentine's Day.

The only restaurant in town with a free table turned out to be the unfortunately named Satist Palace, an Indian place that was completely and depressingly empty, undoubtedly due to its orange leatherette chairs and fluorescent lights and utterly unromantic atmosphere.

"Can you imagine coming here with someone you love?" Anne asked.

"I love you," said Juliette, who was dressed festively in a red shirt and white wool suit, looking happier than she had in months. Years. No, Anne thought: ever.

"Yes," said Anne. "But you're not trying to get in the mood to rip my clothes off at the end of the night."

"This place would definitely not do it for me," said Lisa, looking around. "Is Deirdre coming?"

"She said she was," said Juliette. "I'm sure she'll be here any second. In the meantime . . ."

She rooted around under the table and came up with a bag that obviously held a bottle in the air.

"Da da!" Juliette said, taking a bottle of sparkling cider from its brown paper wrapper.

"How festive," said Anne. "If not alcoholic. What are we celebrating?"

Juliette leaned in closer. "I should wait for Deirdre to tell you this, but I can't keep it in any longer." She grinned. "I'm pregnant!"

"Oh, Juliette, that's fabulous," Lisa said, getting up from her chair to hug her friend. "I'm so happy for you."

When it was her turn, Anne hugged Juliette and kissed her on the cheek. It was so cheering, in this season of upheaval, to have something go right for one of them. Anne knew how Juliette had been longing for this, how despairing she'd felt when it seemed as if it wasn't going to happen, how hard she'd worked to get Cooper on her side. And now it was a reality.

"When are you due?" Anne asked.

"Gee, it's so new," Juliette said. "I've got an appointment to confirm things with Dr. Kaufman in two days, when I'll be offi-cially overdue. But I'm always so regular, and I *feel* completely pregnant—tender breasts, falling asleep right after dinner. I fig-ure the baby will be here around Thanksgiving."

"So, is Cooper excited?" Anne asked.

"He was totally beside himself," Juliette said. "He kept say-ing he couldn't believe it had really happened, the first month we tried."

"That is pretty fast."

"I think it happened that night I rented the hotel room in the city, when I first promised Cooper I would meet him halfway," Juliette said happily. "I timed that night for when I was ovulating. I even put a pillow underneath my bottom when we were finished. I'm sure it happened that first night."

"It's going to be so much fun to have a baby in the group again," Lisa said, sounding so enthusiastic that Anne wondered whether Lisa might want another one herself.

And then, thinking of all of them sitting together as they used to do so long ago, passing a brand-new baby from one to the other, Anne felt a stab of something so unexpected she had to think for a minute before she was able to name it. What she felt was jealousy—not of the new closeness in Juliette's marriage, but of the pregnancy. Anne was astonished to find that she wished it were she who was, with or without Damian, expecting a baby.

"Where is Deirdre, anyway?" she said. "I want some of that faux champagne."

"Let's open it," said Juliette. "I'm sure she'll be here any sec-ond. I would have bought real champagne, but this way I can have some of it too."

Sipping the cider, which was so sweet it made her teeth hurt, brought Anne back to the early days of her pregnancy with Clementine. They'd still been in England then, and she'd been so excited, savoring every moment because they'd agreed there would just be the one. She'd even been sentimental about her brief bout with morning sickness, knowing she'd experience it only once, and still remembered her food cravings: Ribena, which was a strange black currant juice everyone seemed to drink in London, and vinegar crisps. Yuk.

Why had she gone along with Damian's insistence that they have only one child, as she'd gone along with so much else? It seemed to her now it was almost as if she'd been hypnotized, so thoroughly had she been under his power, so completely had she bought into his vision of the world and their future in it. But she was the one making the money and paying the babysitter; having more children would have had a greater effect on her career and life than on his. Yet she'd allowed him to make the rules.

"I wanted more than one," she said. When they looked at her in confusion, she realized she hadn't been saying her thoughts out loud. "Child, I mean. It was Damian who only wanted one."

"Tommy wanted five," said Lisa. "I thought we might actually get that far, but now it's not going to happen."

"Why not?" said Juliette. "You should. We could push strollers together. Start a new play group."

"Because—" Lisa began, and then stopped. "We just decided not to."

"Well, I wish I'd overridden Damian," Anne said. "I'd love to have had another child or two."

"But maybe it's better . . . ," Lisa said. "Considering . . ."

"Considering that we've broken up?" said Anne.

"I'm sorry," Lisa said. "I didn't mean to upset you."

The door of the restaurant opened, and they all looked up, expecting Deirdre. But it was a young couple—at last some Valentine revelers—who headed to a booth in the corner.

"Where is Deirdre?" said Anne. "I'm getting hungry."

"I'll try calling her cell," said Juliette, getting out her phone. "I think we should go ahead and order."

Deirdre's cell yielded no response, and at her home Paul said a sitter was there with the kids when he got home from work, so he assumed Deirdre was with them.

"Hmmmm," said Lisa. "Maybe she's off getting it on with that music guy."

"I don't think so," Juliette said quickly.

"What makes you so sure? Did you go into the city to see her show that night?"

"Yes, and she was fantastic," said Juliette. "There was even an agent there who said he thought he could get her work, so it looks like this thing is really taking off."

"That's amazing," Lisa said. "Look at the two of you, with all this great stuff happening. It gives us hope. Right, Anne?"

Anne looked away, and unfortunately her eyes fell on the couple in the corner. They were young and delighted-looking—if a collective two hundred pounds overweight—and they were sitting on the same side of the banquette with their arms wrapped around each other, heads together so that the heavy black frames of their twin eyeglasses were nearly touching.

"I don't know about hope," Anne said. "At least when it comes to Damian."

"What do you mean?" said Juliette. "I thought you and Damian were talking. I know you said . . ."

Juliette hesitated. Anne had told her that she'd slept with Damian—she'd talked to Deirdre about it too—but she'd asked both of them not to tell Lisa. It wasn't that Anne wanted to keep secrets from Lisa, but that night at the hospital, Lisa had seemed so disapproving. But now she was beginning to think Lisa had been right. What was it she'd said? Oh right: missing him doesn't mean you should take him back. She wished she'd considered that before she'd screwed him on the cellar stairs.

Maybe, Anne decided, as much as her opinions might sting, Lisa was the one she *should* be confiding in about Damian. The one in the group who would do the most to bolster her new-found resolution to press forward with a divorce.

"I slept with Damian," Anne said, trying to keep her gaze steady as she looked at Lisa.

"Oy," said Lisa. "You violated rule number one."

"What's that?" asked Anne. She could never keep up with Lisa's rules.

"Protect yourself!" cried Lisa. "You need a mommy."

"You're right," said Anne. "I do. And guess what, I'm available for adoption in case anybody's interested."

"Just listen to me," said Lisa. "Get over that guy."

"But don't you think for Clementine's sake," Juliette began. "I mean, I know you're discouraged, but if there's even the slightest chance . . ."

"That we could make our marriage different?" said Anne.

Juliette nodded. "Like me and Cooper."

"I know. I wanted that to be true. Even after I made him leave that night, after I had sex with him, some part of me wanted it to be true. But I've been poking around this month, going through old records, all the junk of Damian's that's still in the house."

An exercise that brought her more than she'd bargained for. From the sketchy but voluminous evidence that she could piece together—everything from old credit card receipts from his business to preserved love notes—Gwendolyn had not been the first colleague Damian had had an affair with. It seemed his on-set dalliances, with makeup artists and costumers and screen-writers as well as actresses, stretched all the way back in an unbroken line to the beginning of their marriage. When Damian had claimed he hadn't changed, he'd been telling the truth: he'd always been a monster.

"He's cheated on me all along," Anne said now, the moment that the papadams they'd ordered to tide them over until Deirdre's arrival showed up at the table. She'd thought she was starving, but now she felt a queasiness rise up in her throat. "I have no doubt. I'm filing for divorce."

"But you were happy before you found all this stuff out," said Juliette. "Maybe if you could try to forget it, to pretend it didn't happen, you could get back together and everything would be the same."

Anne shook her head forcefully. "I could never do that," she said. "It would be like walking with a thorn in your shoe and claiming you didn't feel it. Could you do that?"

Juliette sighed and shook her head, pressing her lips together.

Lisa reached across the table and squeezed her arm. "I know it's rough," she said, "but I really think you're doing the right thing. And I think you'll be better off, you'll see."

Anne managed a smile. "Thanks, Mom."

Juliette looked at her watch. "She's almost an hour late now. I'm getting worried." She took out her cell phone and dialed, and then they heard her say, "Deirdre! Where are you?"

They listened, although Anne couldn't tell much from just Juliette's side of the conversation.

"You're kidding," Juliette said, sounding truly floored.

Then, "Did you talk to Paul?"

Then, "Why didn't you tell me?"

Over in the corner, the couple kissed.

"All right," Juliette said. "All right. All right."

She snapped the phone closed and looked at Anne and Lisa.

"She's in New York," Juliette said. "She's got an audition tomorrow morning, for that agent I told you about. She's staying over—Nick's out of town."

"Wow," said Lisa.

"Yeah," said Juliette. "She already called Paul and told him, but she was afraid if she told us, we would think she was picking her new singing career over our monthly dinner."

"Which obviously she was," said Anne.

"It's amazing how everything is changing," said Lisa.

"Expect the unexpected," said Anne.

"I wish she'd let us know so we could have started eating," said Juliette. "I'm so hungry these days, and now I don't feel well. Excuse me just a minute."

When Juliette stood up and headed toward the ladies' room, Anne nearly screamed at the sight of the back of Juliette's white wool skirt, soaked in scarlet blood.

CHAPTER 17

Deirdre

Deirdre walked west along Forty-fourth Street, west and farther west, swinging her arms and sashaying her hips. Swing swing, she told herself. Wiggle wiggle. She made herself smile and felt it was true what she'd read in *Glamour* yesterday: doing the action can make you feel the feeling, in her case, happier and sexier. She was wearing a new tight black suede skirt, shorter than any skirt she'd owned since seventh grade, and it was freezing, so she was walking very fast. Under her arm she carried a portfolio holding the head shots she'd had taken three days ago; her newly straightened hair slid—as opposed to bounced—against her cheek. A good-looking businessman standing on the corner of Eighth Avenue turned to watch her as she passed. Swing swing. Wiggle wiggle.

She was going to see Elliot Lesser, the agent who'd given her his card that night when she did the show with Nick. She'd called him the next day, and he thought she could have a real career. Very talented, incredibly versatile. He saw tremendous commercial possibilities, character parts on Broadway, touring dates with top bands, maybe even a solo appearance at one of the major nightspots. Did people use the word *nightspot* anymore? Never mind, what did she know? Elliot Lesser had told her that he was a veteran of one of the major show business agencies and an entertainment lawyer to boot. And he was interested in taking her on as a client. Having an agent, someone who could send her to closed auditions and recommend her for roles, would be a huge step up from the cattle calls she'd been going on.

As she continued to walk west and the streets became both scrubbier and more deserted, she felt sweat spring to her palms as her heart began to thump in her ears. She opened her mouth to take in more air and felt her throat go dry, that arid feeling she woke up with in the middle of the night for all those months after the twins were born when she was on antidepressants, the feeling that was death to her voice. Just the hint of that feeling—the memory of the depression and the fear that she would never be able to sing again—made her panicky.

Swing swing, she told herself. Wiggle wiggle. But it had stopped working. She even tried to smile but felt her teeth clench in a grimace. Her mind had swung to the twins. She hadn't been home for three days, and she missed them so sharply she could have doubled over there on the sidewalk. They were at an age now when they were away from her far more than they were in her arms or on her lap, even when she was at home, but she realized how much she counted on their first-thing-in-the-morning snuggles and their good night kisses, their full-body hugs at the end of the school day and their drowsy heads in her lap as they watched TV together at night. Of course she could still talk to them on the phone, of course she could gaze at their pictures, but she was stunned by how unmoored she felt without these physical touchstones.

Focus, she told herself. This was only making her more nervous, when she needed to feel as positive as possible. She reminded herself that the separation seemed to be harder on her than on the twins themselves. The kids were being showered by attention from Paul, who had indeed joined the family practice in Homewood, and Juliette, who said being with them was helping to cheer her up, since it turned out she had not been pregnant after all. She needed to stop worrying about the children and focus on her interview with Lesser, which might be the biggest thing ever to happen in her professional life. But just thinking that made her feel even more nervous, and she felt her stomach cramp and acid shoot toward her mouth. Wildly, she looked around at the street of unkempt brownstones, panicking further at the idea that if she ended up needing a bathroom, there was not one in sight.

Beginning to trot, she took some comfort in noticing that the gap was closing between the street number on Elliot Lesser's card and the numbers on the town houses. There it was, at last, the place she had dreamed about ever since he'd handed her his card. Only, in her fantasies, it had been a tall gleaming building and she'd ridden in an elevator up many floors to his spacious offices, the chrome and white marble front desk manned by an equally sleek receptionist. She'd realized that vision wasn't going to come true once she crossed Broadway and moved from the land of skyscrapers to that of four-story century-old buildings. Even then she'd imagined a polished brownstone with a coal-shiny black door, all of its elegant stories thrumming with the creative life of the agency. She certainly hadn't guessed she'd find herself in front of a crumbling brick tenement, picking her way over discarded fast-food containers and knotted plastic bags of dog poop to get to the grate guarding the basement entrance to Lesser Management.

At least this made her less nervous. Or was it more nervous? Less intimidated, more skeptical. Still sweating and having trouble breathing. She reached out and pressed the greasy bell and then, when she heard the buzzer, leaned her shoulder hard into the flaking black bars of the grate.

It was dark inside, and cramped. Deirdre found herself in a tiny anteroom reeking of nail polish, populated by a young woman with blonde hair bunched atop her head and pinned with a white plastic butterfly clip. The woman was pretty, which was reassuring to Deirdre after the shabby appearance of the building. You had to be somewhat successful to have an attractive assistant, didn't you?

"I'm Deirdre Wylie," Deirdre said. "I have an appointment."

"Oh, yes," said the blonde woman, eyes instantly glazing over. She lifted the applicator from a bottle of sparkly lavender polish. "Elliot's on a conference call right now."

Deirdre sat in a gray metal chair with a gray plastic seat, her short shearling jacket—another new purchase—still on and her portfolio grasped in her still-gloved hands. She saw that the portfolio's red ribbon had come unknotted and fumbled to retie it, an impossible task while wearing heavy suede gloves. But in struggling to pull off the brand-new gloves the portfolio slipped off her lap onto the grimy floor, spilling her expensive new photographs—sultry black-and-white Deirdres times twenty—across the linoleum.

"Shit," she said. Then, for the receptionist's benefit: "I'm sorry."

She tugged off her gloves and shrugged off the heavy coat, crouching down to retrieve the photos and wondering whether the receptionist could see straight up her skirt. Oh, no matter, the girl was staring at her own cuticles, not at Deirdre anyway.

Deirdre gathered her things, anxious now that Elliot Lesser was going to emerge from his office to find her scrambling on the floor. But she had everything back in order and was sitting with her legs crossed once again on the gray chair and there was still no sign of him. She noticed she was jiggling her bottom leg and willed herself to stop, but two minutes later it was jiggling again. The receptionist's manicure was proceeding at an excruciatingly slow pace. The smell was making Deirdre dizzy, and each time she let herself watch as the girl dragged the brush, millimeter by millimeter, up her nail, she found her leg bouncing again.

"I did have an eleven o'clock, didn't I?" Deirdre said finally.

"He should be with you shortly," the girl said, without looking up.

Ten more minutes went by. Twenty. Deirdre felt her stomach growl; she hadn't eaten breakfast for fear of how it would affect her stomach, and now, despite feeling ill from the combination of nerves and acetone, she was afraid her stomach was about to launch into its noontime wail. She wished at least that the nail polisher wasn't sitting right there so she could use her cell phone to call Paul and ask his advice on how to handle this. Nick might be the one who had more experience in the music world, but Paul was so good at being calm, she found to her surprise that whenever she was unsure how to handle something, it was Paul she wanted to call, not Nick.

"Is Mr. Lesser still on that call?" Deirdre asked.

The girl glanced toward the phone. "It looks like he's off."

"Well, can you let him know I'm here?" Deirdre said, feeling her temper rise. Don't say anything, she told herself. It won't get you anywhere and it might screw things up. "If it's not too much trouble," she said, trying to keep the edge out of her voice but wanting the girl to know that even if she was the needy one here, she knew when she was being treated badly.

Sighing deeply, the girl picked up the phone, punched some buttons, and mumbled something. Then she set down the receiver and looked straight at Deirdre.

"He says to tell you he's sorry, but he's been unavoidably tied up. He says you can leave your head shots if you want and come back next week."

"But I had an appointment," Deirdre said. "It was for eleven o'clock, and I've been waiting almost an hour."

The girl shrugged. "Sorry," she said.

"No, not sorry," Deirdre said, rising to her feet. "I've been waiting all this time, and I've done all these things he told me to do, and now I want to see him."

"He's not available," the girl said.

Deirdre was looming over the receptionist now. She had a vision of herself snatching up the nail polish bottle and hurling it across the room, lavender crystals spraying through the air. She felt herself vibrating, and it was very difficult to keep from opening her mouth and screaming as loudly as she could. She could access a vision of how she was supposed to act—professional and poised despite her disappointment, willing to leave some photos but firm about rescheduling the appointment—but she couldn't get anywhere close to feeling as if she could behave that way.

"You listen to me," she said to the girl. "I spent two thousand fucking dollars getting ready for this appointment. I've done everything he told me I needed to do. Do you understand what I mean? Do you understand me?"

The girl just stared up at Deirdre, her mouth slightly open, her eyes as blank and dumb as a cow's.

"Oh, fuck," Deirdre said, realizing she was taking out everything on this girl who was nobody, who had no power and who didn't give a fuck about her or even about Elliot Lesser or the music business. There was only one productive thing to do. "I'm going in there."

Deirdre still half-expected the girl to fling herself across the entrance to Lesser's, but the only sign of life she showed was to follow Deirdre with her eyes as Deirdre strode across the room and slammed open the door to the inner sanctum. There was Lesser, hunched at a desk piled with papers and CDs and cassette tapes, eating a sandwich. The smell of tuna was as pungent as the smell of nail polish in the reception area.

"You have to see me," Deirdre said.

He blinked up at her, chewing.

"Who are you?" he said finally.

"Deirdre Wylie! Deirdre Wylie! Your bimbo just told you I was waiting out there! Don't you remember? You gave me your card! You saw the show I did with Nick Ruby and you told me I could have this big career, you made me buy all these clothes and spend all this money on pictures and sign up for these expensive voice lessons!"

"I *made* you?" Lesser said, as if the idea were preposterous.

"Yes, you made me! You made me change my entire life!"

There was the dental work she'd put off so she could pour the money into her career, even though her teeth were aching right this very minute. There was Paul's job change and the twins' tears each time she left for more time away. And why had she done all this, asked all this of the people who loved her? Because she'd been ready to believe, on no evidence whatsoever, that this little weasel had the power to transform her life.

"You don't give a shit, do you?" she said, surprised by the calm in her voice.

He studiously wiped his fingers on a crumbled paper napkin, his eyes relentlessly averted. "Who said that?"

"All right, so here I am," she said, feeling the emotion rise up within her again. But now all her feelings seemed more cohesive, somehow, twining around one another to form a cord that seemed to operate as a second backbone, making her stand strong and tall.

"This doesn't seem to be the—"

"I'm here," she snapped. "Listen to me."

And then she opened her mouth and sang. She had prepared three songs for today, but the one she found coming out of her mouth wasn't any of them. "Tell her she's a fool, she'll say Yes, I know, but I love him so. . . ." She closed her eyes, flung out her arms, threw back her head—exposed her throat to him. This is it, she thought as she heard her own voice, lush and gorgeous, fill the room. This is the best I've ever sounded.

When she finished, there was silence for longer than was comfortable. She didn't want to look at him, but then she began to feel as if there might be something further required of her. Was she supposed to bow? Roll right into another number?

Lesser cleared his throat. "That was," he said, "very nice."

"Very *nice?* That's what you call *nice?* Who else comes in here to sing for you—Callas?"

"I don't like your tone," he said.

"You don't like *my* tone?" She snatched her portfolio from where she'd set it on his desk. "Well, I think you're a total liar and a phony."

Great, Deirdre, she thought. A liar and a phony. Why don't you just stick out your tongue at him and blow him a raspberry.

"Wait a minute, now," Lesser said, swaying to his feet. "I think you have potential."

"Potential? Potential is what you tell someone they have when you're talking to them on the phone. Not after what you just heard."

"You keep up with the lessons, maybe take off a little weight . . ."

That was the end. "Listen," Deirdre said, "I could be Christina fucking Aguilera and you wouldn't know what to do with me. You're the one with the problem, not me."

She whirled around and headed away from the tuna fish and

into the relatively fresh nail polish air of the waiting room, which is where he caught up with her.

"Wait," he said, breathing heavily. "There's something you might be perfect for. But I don't know whether you're interested. It's the role of a mother."

Deirdre frowned. "What's the problem? I'm a mother."

Elliot Lesser shrugged elaborately. "Some women, they don't want to play mothers. But if you're interested, I could send you to this audition. As my client."

On the one hand, she wanted to continue her current trajectory and tell him to fuck off, that she was going to find somebody better. On the other hand, this was it: she could right now, right this minute, have a real agent and an in at a real audition, not just a cattle call. She thought of what Nick had said to her that night, that she had to be tough.

So she told Lesser she'd do it, and then he made her sign a paper that seemed to say she'd give him 15 percent of everything she earned from now until forever. She read the contract quickly, not really taking it in, and then shook Lesser's fragrant hand. She couldn't wait to be outside, and on her own.

Once she was there, walking down the street on the clear and frigid afternoon, she breathed in deeply and closed her eyes. This is it, she thought: this is as good as it gets. She had the impulse to call Paul, who she was surprised to find she missed almost as much as the kids. I'll call him, she thought, but first I want to walk alone for a minute with my future. Swing swing, she reminded herself, beginning to smile. Wiggle wiggle.

CHAPTER 18

Lisa

The bedside alarm sounded. Damn: 2:50 already. Hadn't the kids just *left* for school? And on the television, the guy with the skinny dark mustache was about to reveal whether he preferred the mother or the daughter, both of whom he was dating. But even more compelling was the certain knowledge that Anne's babysitter Consuelo, who was driving the carpool today, would be pulling into the driveway in less than five minutes.

Lisa rolled out of bed, upturning the notebook that had lain, open but untouched, on top of the covers all day, and scrambled to the closet to get dressed. The clothes she'd put on that morning, the cream cashmere turtleneck and trim khakis she'd worn while she cooked breakfast for everyone and kissed Tommy good-bye and ferried the children to school, were folded neatly on the floor, the pointy-toed brown boots beside them. She'd thought today might be the day she actually got to the gym before she turned to her book, but then she decided just to come home and work, and then ended up changing out of her clothes and back into her sweats and climbing into the bed with her notebook. And watching television, dozing on and off, instead of writing.

She knew by now how to pull herself together near-instantaneously, and she was standing ready by the front door, checking her freshly brushed hair and newly applied lipstick in the hall mirror, when Laddie barked excitedly and she heard the toot of Consuelo's horn in the driveway. She opened the door and leaned out with a huge smile on her face, waving energetically. Matthew knew that he was supposed to help his little brothers and sister from the van, and he stood there dutifully in the cold and darkening afternoon, helping each of them down into the snowy driveway while Lisa stood at the door, grinning and hugging herself. She got chilled so easily now and already felt her arms starting to quake as her teeth chattered and her knees trembled.

"Hurry up," she called to the kids, maintaining her smile but at the same time waving good-bye to Consuelo and breaking eye contact, trying to back imperceptibly into the warmth of the house without betraying any weakness. The important thing was not to give Consuelo anything negative to report to Anne.

The kids knew the drill. They hung their backpacks and jackets on their color-coded hooks and came inside, embracing her one by one.

"How was your day?" she asked them.

Matt and Will mumbled that it had been fine, and Daisy scampered without a word into the playroom, snapping on the television and settling in on the floor, her thumb in her mouth. For the first several days after coming home from the hospital, Lisa had held the line on her ban on after-school television, but then she'd relented, only cautioning the children not to tell their father. "If you tell Daddy," she said, "I won't let you do it anymore."

The two older boys joined Daisy in front of the television. Only Henry lingered in the front hallway, wrapping his arms around Lisa's thighs and resting his head on her hip.

"How was your day, Mommy?" he asked.

God, what other four-year-old asked his mother how her day was? Tommy didn't even remember most of the time. Lisa reached down and ran her fingers through his hair, and her light touch was all the encouragement the child needed to squeeze tightly with his little arms and press his head so fiercely into her side that it felt as if he might pop right through her skin to the hollow place where her womb had been.

She gripped Henry's shoulders and propelled him away from her.

"Now you go in and watch TV with the other kids, you hear me?" she said, trying to catch his eye so he would know she was serious. But he looked away, blinking back tears.

"I just want to be with you, Mommy," he said.

Every day it was the same thing. He was gentle, too vulnerable for his own good, but astonishingly persistent, she had to give him that.

"Mommy has things to do," she said. "We've talked about this. Mommy is working now. Would you like it if instead of watching TV down here with your brothers and sister Mommy left you with a babysitter?"

Henry sadly shook his head no.

"Well, then go watch television," Lisa said, nudging him softly on the shoulder. "Go on."

Her heart seemed to drain of blood as she watched his defeated little figure trudge away. She sucked in a chest full of air and whirled around, heading up the stairs before she had to look at him for one more minute, which might just be her downfall. And his downfall too. It was vital that the entire family grow accustomed as quickly as possible to the new order of things. The children had to learn to be more independent, to rely on themselves and one another for entertainment and basic necessities like snacks and comfort. And Lisa at the same time had to give herself permission to get her work done so she could move into her new life as well.

Sitting back on the bed, she opened the notebook on her lap with a new sense of purpose and lifted the remote control, intending to turn off the TV. The show featuring the mothers and daughters in love with the same guy had ended, and a new one had begun. A heavy-breasted woman in a tight white blouse and large gold hoop earrings sat implacably in a red swivel chair, while beside her a man with a crew cut was slumped, his knees spread above a pair of pristine work boots. Across the bottom of the screen was printed the words: "I never told you this but. . . ."

"Ramona," said the host. "Is there anything you want to tell Darren before we open the curtain?"

Ramona looked toward the ceiling, as if she'd never considered this question before.

"No," she said finally.

Was there anything that Lisa had never told Tommy? What would be behind the curtain if they were on this program?

This.

The TV watching.

The days she was claiming to work but instead did nothing.

The dirty laundry, which she'd been hiding in the old coal bin in the basement.

The kids' teeth, which hadn't been brushed, not once, since she'd been home.

The pain that crippled her if she tried to do anything more energetic than climb the stairs to watch more TV. That sometimes crippled her even then.

The calls from her friends that she never returned, even though she knew Juliette was crushed about the pregnancy that wasn't, and Anne was struggling to make a final break with Damian. And then there was Deirdre, who left long rambling messages on the nights when she was alone in the city, talking about her adventures but also inviting Lisa to call and talk about how she was really doing.

She felt a tug on the covers beneath her and looked down to find Henry trying to haul himself onto the bed.

"Henry, go back downstairs."

Henry kept standing there. "No," he said finally.

"What do you mean, no?"

His tears had left grimy tracks on his cheeks. There was chocolate milk crusted into the corners of his mouth and sleep still in his eyes, even though night was falling again.

"I want to stay with you," the little boy said.

He hesitated near the edge of the bed, and then suddenly

lunged again, grabbing two fistfuls of the bedspread to hoist himself up.

"I told you no," she snapped, squeezing her hands into fists and stuffing them under her thighs. "Go back downstairs with Matty and Will."

Henry didn't respond but kept crawling onto the bed, his knee digging in her ankle, his hand gripping her knee.

"You can't be up here," Lisa said.

Heaving a sigh, he hurled himself onto his side, his dark head—he was the only one of the boys with Tommy's coloring—heavy on her thighs and his face away from her and toward the TV, where Ramona seemed to be revealing that she had once been Ramon.

"Matty!" Lisa shouted, thinking wildly that her oldest son might be able to pry his little brother loose and bring him downstairs.

She turned down the volume on the television, aware of how warm and solid Henry's head felt on her lap, and heard the commotion downstairs. There was squealing and there was the thump of feet tearing across the living room.

"Are the other kids going wild down there?" Lisa asked her son.

Henry's little shoulders heaved a shrug. She heard a door slam and then Daisy's crazed laughter.

"Are you feeling tired today?" she asked him. It was taking all her energy to keep from reaching out and stroking the boy's dark matted hair.

He shrugged again, but then he said something so softly that she had to ask him to repeat it.

"I miss you, Mommy," he said.

She did reach out then and touch his shoulder.

"I'm right here, baby."

She felt him shake his head no, and she tightened her grip.

"Yes," she said. "I'm right here."

He sighed deeply at that and settled even farther into her thighs. Drawing a breath in through her nose, Lisa flicked off the TV and sank back into the pillows, closing her eyes. Tommy would be home by six, but there was time before that to rest for just a minute. It was quieter again downstairs—Yu-Gi-Oh must be on—and Henry was so warm on her lap.

She wasn't aware that she'd fallen asleep, but she opened her eyes to see that it was black outside the windows and the other three children were standing solemnly by her bed gazing at her. Henry snored in her lap, his little body soft and warm, wrapped around her outstretched legs.

"How come he gets to be up here?" Will asked.

Daisy didn't wait for an answer. She vaulted onto the bed and snuggled into Lisa's side, lifting the remote control and switching on the TV. After a moment, Will followed his sister's lead, burrowing into Tommy's side of the bed. Matt waited, peering at Lisa with a frightened look on his face as if he expected her to start yelling, but when she didn't say anything he sat gingerly on the foot of the bed.

"Matty," Lisa said. "You can come sit here next to me."

He looked back at the full bed. Only when she scooted toward the center and held out her left arm did he shamble back and perch beside her, and then allow her to pull him closer.

The only time they had ever been all together in bed like

this was when Daisy was born, and that was only long enough for Tommy to snap a picture. There had never been time to just *be*. How was it possible, she wondered, that it had taken every available instant to do all their activities and keep the house running smoothly? How could she have been so sure she was doing everything she was supposed to do, and left out this?

CHAPTER 19

Anne

With a huge sigh, Anne heaved herself up from her office chair and retrieved her coat from where it hung on the back of her door. It was physically painful, almost, for her to leave work at the end of the day. As long as she was in the office, she could put Damian and their separation out of her mind and out of her heart. As long as she was in the office, she was Anne Dobrowski, senior vice president, safe in the world of marketing reports and efficiency studies. But even as she walked toward the door, she felt the layers of protection her job afforded her peel away and the pain rise up again.

There was the pressure now too to leave work in time to let Consuelo go home, but that meant trying to sneak out without the even more senior executives seeing her. And at home, there was more to do than ever before, more responsibility to be everything for Clementine and to keep the house running smoothly as well. Had Damian really done so much? It had never seemed like it, but still Anne missed his help.

An icy wind whipped down the canyon of Forty-second Street from the Hudson and Anne clutched her collar more tightly around her throat, tucking her chin and mouth down into the soft fabric as she made her way west from Times Square to the bus terminal on Eighth Avenue. She hated being in this anonymous crowd, her proximity to all these untouchable bodies underscoring her physical isolation. Sometimes, she moved her hand at the moment the deli counterman gave her her change so that his fingers would brush her palm, and she'd taken to snuggling with Clementine so much that the tables had turned and it was her little girl who always pulled away first.

It was inside Port Authority, stepping onto the escalator up to the second level, that she felt someone close behind her. Too close. Her heartbeat jumped and she sprinted up the moving stairs, but he—she somehow knew it was a he—quickened his step to keep pace with hers. It's someone trying to catch his bus, she told herself. There are people all around; this will be okay. But in the wide and crowded hallway, when she took off at a run as if she were late for her own bus, she could hear his footsteps pounding behind her.

"Anne."

She heard her name and then almost instantly felt the fingers dig into her arm. Opening her mouth and feeling a scream gather in her throat, she whirled around. But the second before her eyes locked on his she realized what of course she'd known on some level all along: it was Damian.

"No!" she cried, wrenching her arm away. "Leave me alone."

"Anne. Please."

He looked terrible, hollow-cheeked, unshaven, his brown hair greasy and his skin the grayish pale of day-old pancake batter. He'd been calling her, first just at home but lately at the office too, even more insistently after she'd confronted him with the evidence of his long trail of affairs. But the evasions and rationalizations he'd offered in response had only made it more clear to her that he would continue to be who he had always been. He was not going to change, their marriage was not going to change. The only hope for change was in her.

"Anne," he said again, holding out his hand like a beggar. "Have some mercy."

"It's over, Damian," she said, swiveling around and walking fast to the next escalator.

But she could feel him following her and she knew this encounter wasn't over. She knew she didn't even want it to be over. She hated him, she was terrified of letting him back into her life, and yet she missed him so much, longed for him after Clementine was asleep and she lay huddled alone under the comforter, unable to stop shivering.

"Anne." His voice was behind her, his breath against her hair. "Darling."

She wouldn't turn around but just kept moving up the escalator, increasing her pace. The escalator reached the landing and she clicked off down the hallway, focused on the bus that was waiting to take her home.

"Anne, won't you even speak to me?" he said, the tiny edge of a whine creeping into his voice. "I got those papers, the divorce papers you sent, and you can't really want to go ahead with this."

Up ahead was the end of the long line of people waiting to get onto the 6:10 bus Anne took home every night, the one that pulled up to the corner around from her house at three minutes before 7:00. Anne joined the bus line and felt Damian slip into the line behind her.

"Doll." He touched her shoulder, and she flinched, inching forward to the bus door, still keeping her head turned resolutely to the front.

"Can't we go somewhere and have a drink? Talk about things."

"I have to get back for Clementine," she said. The readily acceptable explanation.

"I'll go with you," he said eagerly. "We'll have dinner together, the three of us, she'll love that, and then we'll put the sprog to bed and have a good chat, you and me."

She looked at him now while continuing to move toward the bus. He was last in line. She could imagine how it would be: the delighted Clementine springing into her father's arms, chatting excitedly as she showed him her new drawings and homework projects while Anne fixed their customary pasta for dinner, the three of them sitting together at the round oak table just as always. Damian would insist on being the one to put Clementine to bed, and then he and Anne would sit on the sofa, begin talking, end up in each other's arms. She could almost imagine that she wanted him to come back home.

"I'm so angry at you, Damian," she said, turning to him.

"I know, doll," he said, seeming to try and rise to the opening she'd given him. "And I'm so sorry about everything. I've been such a fool. I love you and Clem so much, and all I want to do is make up for everything so that you'll let me come home."

She was listening, and although all those words sounded right, although anybody might have guessed that those were precisely the things she needed to hear, they weren't doing it for her.

"Please," he said for what seemed like the twelfth time. "Just let's talk. You owe me that."

Owe him? She felt a tiny explosion, like a blood vessel bursting in her temple. She *owed* him? She had just paid the MasterCard bill, on which he was charging his meals and his dry cleaning and even pharmacy purchases—what was he buying, anyway? antidepressants? *condoms?*—since their separation. Despite being the highest-earning woman at her firm, her house was mortgaged to the limit and her bank account was depleted. Even her retirement account as well as Clementine's pitiful college fund had been raided to underwrite his films. Including the film starring his prostitute bride.

It was her turn to climb the tall stairs onto the bus and she suddenly felt panicky, realizing that all she wanted was for him to not be there, for her to not have to make this choice, to make and remake this awful choice. But here he was, following her onto the bus. She looked from the driver to Damian and back again, calculating what she was willing to do to get rid of him. Scream? Tell the driver he was harassing her? If she just told Damian to go, would he listen?

She ripped a ticket from her little blue booklet and handed it to the driver.

"Ticket?" the driver said to Damian, who was right behind her, up on the stairs.

"Anne?" said Damian.

He didn't have a ticket, and the bus drivers didn't take cash. Anne remembered someone at a dinner party teasing him once about his refusal to buy a monthly supply of bus tickets like ordinary commuters, saying, "Wow, that's incredible optimism, to believe every day that something might happen that will mean you won't have to ride the bus home."

Or even go home.

The driver was impatiently holding out his hand. Damian looked beseechingly at Anne.

"Come on, darling," he said, but betraying the "darling" by letting the old wheedling edge back into his voice. "Give us a ticket."

Anne didn't say anything, just turned her back and moved down the aisle, into the depths of the crowded bus.

"Make up your mind, buddy," she heard the driver say in his cranky voice. "You either got a ticket or you got to get off the bus."

"Anne, please!" Damian yelled.

Anne tucked her head back into her collar, avoiding the eyes of the passengers who stared up from their seats at her. She hated the idea that these people she didn't know but saw nearly every day would now have this in their minds every time they looked at her.

"All right, that's it!" the driver said, and then she heard the decisive clap of the bus door slamming shut.

Anne sank into the middle seat of the very back row, her head still bowed. The bus jerked and its lights dimmed and it pulled back from its stall and then lurched forward toward home, fumes and icy air seeping through the windows. Outside the tinted glass, all was dim and shadowy. From the corner of her eye, Anne could barely make out the figure of a man leaping and waving and running after the bus, a man who might have been calling her name.

CHAPTER 20

Juliette

Juliette sat in the gray and chrome waiting room of the best fertility specialist in Manhattan, trying very hard to concentrate on the *Vogue* in her lap and to ignore the fact that Cooper was now a full forty minutes late.

"Mrs. Chalfont?"

Just keep reading, she told herself. His meeting ran late, he was tied up in traffic, he'll be here any second.

"Mrs. Chalfont!"

The nurse was standing over her now. When Juliette looked up, she saw for the first time that she was the only one left in the waiting room.

"Mrs. Chalfont, we're getting ready to close down for lunch."

"I'm sure my husband will be here in a minute," Juliette said. "Couldn't you get started with me until he arrives?"

"I'm sorry, Mrs. Chalfont, but our initial testing is always done on the male partner first, as that procedure is simpler and less invasive."

"Please," Juliette said, frantic at the idea that she was going to lose this appointment. When she turned out not to have been pregnant after all last month, she'd decided that she had to act to make sure she conceived while Cooper was still in a cooperative frame of mind. She'd used every possible connection, from the president of the hospital where she headed the volunteer board to Paul's Manhattan doctor friends, to get this practice to squeeze her in. Where was Cooper? She kept getting voice mail on both his cell and his office phone; he had to be on his way uptown, stuck in a cab. "Won't you let me try to phone my husband one more time and see where he is?"

Fumbling with her cell phone as the nurse loomed over her, Juliette dialed Cooper's cell only to get his voice mail. Then, thinking his assistant would at least be able to tell her when he'd left the office, she called his work number. But it wasn't his assistant who answered. It was Cooper himself.

"What are you doing there?" she managed to choke out. "I've been waiting for you for nearly an hour at the doctor's office."

"I'm sorry," he said lightly. "I'm afraid I won't be able to make it."

"You won't be able to make it! Cooper, I reminded you twelve times about this appointment. I called you two hours ago when I left home to make sure you were going to be here. Don't tell me you can't make it!"

"I said I'm sorry, sweetie. It was unavoidable."

Juliette swiveled away from the nurse. "The next opening they have is in June, Cooper. June!"

"I don't know why we have to rush into this, anyway. I have an idea. Why don't we go to Paris, just the two of us. That will probably get us closer to having a baby than a whole team of doctors."

"Cooper, no!" Juliette cried, completely horrified. For the past two months, their marriage had seemed to be on a totally different track. They were both making an effort to be loving and affectionate with each another, even romantic, even sexy. She had believed they were on the same page now in pursuing the pregnancy, not only in trying for another baby, but also in revving directly to the fertility doctor. This was the first time he'd given even a hint of backtracking.

You have to meet him halfway, she reminded herself. "If the doctors don't find anything wrong, then fine, I'll give it six months or a year to happen on its own," she said, in a more conciliatory tone. "But if I don't get pregnant and we start infertility treatments when I'm thirty-seven or thirty-eight, it's going to be that much more difficult."

Up until this point, she was annoyed with Cooper but still felt fairly reasonable. She told herself to be realistic: Cooper was always getting held up at work, no guy likes to be examined down there, and he wasn't so keen on this baby thing in the first place.

"Okay," she said, working to keep her voice calm. "I'll reschedule. Maybe I'll look around for another doctor, someone who can get us in sooner."

She noticed that the nurse had padded away and heard the

sound of the frosted glass barrier between the waiting room and the inner sanctum sliding shut.

"The thing is," said Cooper, "I don't think I'm as ready as you to go the high-tech route."

Everything went still. "When do you think you'll be ready, Cooper?"

He cleared his throat. "See, my feeling is, about the baby, if it happens, it happens. But I'm not interested in taking any extraordinary measures to get you pregnant."

"Never?" she managed to say.

"I suppose that's right. Never."

Juliette stood up, as if commanded by a hidden force. She pushed through the heavy glass door out onto Park Avenue and sailed her cell phone, with Cooper's voice still squawking from it—"Juliette! Are you there, Juliette?"—into the street. She watched it skitter across the pavement and splinter beneath the wheels of a speeding taxi. Instantly, she felt freer, if slightly panicky that now Heather wouldn't be able to reach her if there were a problem with Trey. If Heather really needed someone, Juliette reminded herself, she knew where to reach Cooper. Cooper was, after all, Trey's parent too.

The sun was beaming down from a cloudless sky, the air freakishly warm for February. People had left their offices for lunch wearing only suit jackets, and soon, walking fast, feeling sweat break out on her upper lip and under her arms and along the waistband of her snug, Cooper-friendly skirt, Juliette took off her own coat. She carried it for a few blocks but then, on impulse as she was passing an overstuffed city-regulation garbage can, she laid it on top of the mound of paper cups and fast-food bags. Halfway down the block, she had a moment of regret—that coat had cost $700, on sale!—but by the time she looked back, a twentysomething fashionista was already examining the coat's Dolce & Gabanna label and looking around as if for a hidden camera.

Like the phone, she felt better without the coat, faster, more adventurous. She wished she were wearing her old loose-knit clothes and flat comfy shoes, but then again her anger at Cooper compensated for the drag of her tight skirt and high heels. She was flying; she was just afraid of what might happen if she stopped.

Weaving along the city streets, oxygen filling her lungs, she found herself wishing she could talk to Nick. He continued to call her, during the day when she was home alone, whether he was in the city or on the road. He let her talk about Cooper, about the baby; he'd been the only one, in the end, who expressed much real sympathy when she turned out not to be pregnant after all. She couldn't believe she'd even told him about that, but instead of backing off when she revealed the details—the bloody skirt, the sense of everything inside her flooding out—he'd kept asking for more. He'd want to know what had just happened, how she felt now. No phone, she reminded herself. Plus he's gone, off in Detroit or Chicago or Miami, being a musician, living his real life, the one that didn't include her.

As her real life certainly didn't include him. She'd made it clear that she wasn't going to sleep with him, get involved with him, even see him one on one. Still, she found herself feeling closer and closer to him. But he was like an imaginary friend, one who she could reveal everything to, with whom she could be her true self, but who wasn't going to pop up at the dinner table.

Below Fourteenth Street, she caught sight of herself in the broad windows of a salon, mascara smudged beneath her wild eyes, reddened lips open like a wound. Her long hair was wind-blown and frizzed, disheveled as a witch's wig. She stopped and stood rooted to the dirty sidewalk, staring at her reflection. Who was this person? Not anyone she wanted to be.

Without consideration, Juliette flung open the door of the salon and marched over to where a very young, very slender, and very frightened-looking young man stood beside a hair-dressing chair.

"I want you to cut it all off," she said.

At that, he looked even more frightened, as well as confused.

"My hair!" she cried, throwing herself into the chair. "It all has to go!"

He took a timid step forward, and gingerly lifted a strand of her thick hair.

"Are you sure?" he said.

Was she sure? She had never cut her hair, not short anyway. It was long in her first school photos, it was long in her graduation pictures, it was long in her wedding album, it was long now. She had always thought she would sail into old age with her long hair intact, silver and piled majestically atop her head. Surrounded by children and grandchildren.

She squeezed her eyes shut. "Cut it," she commanded.

"Oooh," the stylist said, gathering enthusiasm as his scissors moved over her head, sending substantial lengths of hair to the floor, "wait till you see how you look with this cut. You are going to look *hot.*"

"I don't care about hot," Juliette said, wiggling out of her shoes and leaning back in the chair. "I just want it gone."

She kept her eyes closed for the whole thing. The more he cut, the better it felt. She didn't look when he finished cutting and started to blow-dry and chattered about his trip to Barcelona. She didn't look until he was finished and insisted, holding up the small mirror so she could see the back of her head.

And then she burst out laughing. She didn't know what she expected, but with her hair cropped and artfully disheveled, she looked younger, freer, sexier. And with her hair gone, she realized, she looked exactly like Trey. Like her own little boy. She'd always said he looked like Cooper, but now she realized she'd just been saying that in a vain attempt to make Cooper feel closer to his son. It was she that Trey looked like. She who looked like Trey.

Out on the street again, she felt like some twisted version of Superman: that transformed. Her head, her entire body, seemed supernaturally light, and she felt more energetic, clearer of vision. She looked up at the buildings rising along the other side of Broadway, and suddenly she saw it: NYU. A mere few blocks west of here was the Education Building, which housed the Occupational Therapy department. The application deadline was—oh my God, it was tomorrow. Since November, the push toward having another child had put the school idea so far on the back burner that she'd nearly forgotten it. She'd done nothing to prepare to apply, had even recycled all her pamphlets and forms on mixed-paper day. But she could pick up a new set, get busy right away, work on them all night, bring them back down here herself. She could at least try.

But Cooper would disapprove. Even before she'd introduced the possibility of another child, Cooper had not been thrilled by the idea of her going back to school. And if she and Cooper stayed married, chances were she'd get pregnant eventually, even without the intervention of a fertility doctor.

If she and Cooper stayed married.

She had come this far and continued to go through the motions of entering the university building, finding her way to the OT department, gathering the material she needed. But she found herself, for the first time all day, gripped by doubt. Her hair was gone, she had decided to apply to school, Cooper had drawn a line about how far he would go to have another baby, but did this really mean her marriage was over? Was she in any way prepared to strike out on her own? Thinking about how much Anne missed Damian, how tough it was for Deirdre to put herself out there every day, made her panicky about how difficult it would be to go it alone. And she didn't even have a talent like Deirdre or a career like Anne, just an interest it was going to take years of school to turn into anything that would earn her a living.

But this wasn't about money, was it? She remembered what Cooper had said to her that night, about how it was his money, and the reality behind that statement, that she was in fact entitled to half of everything he owned. There was no practical reason for her to be worried about money; even if she left Cooper, there would be enough for her to spend the rest of her life shopping and lunching and going to the theater, if that's what she wanted to do.

But that *wasn't* what she wanted to do. She didn't care about money; she certainly didn't care about the big house and the fancy furniture, about the cars or the jewelry. What she'd wanted all along from Cooper, from his money, was not a fat bank account or lots of things, but security. And so why, the longer they were married, did she feel less and less secure?

She had to talk to Deirdre. Deirdre and she may have grown distant from each other over the past few months, but Deirdre knew what it felt like to wrestle with doubts about your marriage and the desire to be someone that the world didn't necessarily want you to be. She had tried to arrange a lunch in the city with Deirdre today, but Deirdre had said she was going to an audition, suggesting they get together instead late in the afternoon in the East Village near Nick's place. Or even at Nick's place itself—Deirdre was spending the night in the city again, headed to another audition first thing tomorrow morning. Juliette had begged off, assuming she'd be heading out to Homewood to beat the rush hour. But now seeing Deirdre seemed more important than hurrying home.

With her cell phone gone, she was forced to look for a pay phone, never an easy task in Manhattan but especially difficult now that most of the world no longer needed them. She walked four blocks before she found one, and another four before she found one that worked—and then dialed Deirdre's cell number only to reach her voice mail. Damn. After two more unsuccessful tries, plus two to Nick's home phone, where she encountered a busy signal, she decided it would be faster for her to walk over to the apartment than to keep standing there dialing the germ-ridden pay phone.

Three minutes later she was standing on Nick's brownstone stoop, ringing his bell. The intercom crackled, but nothing else.

"Deirdre?" Juliette said, into the tarnished brass loudspeaker. "Deirdre, are you there?"

And then suddenly, the shiny black door swung open and there stood Nick Ruby, looking as surprised to see her as she was to see him.

"You're finally here," he said.

"I'm not here to see you. I thought you were out of town."

"My gig got cancelled," he said. "Deirdre decided to head home for tonight."

He stood there staring at her and then, without a word, reached out and touched her short hair.

"You hate it," she said, bringing her own hand to her head.

"On the contrary." He smiled and kept his hand where it was.

"It was an impulse." She looked him directly in his dark brown eyes, which was not easy, considering how distracting it was to have his fingers against the side of her bare neck.

"It was a very good impulse."

"Cooper's not going to like it at all."

"Yes," he said, "but I like it a lot."

"As much?" she whispered.

"More," he said, leaning in and bringing his lips to hers in a kiss she would feel for days.

CHAPTER 21

The March Dinner

For Deirdre, the snow that began falling unexpectedly, so thick that it blanketed the sidewalk in the time it took her to walk from the Lafayette Street subway stop to the restaurant on Second Avenue, only confirmed the magic of the day. It had happened. It had *really* happened. She had gone to the audition as Lesser arranged, she had sung, they had asked her to stay and sing again, and then again, and then they had offered her the part, there on the spot, one of the leads in the touring company of a Broadway musical.

She flew out of the audition and called Paul on her cell phone as soon as she was on the sidewalk, her racing feet barely making contact with the cement.

"That's great, sweetie," he said. "Everything you wanted."

"And you?" she asked him. "It would mean I'd have to be on

the road all week, home for probably just a day and a half. Can you really handle that?"

"Can you?" he said.

Thinking about being away from the kids for that much time, that consistently, filled her with dread. *They* seemed to be doing fine: they were thrilled to have more time with their dad, delighted with the after-care program at their school. Half the time when she was home, they were too busy with sports and friends and computer games and books—the entire world that seemed to open up to them now that they were no longer babies but full-fledged kids. It was she who found herself missing them more than she'd ever expected.

But that was part of having a career like the one she'd set out to make for herself. Here she was, exactly in the spot she'd been in way back when she quit singing, with another chance to take the path she'd decided not to follow the first time around. Thinking about it like that, all she felt was wonderful. And the rest of it, she told herself, was only fear.

As she approached the restaurant, she saw Anne and Lisa and Juliette were huddled beneath its awning, all peering anxiously at the sky and the snow.

"This wasn't supposed to happen," said Lisa, looking up, blinking hard against the snowflakes.

"I've been in an audition all day, so I had no idea what was going on in the outside world," Deirdre said, bursting with her news. "Let's go sit down. I've got something I'm dying to tell you."

She hadn't seen any of them in the month that she'd been staying part-time in the city. When she was here, every minute was filled with voice lessons and auditions and getting ready for auditions and going to see other musicians and shows. And when she was home, she was always going crazy trying to catch up on everything that went undone during the time she spent in town, including lavishing the twins with attention and talking with Paul. She and Juliette had talked on the phone—she'd heard about the haircut—but this was the first time she'd seen the results for herself. Actually, she thought, Juliette looked better now than she ever had, more natural than when she'd gotten herself all done up for Cooper's benefit, livelier and even sexier than she had in her dowdy bun and baggy clothes.

As they sat down, she noticed that Anne, too, seemed transformed, rounder and pinker; even her hair looked thicker and infused with health. She was wearing her old red lipstick again, the same vivid color as a tight turtleneck that outlined what looked like actual curves under Anne's suit jacket. Sometimes when she looked at Anne in the past, she'd think—you know, maybe you *can* be too thin. But now Anne seemed just right, and happier to boot.

Only Lisa seemed somehow diminished, peering outside at the gathering blizzard and looking pinched and anxious.

"I'm worried about getting home in this snow," Lisa said.

"The buses always run," said Deirdre. "Or the train."

She hadn't noticed this about suburbanites when she was one of them full-time, but they were always worried about how they were going to get into the city, and then as soon as they got there they began worrying about how they were going to get out.

"No," said Lisa, continuing to look out the window. Her

blonde bob was longer and no longer perfectly even at the ends, Deirdre noticed. "I drove. I think I'm going to have to get out before this gets any worse."

"Oh, no!" Deirdre cried. "I mean, can't you see how it goes? You can always leave the car here overnight and take mass transit—I'll drive it back to Homewood for you tomorrow or the next day."

"I don't want to have to do that," Lisa said flatly.

"Okay, well I was saving this news for dessert," Deirdre said, "but I'll say it while you're all still here." She drew in her breath and spread her arms for her big announcement. "I got a part!"

There was general squealing and hugging and kissing, and Deirdre had just launched into a description of the part and how she got it when Lisa interrupted her.

"I'm sorry," she said, tension still constricting her voice. "I'd love to hear about it. But I really have to go."

Lisa was already standing up, already fishing in her bag for her keys.

"But I don't want to leave yet," said Anne. "Clementine's with Damian this weekend so I don't have to be home at any special time—or really at all until Sunday afternoon."

"I know," Deirdre said, feeling inspired. "We can all spend the night at Nick's place. It'll be a pajama party. You too, Lisa."

"Thanks," Lisa said. "But I'm still heading back to Homewood."

"I'm going to go with Lisa," said Juliette. "It sounds like it will be way too crowded at Nick's."

"No, no," said Deirdre. "Nick left for Chicago today. It would just be the three of us."

"I hate to leave Lisa to drive home by herself," said Juliette.

"I don't mind going alone, honestly," said Lisa. "I just want to get a move on before this gets any worse."

"Okay," Juliette said. "If you're sure."

Deirdre was happy Juliette and Anne were staying. But watching Lisa hurry outside, looking so frail and battling to raise her umbrella against the storm, she felt a pang of concern. Guiltily, she realized that she'd barely given Lisa's health a thought in the past few months. She'd been so wrapped up in her own world. When she called and Lisa assured her she was fine, just busy, Deirdre had been happy to accept that explanation. She'd been happy, almost, to be rebuffed.

Deirdre leaned across the table.

"What's going on?" she asked. "Is she okay?"

Juliette shrugged. "She seemed fine on the drive in, talking about the house and the kids."

"But in general," Deirdre said. "She doesn't look good. Have you noticed anything?"

"I've been calling," Anne said, "but she keeps claiming she's too busy to see me."

"Me too," said Juliette.

"I don't know," said Deirdre. She had always liked it that Anne and Juliette were the kind of friends who didn't push, who weren't judgmental, who made her feel loved and accepted. But maybe someone should be challenging Lisa more, she thought. If she were in Homewood more these days, she knew, she'd be the one to do it.

She couldn't think about that now, though. This was her night, a time for celebrating. She waved for the waiter and ordered a bottle of champagne, along with their meals. When the bottle had been popped with a flourish and three glasses filled, Deirdre lifted her own glass to her friends.

"Here's to success," she said. "For all of us."

She could see through the bubbles in her glass to the restaurant's window and the snowy street beyond. Growing up in San Francisco, she'd never lost her sense of wonder at finding herself in a place where snow came down as uneventfully as sunshine. But this snowstorm looked like something else already, denser, more insistent, already mounting on streetlights and parked cars and on the shoulders of the pedestrians hunched against the storm.

A month ago, she'd been so nervous, spending her first night in Nick's apartment alone. And now she felt like the city belonged to her. She imagined her picture on the cover of the *Times* arts section, the money mounting up in the bank as record producers and movie directors came calling, an apartment for the whole family high in a building overlooking the Hudson, looking at New Jersey rather than living there.

She brought her glass to her lips and took a deep swallow. It was only then that she realized no one else was drinking.

"What's wrong?" she said. "Aren't you two happy for me?"

At that, Juliette burst into tears. "I'm sorry," she said. "I'm happy for you. I guess. But I miss you. I want you down the street from me, in Homewood. Not off in Cleveland or Pittsburgh or somewhere else every night."

Deirdre felt as if she'd been stabbed in the heart. She missed Juliette too. She missed all her friends. But did that mean they couldn't ever make changes in their individual lives?

"I have to do this, Juliette," Deirdre said. "You of all people know how much I've wanted it. We won't see each other as much, but we'll still be friends."

"Sure," Juliette said, trying to dry her tears, although new ones kept coursing down her cheek. "I know. I just . . ."

Her tears came harder again.

"Is it the baby?" asked Deirdre.

"What baby?" said Anne. "Do you think you're pregnant again?" She looked at Juliette.

"No, no. I meant the baby she wants to have," Deirdre explained. "Is that what's upsetting you?"

"I guess so," said Juliette, attempting to dry her eyes again. "I don't even know anymore." At that, she knocked back her entire glass of champagne, poured herself a refill, and drank that down too. "See. I'm happy for you."

Anne took a sip of her champagne. "I'm happy for you, too. See, this is one thing city restaurants have going for them as opposed to so many restaurants in New Jersey: liquor licenses. That's how they make all their money."

"What would it take to get a liquor license in New Jersey?" asked Deirdre.

"Money, and lots of it. I don't know how I'd ever swing it."

"So you're really thinking about doing the restaurant thing?" Deirdre asked.

"Oh, there's no way right now. I'm feeling more financial pressure than ever, without anything at all coming in from Damian, and I need the medical insurance. But I'm thinking about it all the time."

Deirdre looked at Anne with interest. Anne had been so forlorn for months now about her relationship with Damian. But even before that happened, she'd never been prone to doing wild and crazy things. In fact, taking Fridays off to be part of their moms' group seemed to be the most radical departure Anne had ever made from her workaday routine.

"What's going on with you?" Deirdre asked. "You look, I don't know—glowing."

Anne just smiled and shook her head. "Nothing definite. I'm not ready to talk about it yet."

Suddenly, Deirdre knew. All the pieces fit together. Anne loved sex and missed being in a relationship, but her marriage was over. Ergo: "You're in love, aren't you? You've got a new guy."

Anne shrugged and kept smiling. "Don't worry. If anything serious is happening I'll tell you soon. But what makes you think it's not a girl?"

"Whooo!" said Deirdre. "You're going lesbian! That'll show Damian."

That got a smile even out of Juliette.

"Can you imagine?" said Anne. "He'd probably want to watch."

"A girl tried to pick me up the other day," said Deirdre. It was at a breath class; the girl was young and blonde and dressed in pink, and Deirdre had been stunned to feel the girl's hand on her hip.

"When Damian and I were first together," Anne said, "we had a threesome with this nympho Australian girl he tended bar with in London."

"That should have been your first clue," said Deirdre.

"Oh, God, that was *far* from my first clue, and we'd been together only a few months at that point."

"So how was it?" said Juliette.

"It was, I don't know." Anne grimaced and smacked her lips. "Salty."

"Ew," Deirdre and Juliette said in tandem, making faces at each other.

"I know," said Anne. "And if you're not into that, the party's just about over."

"I'm not sure," said Juliette. "In eighth grade I had the strongest desire to touch Mary Pat McGillicuddy's boobs."

Deirdre burst out laughing as the waiter slid a steak in front of her. A steak so enormous it seemed designed to make the person eating it feel like a leader of the free world.

"Well, I did!" Juliette said. "Once, when we were sneaking cigarettes in her garage, I nearly asked her if I could."

"So what happened?"

"I chickened out," said Juliette.

"Which, in this case, was probably a good thing." Deirdre cut herself a piece of her monster steak and chewed. Why was something as simple as a steak so much better in the city than in the suburbs? "Too bad all this happened before you girls had your Pocket Rockets."

"I still haven't tried mine," said Juliette, draining the champagne bottle and ignoring her food.

"Me neither," said Deirdre. "At home Paul and I never get around to having sex, and if I packed it when I came into the city, I'd feel guilty, like I was having an affair."

"You can't have an affair with something that's four inches long and made of plastic," said Juliette.

"Catholicism," said Deirdre. "You should know about that."

"Well, mine's been working overtime," said Anne, bringing

a forkful of creamy pasta to her mouth. "Poor little thing. Now that I'm single I think I'm going to upgrade to a model with more horsepower."

"Wait a minute," said Deirdre. "I thought you said—"

"No, *you* said," countered Anne, looking around the restaurant, which, if anything, was more crowded than ever. "God, there are a lot more cute guys in here than you ever see in Homewood. Look at that guy over near the bar, the one in the dark blue jacket."

Deirdre looked and was amused to see that the man that Anne had picked out could have been Damian's twin. Damian's homosexual twin. "Gay," Deirdre said. She pointed at the best-looking men around the room: "Gay, gay. Gay. Gay."

"Ugh," said Anne. "That's so depressing."

"Yeah," said Deirdre. "Sometimes I think Nick Ruby is the last straight man below Fourteenth Street."

"How *is* Nick?" Anne asked. "What's happening between you two?"

"We almost never see each other," said Deirdre. "I only stay in his place when he's out of town, and when we're there together for more than a few minutes, all I can think about is how we could never live together. He would drive me absolutely out of my mind."

"Why's that?" said Juliette.

"He's a neat freak, for one thing," she said. "I mean, Paul is more organized than me, but if you put some change on a table in Nick's place, you turn around and it's gone. Cleaned up."

Juliette smiled. "That sounds good to me."

"Well, you can have him," Deirdre said.

Juliette flushed and fanned her neck with her hand. "Is it hot in here? It feels like they turned up the heat."

"You're supposed to feel cooler when you get your hair cut," said Deirdre, smiling. She turned to Anne. "How are you doing? How's Clementine handling the separation?"

"She's okay," Anne said. "We're both trying to shield her from tension between the two of us, or at least I am and I hope Damian is."

"When she was over the other day after school," said Juliette, still fanning herself, "when Zoe and Zack were there, she and Zoe were debating the merits of being with moms versus dads."

"My Zoe?" said Deirdre. "You heard my Zoe say this?"

Juliette nodded. "Zoe said that moms were better cooks, but dads were more fun because they didn't make you take a bath."

Wait a minute, Deirdre thought. Paul didn't make the kids take a bath?

Anne said, "Clementine's thrilled that Zoe's taking ballet with her now."

"Zoe's not taking ballet," said Deirdre. In fact, she'd told Paul specifically that she wanted Zoe to stay in gymnastics.

"No, they started this week," said Anne. "Zoe looked so cute in her tutu. I told her I'd take a picture for you so you can see her."

"Which reminds me," said Juliette. "I saw Zack's teacher when I picked the kids up from school the other day and she told me Zack had had that big breakthrough with his reading, which is fabulous."

Deirdre was speechless. Zoe had been reading by the end of kindergarten, but they'd been worried because here it was the middle of first grade and Zack still didn't seem to get it. Or at least he hadn't the last time she'd heard.

"But Paul probably told you all this."

"No," Deirdre said. "Paul hasn't told me any of this. Excuse me. I just have to go to the ladies' room."

But instead, she took her purse and went to the door of the restaurant, and when that was still too noisy, she ducked outside and huddled against the building while she dialed her home number. The entire city was hushed now, with almost no traffic on the streets. The few people who were out seemed to float along the wave of snow. When Zoe answered the phone, she panicked for a moment and nearly hung up because she felt that if she had an actual conversation with her daughter, she would start crying. Instead, she asked for Paul.

"I hear Zack is reading," she said without preamble when he came on the phone.

He hesitated. "Oh, I guess Juliette told you."

"And Zoe's taking ballet and you're the better parent because you don't make her take a bath."

"This isn't about who's the better parent, Deirdre," Paul said. "It's about who's here."

"And just because I'm not there full-time means I don't get to know what's going on, I don't get a say?" she demanded. "There were years when you were gone all the time, during your residency, when you first went to the clinic."

"And you made all the decisions then," Paul said. That was the maddening thing about him: he was invariably so calm, so rational.

"So if I go ahead and take this part, that means when I'm home I'm like, I don't know, a visiting aunt?"

"Is there an if?" Paul asked.

Was there? "I didn't think so before I heard all this," she said stonily.

"I'm not going to tell you what to do, Deirdre," Paul said, "but there are trade-offs. If you're home, you're itchy to sing. If you're singing, you have to let go at home. And if you let it bother you too much, you're in trouble."

"I need stronger boundaries," she said.

That's what Nick had told her, that if she were going to be a singer she had to get tougher about rejection, to be less vulnerable to what people thought of her, had to keep her emotions from contaminating her career and vice versa. So easy for him to say, he who'd never had babies and had those boundaries pierced and poked and shoved aside. Her boundaries were like the lungs of an emphysema patient, Deirdre thought, remembering how the doctor had described her grandfather's lungs: like lace.

CHAPTER 22

Juliette

Standing in the dingy hallway, waiting as Deirdre struggled to undo the three locks to Nick Ruby's apartment, Juliette held her breath, not knowing what to expect. That day on the stoop, the day of the kiss, she hadn't even stepped inside the building. There'd been a line then, the line between the public place of the street and the privacy of his apartment, that she hadn't been willing to cross, especially not after she'd strayed over the last line she'd drawn, the one dividing talking and touching, the one separating fantasy from reality.

Now she was redrawing the line again. It was all right to go into his building, into his apartment, because he wasn't there. But when the last lock finally loosened and the door swung open, Juliette was so stunned she kept standing in the hallway, unable to believe her eyes. The only grown-up apartments she'd been to in New York—the only apartments she'd been to since her fashion school and early career days, when everyone lived in tiny bare rooms—belonged to Cooper's business associates, and they were huge lavish affairs, horizontal mansions. Or they were entire town houses, ranging up several stories, seemingly to the sky. Juliette felt as poor in these places as she usually felt embarrassingly rich in the house she shared with Cooper—rich compared with most other people in Homewood and especially rich compared with the way she'd grown up.

But what she felt gazing around Nick's apartment for the first time wasn't poor and wasn't rich but at home. There was something about it that reminded her of her mother's apartment in Paris, even the little house where they'd lived in Pennsylvania when she was very young: the cleverness about making a small space look beautiful, look like a home, look *expensive*. And then there was a sophistication of taste that Juliette thought of as French or at least European. Nick was obviously a minimalist, but each thing he had—the single cushion on the only chair, for instance—was perfect.

And yet there was something else, some level of comfort combined with an individualism that signaled this place was constructed for his eyes alone, that he did not care what anyone else thought of him or his home. The one beautiful room in the Pennsylvania house was designed for show, to let the world know that Juliette's mother was a woman of culture and style, a woman from an old family with great theoretical wealth. If little actual money.

But this room . . . Juliette imagined Nick alone here, his length sprawled down the charcoal flannel sofa, his great head on the blue silk pillow, gazing at the ceiling while he listened to one of the thousands of CDs that filled the shelves that covered the longest wall of the living room.

"This place," she breathed, taking it in, searching her mind for the right word, " . . . is spectacular."

Deirdre gave her a strange look. "You think?"

Juliette looked at Deirdre, not attempting to hide the puzzlement on her face. "Of course, don't you?"

"I don't know," Deirdre said. "To me it looks a little . . . empty."

That made sense, Juliette thought, considering that every surface in Deirdre's house seemed to be covered with a pillow or a painting or a bowl or a stack of books.

Juliette shook her head and said, "I've got to call Cooper."

She slipped into the bedroom with her cell phone to make the call. This would be the first time she'd ever left Trey overnight, but she thought, Cooper has to learn to deal with his son. If he won't have another child, at least he can be a father to the one he's got.

But she had not finished dialing the number when she heard the sound of a door and then voices, Deirdre's and a man's, in the next room. She clicked off the phone and stood in the bedroom listening, refusing to believe what her ears were telling her. Deirdre had sworn Nick was in Chicago; how could he possibly have gotten back in this storm? Juliette stood frozen behind the closed door, listening to the voice that had become so familiar. Juliette heard Deirdre say her name, and then silence, and then, just as she was about to open the bedroom door and see the scene for herself, the door opened upon her and there stood Nick Ruby, gazing at her as if she were an apparition.

"You're supposed to be away," she blurted.

"I tried my best," he said, smiling a little. "My plane was grounded."

"He was at the airport for seven hours," Deirdre said behind him.

"Well, I'm leaving," Juliette said, pushing past the bulk of him, doing her best not to look at him.

"You can't leave—" Deirdre started to say.

"Watch me," said Juliette, knowing she sounded harsh when what she felt was panicky, flummoxed by seeing Nick Ruby and by the idea that she might be forced to not only spend the night in his company but also hide what had passed between them. She had shrugged on her coat, grabbed her bag, tied her wool challis scarf tight under her chin like a grandma going off to market.

"Juliette, this is nuts!" Deirdre called after her.

She was already flying down the stairs, her fingers light on the metal banister.

"Juliette!" Now he was coming down after her, his feet surprisingly light and quick on the wet stone. Juliette had a flash of her father, a moment she had not remembered for years, singing "That Old Soft Shoe," and shuffling in his Italian leather slippers across the tile of the Pennsylvania kitchen floor. "Juliette, wait!"

"Don't!" she barked, stopping in her tracks and swinging around to face him, brandishing her hand at him as if it held a knife.

"I didn't mean . . . ," he began. "It's just, the snow."

"Don't move another inch," she said. "I am going down the stairs now, and I don't want you to follow me."

The door of another apartment clicked open, and a pair of eyes peered at them through the crack.

"Stay there," Juliette ordered, thinking he was so much more handsome than she had ever noticed before. And larger too, and more threatening in his persistence. But what felt truly threatening was herself, the feeling in her chest. It was that feeling that she had to escape.

Slowly, she began backing down the stairs away from him, and then swiveled and began walking at a normal pace, all her attention trained on listening for him behind her. If he followed her even one step, she thought, if he spoke so much as one word to her, she felt as if she would explode. Or rush into his arms.

But she heard nothing. She reached the little lobby with its white and brown tiled floor and brass mailboxes and heavy glass door. Outside, the snow still fell, consuming all the lamplight. The street was near deserted, snow mounded on the parked cars, the pavement covered with white in the absence of traffic, what footprints there were on the sidewalk filling rapidly with the white powder.

It felt different outside, different from the way New York had ever felt, and suddenly Juliette knew why. It was the silence, the nearly total silence, which combined with the whiteness made the city that much more beautiful, that much more magical. She was not frightened being out there alone, as she had expected to be, and instead felt glad to be away from Nick Ruby's apartment, away from home, to be exactly here in this singular moment.

When she reached the corner of Avenue A, she stopped there not because there was any traffic but just because she wanted to savor the moment of having already left, but not having actively begun to worry about how she was going to get home. She turned around then and looked back down the street, back at Nick Ruby's building, and then up to the top floor where his apartment was. That's when she saw them, all three of them, silhouetted against the golden light from inside, pressed against the window looking down at her.

She arrived home, dozing on and off in the back of the huge car, after more than four hours of traveling, the sky still dark and thick with snow, the roads empty except for the plows. The limousine headlights illuminated one patch of white in the world of white. The driver refused to get out but just sat there, his eyes trained straight ahead while she labored over the drifts toward the dark house. She'd had her key out and in her hand since they'd turned off the highway, maybe an hour ago, and felt as if she were crossing the finish line of a marathon as she slipped it into the lock.

Inside, the house was dark and quiet and cool, the only sound the hum of the refrigerator. Juliette felt like a thief, or a spirit, slipping silently across the carpet and up the stairs, heading directly for Trey's room. There, he was fast asleep, sprawled on his back, his mouth open as if in surprise and his arms flung wide, covers half kicked off. Juliette pulled the comforter close around him and kissed his forehead, and the little boy mumbled, and turned on his side.

Down the hall, she could hear Cooper snoring. Better not wake him yet. Instead of exhausted, what she expected to feel, she found herself restless. She knew what she'd do: she'd shovel the snow.

Now that she was no longer trying to make her way through it, the snow seemed magnificent, epic. It came up over the top of Cooper's tall galoshes, grazed the hem of his jacket, the old one she used to shovel snow. It had stopped falling from the sky but blew up in gusts around her, like little geysers, or ghosts rising from the powdery drifts.

Her goal was to clear a path to the street, telling herself this was a safety basic—what if there was a fire, and the firefighters had to get to the house to rescue them?—and also imagined how pleased Cooper would be to wake up and find he wouldn't have to wait for Crazy Bob to show up with the snowblower to release him from the house so he could head into the city for his usual Saturday morning in the office.

She hoped.

Then she'd be alone at home with Trey. Exactly the way she liked it.

She stood up straight, staring slack-jawed at the expanse of white before her, paralyzed by a sudden piece of knowledge that seemed as solid as a boulder in her path. She didn't want to be with Cooper. Not tomorrow, not ever. Their entire marriage was predicated on his absence, on their physical separation, on their failure to connect on any level. It was only by not seeing each other, not communicating at all, that they could bear to stay together.

That was the real problem with the baby issue. It wasn't, in the end, that they disagreed about whether to have another baby, although that was a problem too, or that they didn't connect in bed, though of course that was also a problem. But the real problem was that deciding whether to have another baby required both of them to reveal their true and important feelings to each other, and they couldn't do that. Didn't want to do it, and never had.

They'd gotten married because all the surface qualities were in sync, and they'd never really had to test whether they agreed in any more essential ways. Even Trey's illness hadn't forced them to look deeper, because Cooper had always simply left Trey to Juliette. And Juliette had liked it that way.

She didn't love Cooper—Juliette saw that clearly now. And now that she'd begun demanding more from herself, she was no longer willing to settle for a marriage that bought her a free ride, and nothing else of value. She wasn't willing to settle for so little on Trey's behalf either. Trey deserved a real father, and if Cooper wasn't willing to do his share while she was on the scene, maybe things would be different when he had no choice but to handle his son on his own.

She began shoveling again, faster than before, her thoughts moving to Nick. Where was Nick in all this? Nick was nowhere. Nick was everywhere. Nick did not exist. Nick was the only man she had ever thought she might love. That truth pierced her like a spear, stopping her cold. Breathing heavily, sweating inside the parka, she stood upright and leaned on the shovel, noticing that the sky was beginning to lighten to dawn.

Suddenly she was tired, so tired she felt as if she could lie down beside the walk and fall asleep right there in the enormous feather bed of snow, like a lost traveler seduced by the illusion of comfort. But she shook herself awake enough to trudge back into the house and slip out of the snow-covered gear, letting the boots and jacket and drenched socks lie near the door, dripping onto the beige carpet. The house was as silent as the blizzard outside, and she tiptoed with her frozen bare feet across the carpet and upstairs through the darkness.

She undressed just inside her bedroom doorway, leaving her sweater and pants in an uncharacteristic crumple on the little slipper chair, and slipped her bra off without actually removing her thin silk turtleneck. Then she tiptoed over to the big bed and slid beneath the feather comforter, reaching a hand out to Cooper.

"Hmmmm?" he said.

Wake him now, or let him sleep and talk later? It seemed cruel to wake him, but cowardly to put off the confrontation.

"Time is it?" Cooper mumbled.

She checked the bedside clock. "Five."

"Hmmmm," he said. "I should go."

She could say nothing and close her eyes, and he'd get up and get dressed and leave the house so quietly she wouldn't even hear him, and maybe he'd end up staying at his club in the city, and soon the memory of tonight might melt away like the snow. Everything would be easier that way, wouldn't it?

"Cooper," she said. "I need to talk with you."

"Oh, God, Juli," he said, groaning and rolling away from her. "Can't this wait for another time? I've got a desk full of work waiting for me and a blizzard to wade through to get to it."

"No," she said simply. "It can't wait."

He swiveled his head back toward her. "This is about the baby idea again, isn't it?"

"No," she said. "It isn't."

"Well, what is it then? Your graduate school idea? Because I've been thinking about that, and I've decided it's all right with me if you want to do that."

"I'll find out April fifteenth whether I'm accepted."

"What?"

"I already applied, Cooper. To NYU. I'll find out on April fifteenth whether I get in, but if I don't, I'm going to apply somewhere else for next year."

"That's good," he said cautiously. "I'm glad you're looking ahead."

"I am, Cooper. And what I want to tell you is, I don't want to be married to you anymore."

It was amazing how easy it felt, to finally get those words out. Easier than it had been keeping them in, pushing them away all this time.

There was a long silence. Cooper was lying on his back now, looking at the ceiling and breathing. The room was getting lighter by the second as the sun rose and hit the fresh snow.

At last Cooper spoke. "I don't believe you mean that," he said.

She had made a mistake, she saw now, to raise this issue in bed. Bed was where you said I love you for the first time, where you proposed, not where you asked for a divorce. But that was, Juliette supposed, further evidence of how little meaning their bed had come to hold for her. Her thoughts darted to Anne: how had Anne managed to cross this divide with Damian, when she still loved him, was still attracted to him? If Juliette felt those feelings, she might never have managed to bring herself to make this move, no matter what Cooper did to her. But she felt no such ambivalence, and only wanted him to know how sure she was.

"Believe it, Cooper."

He shook his head. "What are you going to do?" he said, his voice rising. "You can't do anything on your own. You need me to pay the bills, to maintain the house, to decide for you whether you're going to put one goddamn foot in front of the other."

"That's not true," she said, trying to keep her voice firm, sitting up in the bed.

"It's not?" he said. "The only thing you've ever done without me leading you every step of the way is to cut your hair. Oh, and I guess apply to that absurd graduate program."

This was helping. The ridicule in his voice was something she had long unquestioningly taken to heart—it's true, that graduate program is absurd, I can't do anything on my own! But now she saw that his real agenda was to make her feel helpless, to ensure her continued dependence on him. For years, she had been entirely complicit in this. No more.

There was no point in arguing, though. He could still beat her at any argument, would always be able to, with his MBA training and his corporate experience and, most of all, with his inherent sense of entitlement.

"I want a divorce, Cooper," she said. Unqualified. Irrefutable.

"What is this really about?" Cooper said. "This is about the baby thing again, isn't it? All right then, you've won. If you're really going to insist about that, I'll go along with it. I'll have the baby."

For a moment, her heart rose. He would have the baby. She could put her arms around him right now, and she wouldn't have to sell her house, move her child, start over again on her own.

But now that she knew what she knew, that she didn't love him, that she never really had, it wouldn't be fair to let him do this for her, would it? It felt like a worse kind of trick than getting pregnant without your husband's acquiescence, and then praying his enthusiasm would catch up with his sperm. If she had another baby with Cooper, she'd find herself looking for a way to divorce him three or four years down the road.

"No," she said. "I don't want to have a baby with you anymore."

"Oh, that's rich," he said. "Now you're saying you don't want me to father your child?"

Don't argue, she cautioned herself. "Yes," she said, working to control her voice. "That's what I'm saying."

"That's excellent!" Cooper cried. "Perfect! Because you know what, Juliette, I had a vasectomy a long time ago. I didn't want to *risk* having another child with you."

CHAPTER 23

Anne

Anne awoke, the sun streaming in through Nick Ruby's bare windows, to the absurd idea that she had gone to heaven. It was something about the light, so bright it seemed otherworldly, reflected off the sparkling white that coated every horizontal surface: the streets, the sidewalks, the cars, the windowsills, the roofs. She was wearing a T-shirt of Nick's and her panties, and lying on the sofa in the main room of the apartment, beneath a soft patchwork quilt. The wall behind her went only halfway to the ceiling, leaving what passed for the bedroom open to the light and the air from the windows in the front of the apartment, the only windows in the place. The bathroom, Anne remembered, was through the bedroom.

Nick was propped up in the bed, alone, reading. Anne grabbed her purse from the floor near the door and gave him an embarrassed little half-wave as she shut herself in the white tiled room.

When she bought the pregnancy test kit, on her way from her office to the restaurant last night, she figured she'd be home alone this morning, with a whole weekend of privacy ahead of her. Now, though, despite the altered circumstances, she didn't think she could wait. Her period was more than a month overdue, and she'd spent enough time believing her only problem was stress, and telling herself it was impossible for her to be pregnant. She'd been on the Pill since right after Clementine's birth, was still on it the one and only time she'd had sex since the split with Damian. But between the breakup and the holidays, she'd gotten a little sloppy. Maybe she'd not only forgotten to take her pill every day, but also forgotten to check what safeguards she should take when she forgot. Did that time on the cellar steps happen during a seven-day period when she was supposed to be using backup birth conrol? In the moment, she hadn't even considered that. But now she thought: maybe. More than maybe: probably.

Hands shaking, she ripped the foil open and took out the plastic wand, then held it to catch her pee. Then she waited, looking around the room for something to distract her. There wasn't much. Nick Ruby seemed supernaturally tidy, his possessions honed to a minimum that Anne admired for its discipline but that made her feel slightly anxious. She preferred her nest feathered, not necessarily stylishly or expensively, but with plenty of cushioning against the realities of the outside world.

When she finally allowed herself to look again at the test wand, she was not at all surprised to see that the results were positive. She was pregnant. What did surprise her, what she never would have predicted, was how excited she felt. On some level, she realized, she really wanted this. Because she saw it as a way back to Damian? Because she'd always wanted more than one child and she was thrilled to have been given this unexpected chance? She wasn't sure. She tore open the door of the little bathroom and looked around, blinking as if she'd expected everything beyond herself might have changed as well.

"Where's Deirdre?" she asked Nick, registering fully for the first time that she and Nick were, in fact, alone.

"I don't know," he said. "Maybe she went down to the coffee shop. Or out to look around. See what kind of shape the city is in."

Even reclining on the low bed, he seemed very large. He was wearing a sleeveless undershirt cut skimpily enough to see that his chest, unlike his head, was covered with dark hair. Anne went over to the window, looking down to check whether there was any sign of her friend. Five stories below, people were walking down the middle of the street, which had apparently not been plowed. A couple pulled a baby on a little wooden sled; one man glided into view on cross-country skis.

"There are so many people out," she said.

"Is there still a lot of snow?" Nick asked.

"Tons."

She heard the bed rustle then and his footsteps, and suddenly he was beside her, gazing down at the parade below.

"Wow," he said.

"Have you ever seen anything like this before?"

"I'm from LA," he said. "I'd hardly ever seen snow until I moved here."

"You lived in Paris too, though, right?" Anne had to tilt her head way back to look at him. She tried not to feel self-conscious about the bareness of her legs, or the bareness of his beneath his black knit boxers. Although he was a completely different physical type than Damian, he reminded Anne of Damian in some other way that was harder to pin down. He was an unconventional man, masculine but not at all macho, sexy without being sleazy—a friend, a lover, but never a husband. She'd hit it on the nose, and she had to laugh. She hadn't been crazy for falling in love with Damian, she realized: she'd been crazy for marrying him.

"It doesn't snow much more in Paris than it does in California, believe it or not," Nick was saying. "I've spent a lot of time in Chicago and Detroit, but until this year I'd never been there in winter. No, this is the first time I've been in a big city in a real snowstorm."

"There wasn't a lot of snow where I grew up," Anne said. "And no big buildings and hardly any people, so I've never been in the middle of anything like this either."

Nick looked surprised. "I thought everybody in the suburbs had lived in Manhattan at some point in their lives."

"Not me," Anne said. Damian had always wanted to live in the city, but when they moved here from London she was already pregnant with Clementine, and with only one steady income, Manhattan, even Brooklyn, had been out of reach, to Anne's immense relief. After growing up in a small town in Virginia, she found New York too intense, too noisy and crowded for everyday life.

But now she was delighted to find herself here with the weekend stretching ahead and the usually bustling city muffled by the blizzard.

"I'd love to be out in that snow with my daughter," Anne said, thinking of how awestruck Clementine would be by the drifts, taller than she, and the sight of people sledding and skiing down the middle of the avenues.

"Where is she?" Nick asked.

"She's at my husband's. My ex-husband's. Since we split up, he's been staying at an apartment in Midtown."

"Why don't you call them?" Nick said. "Maybe you could hook up with her, go out for a walk."

"I don't know," said Anne. Since that day at Port Authority, Damian seemed determined to make things difficult for Anne. He refused to make any adjustments to the agreed-upon visitation schedule and would not honor any requests from Anne that he make sure their daughter brush her teeth, say, or work on a project for school. While Anne had to continue to be cordial to Damian for Clementine's sake, the truth was she'd grown afraid of him. A little shiver went through her. She wasn't only pregnant. She was pregnant with the baby of a man she feared. "My ex isn't very accommodating these days."

"But your kid," said Nick. "I thought that no matter how much exes hated each other, they would never give each other a hard time about their kid. I thought the kid was supposed to be sacred."

"You'd think so," said Anne.

"I don't know anything about this," said Nick, "but I think you should at least try to get what you want, even if he doesn't want to give it to you."

Anne looked at Nick, trying to gauge, she guessed, whether she could trust him. When she asked her girlfriends for advice, they mostly confirmed her own instincts to stay as far away from Damian as possible. But here was a guy who was *like* Damian telling her she should confront him.

"So what do I say?"

"Tell him what you told me, that you want to play in the snow with her."

"If I tell him it's something I want, then he'll definitely say no."

"All right, so then you've got to make him think it's something he wants."

Hmmmm, Anne thought. That was interesting. What did Damian want, besides to be allowed to move back into their house? He wanted to be a rich and famous artist, she knew that.

"Maybe I should call them and act like I just want to make sure they're okay, and then offer to take Clementine for a couple of hours while he shoots some footage of the blizzard."

"He's a photographer?" Nick asked.

"Filmmaker."

"There you go. I'll whip us up some breakfast while you go in the bedroom and make the call."

Anne's hands were trembling as she dialed Damian's number. When he finally answered, she tried to keep her voice steady, casual. She could hear the sound of cartoons in the background. "I just wanted to be sure you two were all right."

"Yes, of course we're all right. Don't you think I'm able to take care of my daughter?"

My daughter. This was the way he was all the time now. Then I have to be different, she told herself. Everything is going to be different for me, starting now.

Rather than take his bait, she said, "Isn't the city amazing with all this snow? Have you and Clem been outside yet?"

"How do you know what the city is like in the snow?" Damian asked.

There was a challenge in his tone that made her feel even more anxious than she already was. She'd only been thinking of his response to her request to spend a little time with Clementine during his weekend. She hadn't considered his reaction to the fact that she happened to be in the city in the first place.

"We had our moms' dinner in the city last night and we got stuck in the blizzard," said Anne, trying to stay calm, reminding herself that it was merely the truth. "We had to stay over at Deirdre's friend's apartment."

"What friend?"

"Her musician friend from college."

"Ah," Damian said finally. "The bass player whose apartment she's been kipping at."

Anne didn't respond.

"So all four of you slept there, with the musician," Damian said. "That must have been quite a thrill. Tell me, did you take him on one by one, or did you all just pile into bed with him together?"

Anne sucked in her breath in shock and slammed down the phone. She stood there in Nick's little half-walled bedroom, her heart hammering, breathing hard. From the kitchen, she could hear Nick whistling, and the sound of a fork against a pan, scrambling eggs.

Then the phone rang again.

"Can you get that?" Nick called.

Another ring.

"Anne?" Nick said.

"Okay," she called, battling her ridiculous reluctance to lift up the phone. It was probably Deirdre, calling to say where she was. Or a telemarketer.

When she finally answered the telephone, there was a few seconds of silence, and then a man—she recognized before he even spoke that it was Damian—laughed softly.

"I'm sorry, doll," he said. "You know I didn't mean that."

She held the phone and said nothing. If she hung up, she thought, he'd only call back again, more angry this time. She could take the phone off the hook or unplug it, but he had Clementine. That gave him an enormous amount of power.

"Here's the thing," Damian said. "It's just so bloody fucking difficult here on my own. You're there with our house, with your nice tidy little corporate stock options and 401K, and I figure I'm entitled to at least half of that. In fact, the way I see it, I was the parent who was far more available for Clementine's school functions and such, and I think I could very well be entitled to more than half. A lot more than half."

Anne breathed out until she felt hollow. She knew she should have stayed focused on what he was saying, should even have been writing it down, but all she could think was: how can I have this man's baby? "What?"

"I'm saying I'm ready to make a deal, doll, isn't that what you've been campaigning for? You sell the house and give me the proceeds, you sign over the savings account, and you pay me a certain regular sum, nothing outlandish, say five thousand dollars a month."

Anne was aghast. "You're asking me for *alimony?*"

Damian laughed again, that soft nasty laugh. "Oh, baby, I don't want to call it that."

"Yes," Anne said, her anger gathering force, "but that's what it is. And you're so determined to get back at me you'd actually force your child to leave her own home." In fact, she'd been thinking that the fair plan might be for her to sell the house and split the proceeds with Damian. Then she and Clem could buy a smaller house in Homewood—if a smaller house even existed—and he could get a place of his own where their daughter would be more comfortable on weekends.

"There is another way, you know," he said.

"Oh, right. I can let you move back in."

"No, no, I've come to grips with the fact that you're never going to agree to that. No, I'm talking about you letting me live in the house with Clementine while you move into an apartment in the city. I spend the week with Clem, and you get every other weekend."

Anne gripped her stomach. "You bastard," she whispered.

"Yes," he continued, as if he hadn't heard her, "in fact, I'm considering suing for custody. I've consulted an attorney, who tells me I have an excellent chance. All those teachers who know me so well, and rarely even got a look at you."

"This is not going to happen," Anne said.

"Oh, we'll see," Damian said breezily. "Of course, we could make a private arrangement, settle this out of court. But if not, it will be for the judge to decide, and with the hours you work, I'd say I have a pretty good chance. At the very least I'll end up with the paltry half of everything you've already offered me."

"This is all about money for you, isn't it?" Anne said.

"I've got to go now," said Damian.

"I want to talk to Clementine."

"I'm hanging up."

And that was it. When he had their child in his physical possession, he had Anne too within his control. She would do anything to get her daughter back, to keep her daughter safe. And if she crossed him, what might he do? Take Clementine to England, get his family to help him hide her away there? He was still a British subject; he could find a way to get her out.

"Anne?"

Nick was standing in his sunny living room, holding the pan full of eggs and a spatula. She found herself unable to smile or speak.

"Is everything all right?"

That's when she broke down, the tears flowing that she dared not show anyone else, not her daughter of course, not even her friends. Nick set down the frying pan, crossed the bedroom to where she stood, and put his arms around her. He was so large, so enveloping, that she had the first memory she'd had in years of being held by her father, and remembering the absolute love and safety she'd felt then, and never since, only made her cry harder.

"That's okay," he said, patting her shoulder. "It's all right."

"It's not all right," she sobbed. "He says he's going to try and take her. My daughter."

"Oh, Jesus," said Nick. "You can't let him do that."

I can't, Anne thought. Clementine's all I've got. But then she thought: not all. Not quite all.

"I'm pregnant," she whispered. Wanting to say it, but not too loudly.

He pulled back from her and looked down, trying to catch her eye.

"What did you say?"

"I said I'm pregnant." Now she let herself look at him. He's a stranger, she told herself. I just told this secret to a complete stranger. Not complete, she thought.

"Oh, Jesus," said Nick. "What are you going to do?"

She shook her head miserably. "I have no idea."

"Is it his?"

She looked squarely in Nick Ruby's eyes now. He had very dark eyes, such a deep brown it was almost impossible to tell the iris from the pupil.

"I haven't slept with anyone else since 1993," she said. "It's most definitely his."

"And there's no chance," he said, "I mean that you two . . ."

She shook her head definitively. "That we could get back together? Absolutely not."

"I don't know what your religious feelings are," Nick said hesitantly. "Your ethical feelings."

Anne stepped back and sat down hard on the bed. "You mean abortion," she said.

"Yes," he said gently, sitting beside her. "Abortion."

She was quiet, thinking about it. Of course, she'd considered the issue before, not only when she began to suspect she might be pregnant this time, but also soon after Clementine's birth, in a scare that made her realize she needed to go on the Pill, and also once back in college. She could, she believed, in many circumstances have an abortion—if she were raped or her own life were threatened, certainly, but even if she felt she could not love the expected child.

That was not the way she felt now. If she thought of this

baby as hers and Damian's, she was filled with turmoil. She had no wish to raise another child with this man, and apart or together, she knew that Damian definitely did not want another baby. If she put the matter to him, he would issue an unambiguous directive, the way he had when she thought she was pregnant three months after Clementine's birth: get rid of it.

But for herself—oh, for herself, that was a totally different story. For herself, the idea that she could without design or deviation encounter a new member trying to find a way into her tiny family seemed wonderful bordering on miraculous. The idea that she had lost one of the two living people she loved was heartbreaking nearly beyond endurance; the idea that there might be another love to replace that one felt like a kind of resurrection.

"Do you think," she said to Nick, "that you should go after what you want, even if it makes no sense?"

Nick nodded solemnly. "I do."

"Even if you're not supposed to want it?"

"Yes," said Nick.

"Have you ever felt that way?" she asked him.

He was staring at her, this big man, in a way that was so open, so raw, that she nearly felt she could reach out and touch the muscles beneath his skin. "I feel that way all the time," he said.

That was the moment the door banged open. Neither of them had heard the footsteps in the hallway, the key in the lock. So they both looked up in surprise from where they sat on the bed at Deirdre staring at them from the doorway. Her enormous boots and even her coat, both Nick's from the look of them, were caked with snow, and her cheeks were as red as those of a child running inside after sledding. She was breathing loudly, too, after walking up four flights of stairs.

"How is it out there?" asked Anne.

"It's amazing," said Deirdre, waving her arms around in excitement. Then she clapped her hands, sending a cascade of snow falling from her wooly red mittens onto the shiny floor. "You should check it out. What have you been doing?"

"Talking," said Nick.

"Oh, yeah?" said Deirdre. "What have you been talking about?"

Anne hesitated, asking herself if she was sure she was ready to reveal her secret, but knowing even before she asked that she was. "I'm pregnant," she said. "I found out for sure just this morning. And I was telling Nick that I want to keep it."

Deirdre looked stunned and turned to Nick, as if for confirmation. He opened his mouth and then sat there silently for a moment, as if unsure whether he was actually going to speak.

"And I was just about to tell Anne," he finally said, "that I'm in love with Juliette."

CHAPTER 24

Deirdre

She made noises of congratulation to Anne and murmured something she hoped was neutral to Nick, and then as quickly as she could manage she backed out of the apartment and reeled down the stairs and out into the street, not sure where she was going or what she was going to do. Nick in love with Juliette. Anne having a baby. Her getting offered the part. It was all too much.

She tromped west along the snowy sidewalks, eyes trained on the snow, trying to think. By the time she made it across town, traffic was picking up along the newly plowed streets and shop owners were snapping the icicles from their iron gates, shoveling and salting their sidewalks. Clomping down the stairs to the subway, Deirdre realized that blisters were rising on her feet. She was still wearing Nick's boots, three sizes too big, along with his black jeans and three of his sweaters. His watch cap was smashed down on her head; his big gloves covered her hands like baseball mitts.

Were the department stores open? Was there any way she could stop and buy totally new clothes so she wouldn't show up in Homewood looking like some deranged female Nick impersonator? Was she going to Homewood? That, she realized, seemed to be the thrust. She checked her watch: if she took an express train and caught the next bus, she could be at Homewood within the hour, whereas if she detoured to the stores, it would be afternoon before she'd get there. No way she'd be able to wait that long to talk to Juliette, which she realized suddenly that she had to do.

What did Nick mean, "in love with"? The phrase implied a mutuality: was Juliette in love with him too? Were they having an affair? How had this happened without Deirdre knowing? *Why* had it happened without her knowing?

These questions so occupied Deirdre's mind that it wasn't until she was actually on the bus, hurtling into New Jersey, that she felt the full weight of returning to Homewood. She'd been shuttling back and forth, of course, all along. But this time was different. This time she felt as if she was either going back for good, or going back having made a decision that would alter the course of her life, of her entire family's life.

As the bus raced west along Route 3, past the Meadowlands and Giants stadium, farther from the city and deeper into the suburbs, the snowbanks along the highway grew higher, the hills in the distance more thoroughly white. When they turned onto the narrow streets of Homewood itself, it seemed as if they had entered the land of the Snow Queen, all the trees encased in snow and ice, their branches twinkling in the sun, as if covered with diamonds. The roads there still held a carpet of white, and everything—the SUVs out to prove themselves, the families building snowmen in their front yards or pulling sleds toward the park—was moving even more slowly than usual.

Stepping off the bus, maneuvering down the snowy sidewalks, Deirdre was hit with a longing to see her kids that was so strong, she felt as if she couldn't breathe. It was prompted by the snow crunching beneath her boots, the icy wetness seeping through the legs of her jeans, the distinct scent of the snow-filled world. After her own snowless childhood, searching the rain-sodden winter skies of Berkeley in vain for even one flake, she loved playing in the snow with her own kids. It was a chance to both live that part of her life over and to feel like an unambiguously good mother. Whenever it snowed she'd lead Zack and Zoe outside and they'd build snow forts or go sledding. Almost always, the kids were ready to go back in the house before she was.

Two more blocks and she'd be home. The twins were probably outside right now. If she hurried, she'd catch them before they headed into the house for lunch. She could call Juliette later. It was Saturday, Cooper was probably home now anyway, and Trey, and Heather, the nanny: there was no way they'd be able to talk, even if Deirdre still wanted to stop there.

Deirdre tucked her chin into her collar and deliberately trained her eyes away from Juliette's big gray house, just across the street. She had made it almost past the house's force field when she heard a voice calling, "Hey! Hey! Hey, Deirdre!"

It was Trey, all bundled up in his red snowsuit, standing knee deep in the snow in his front yard, all by himself. That alone was a rarity: normally, if Juliette wasn't with him, Heather was. How had he even recognized Deirdre, in her unfamiliar oversize clothes, from a hundred feet away? She could walk right up to Trey at school or at his own house and say hello and get not a glimmer of response. And now, when she was trying to hurry home, he wouldn't quit yelling her name.

She stopped and faced him. "Hi, Trey," she called.

"Daddy's gone," Trey bellowed.

Well, that was predictable. If Cooper couldn't escape to the office on the weekend, he'd go off to buy himself some books, or pick up his dry cleaning—anything but play with his son.

"Mommy's crying," Trey called.

Juliette was crying? But Juliette was always unfailingly cheerful around Trey, so careful not to upset him for fear of triggering a meltdown.

Deirdre scrambled over the snowdrift at the curb, nearly losing both Nick's boots in the process, and worked her way across the icy street to where Trey stood.

"Where's your mommy, Trey?" she asked. "Is Heather out here with you?"

But now Trey wouldn't look at her. He steadfastly gazed off somewhere in the distance.

"Trey?" she said. "Honey?"

"Hazmat Alert! Call the wrecker!" he cried, scooping up a mittenful of snow and trooping off across the front yard to the driveway, where his sled was perched. Then, flinging the snow in Deirdre's direction, he hopped on his sled and sailed down the driveway toward the backyard.

She didn't know how Juliette did it. Trey was difficult and

isolated enough now, but what about his future? What would become of him when he was an adolescent? An adult?

She walked up the neatly shoveled front walk and rang the doorbell, her mind more on Trey and his report that Juliette was crying than on what was going on with Nick, which was beginning to seem like something that had happened a million years ago, in a distant land.

It took a long time for Juliette to appear, and when she did it was immediately apparent that Trey had been telling the truth. Her nose and eyes were bright red, her cropped hair standing straight up. She was still wearing her nightgown with what looked like a robe of Cooper's, plaid and clashing with the nightgown's flannel flowers.

"What are you doing here?" she said to Deirdre, looking shocked but holding the door open.

"No. The question is what's going on with you?" said Deirdre, kicking the snow off her boots and stepping into the house.

"It's Cooper," said Juliette.

"What happened?" Deirdre asked, the possibilities already racing through her mind. Heart attack? Affair? Huge loss in the stock market or bond market or whatever market Cooper kept his money in?

Juliette shook her head miserably and led Deirdre into the dining room, sinking into an oversize faux Chippendale chair. She didn't seem to notice or care that Deirdre was tracking snow all over the beige carpet.

"It's over, Deirdre."

At first, this didn't compute. "What's over?"

"Our marriage. I asked Cooper to leave."

And then it all moved into line: Nick, the affair, Juliette's flight back home last night, what was undoubtedly her tearful confession to Cooper.

"Oh fuck. You told him about you and Nick."

Now it was Juliette's turn to look confused. "What?"

"I know all about it, Juliette. Nick told me, this morning."

The rest of Juliette's face flushed to match her nose and eyes, but still she said, "I don't know what you're talking about."

Now Deirdre's anger flooded in, full force. "Jesus, come off it, Juliette. I know that you and Nick are having an affair. I can't believe you didn't tell me yourself from the beginning."

"But we're not having an affair," said Juliette. "I don't know why Nick would say that."

"He said you were in love!"

"He used the word *love?*"

"He said, and I quote, 'I'm in love with Juliette.'"

"I can't even believe that," Juliette said. She began crying then and sat there crying for a long time before reaching into the pocket of her robe and extracting a trailing piece of toilet paper, loudly blowing her nose.

"So," said Deirdre, more confused than ever, "are you saying there's nothing going on between you and Nick?"

"Oh," said Juliette weakly, not quite meeting Deirdre's eye, "it depends on what you mean by 'going on.' What you mean by 'nothing.' I mean, he called me. He called me a lot. We talked."

"You talked. That's all."

"We kissed. Once."

Deirdre tried to take this in. "One kiss is a lot, Juliette."

"Oh, I know. I know! But it isn't like I planned it out, like I wanted it. It just was. When I met Cooper, you know, I got together with him because I thought I should. With Nick, should had nothing to do with it."

"Juliette, I just don't understand. Why were you keeping this a secret from me?"

"I didn't know what there was to tell," Juliette said. And then, "That's not quite true. I thought you'd be mad. Or I mean, I didn't want to make you mad over something I thought was nothing."

"I'm still confused," Deirdre said. "I never knew that you and Nick even noticed each other. He seems so not your type."

"Why would you say that?"

"He's the opposite of Cooper."

"It's Cooper who's not my type!" Juliette cried. "Nick is exactly my type."

"But you always said that type was trouble."

Juliette sighed. "They are." She paused. "Did Nick really use the word *love?*"

Deirdre leveled a look at her, realizing that she'd never heard Nick say *love* before. Not to her, not about their relationship. "I wouldn't make that up," she told Juliette now.

Juliette sighed again. "I don't know what to think."

"But if you didn't tell Cooper about Nick," said Deirdre, "what happened that made him leave?"

"We had a confrontation when I got home last night, Deirdre. I told him I wanted a divorce, and he confessed he had a vasectomy. Secretly. That's why I wasn't getting pregnant all this time." Juliette looked out the window, and following her gaze, Deirdre saw Trey spinning around in the backyard, falling, a look of glee on his face, into the snow. "He let me go to the infertility doctor, spend every month hoping, only to be slammed with disappointment."

"But vasectomies can be reversed," Deirdre said. "I mean, if you really wanted to have another baby."

"Cooper has no interest in reversing it, Deirdre, at least not with me," said Juliette, still staring out the window. "He doesn't want to take the chance of having another child like Trey."

"But, Juliette," Deirdre said, as gently as possible, "don't you think that sort of makes sense?"

Juliette looked directly at her then. "They don't know whether Asperger's is genetic," she said, "but it doesn't matter to me. I love Trey, Deirdre. If I had another baby who was just like him, I would be delighted."

Deirdre felt ashamed then, for not having understood that Juliette loved Trey exactly as much as any mother loved her child. Exactly as much as she loved her children, a feeling that welled up inside her again, practically lifting her out of her chair and back in the direction of her own true loves.

"You can still have another baby," Deirdre said. "Maybe with Nick."

"Who knows," said Juliette. "I've got all I can handle here, with working out a divorce settlement, selling the house. . . ."

"Wait a minute," said Deirdre. "You're selling the house?"

Deirdre felt weak. Somehow this news was more upsetting than Cooper's vasectomy, the breakup of Juliette's marriage, or her budding relationship with Nick. Juliette, selling the house. Juliette, not living down the street from her anymore.

"Maybe you should wait," Deirdre said. "Let things settle before you make any big moves."

Juliette shook her head, seemingly more certain about this than about anything else they'd discussed. "Cooper was the one who wanted this enormous house," she said, "not me. I never wanted all this stuff or all this property or all these expenses. That was him."

"Oh, God," Deirdre said. She felt hot, suddenly, in all her sweaters, Nick's sweaters, his scent hitting her now in Juliette's warm house. "You mean just when I'm going to move back home full-time, you're going to leave?"

Juliette grinned. "You mean you're going to move back home?"

And that's when Deirdre knew, for certain, that she was.

CHAPTER 25

Lisa

Lisa sat at her kitchen table, sorting through the stack of dishes. That little plate was part of the creamware set: how did it get separated? No matter, the entire set was going to Juliette, who'd always admired it. The Fiestaware, of course, would go to Deirdre. Deirdre loved those bright colors, and now that she was back home—or at least that was the report Lisa had heard via Tommy—she'd appreciate having them. The painted German dish that had come from her grandmother would get packed away for Daisy. Lisa put that to the side and made a note. She had to make sure Tommy knew which things she wanted saved for the kids so they weren't accidentally thrown away over the years. Maybe they should be stored in a separate place. That was a good idea. All the kids' boxes could be put in that cedar storeroom in the attic, so there would be no confusion after she was gone.

Far away, she heard the telephone ring. Was it ringing more these days or did she just find it more annoying? When Tommy was at work, she simply unplugged it, but that kind of maneuver upset him. It made him more concerned than he already was, and that was exactly what she was trying to avoid.

She heard his footsteps approaching the kitchen. His face looked so beefy to her these days, so fleshy and red. He had put on weight in this past month, ordering too much pizza, cooking too much pasta, sacrificing his hockey nights and squash games. Well, this she could not concern herself with. As long as he stayed healthy for the children, that was all she wanted.

"Yes?" she said finally, when it was clear he was just going to keep standing there. "Was there something you wanted?"

"Anne is on the phone."

Lisa sighed. "Tell her I'm not here."

"I already told her you are here."

"I can't talk now, Tommy. I'm right in the middle of this."

"She's called here, I don't know, twenty times in the past two weeks. What's going on with you? Your friends are worried about you, *I'm* worried about you."

"There's nothing to worry about."

"There's something to worry about," Tommy said. "We keep trying to talk to you, you won't talk to us." He waved one of his meaty hands over the table where the dishes were stacked. "This. I don't know what this is."

"I just need to get rid of things, that's all."

He went rigid. "Why do you need to get rid of things, Lisa?"

"Spring cleaning," she said. "Time to clear out."

"I've seen you do spring cleaning, and that's not this."

She forced a laugh, stood up, and went over to the sink so she wouldn't have to look at him any longer. She was afraid that his dark whiskers, the black hairs sprouting from his hands, were going to make her sick.

"I don't think you were ever paying attention, Tommy," she said.

From the double window over the sink, she could see out to the backyard where the kids were playing. The blizzard that had seemed so absolute just two weeks before had melted within days, and now it was suddenly almost hot, the mud drying and the grass turning a bright green. Yesterday the forsythia had popped, and Lisa watched as Daisy streaked past the bush, her blue shirt and red pants vivid against the bright yellow.

"Lisa," Tommy said.

She turned to face him. He had been so handsome once, not that long ago. Why had she ever cared about such a thing?

"I'm paying attention now, Lisa," he said.

She didn't understand: Why did he consider it so important suddenly to connect with her? He'd always said that he liked her because she was so much like a guy: she never wanted to talk about it, she always preferred action to rumination. And that was precisely why she liked him too, because he was a big handsome happy smart-enough-but-not-too-deep guy who believed in fun, fucking, having lots of kids, and making lots of money.

Except now he was turning all wussy on her. Now when she needed him to be her buckaroo and take over for her. If he had been the one who was—What should she call it? Changing directions—she could have taken over for him. Run Reed Jeep-Honda and taken care of the house and the kids.

"I'm just trying to get the house in order, Tommy," she said, trying to invest her voice with strength so he would be convinced. "I'm just trying to regain some control."

He crossed his arms over his belly. "I don't believe you."

"Hey!" she cried. "Isn't Anne waiting on the phone?"

"I'll tell her I can't find you," he said, pushing off from the counter. "But I'm not going to go away."

As soon as he left the room, she was on her feet and out the door. The kids were racing through the backyard, down the hill as far as they could go before they hit someone's fence, and then back up again. Lisa ignored them, the color and the noise, and trudged toward the back hedge, thinking vaguely that she would cut through the Howes' driveway, jog down Dean Street toward the village, maybe get a coffee, stop at the library, duck into a movie. And then what? she wondered. Then what?

She was squeezing through the hedge, aiming for the driveway, when he caught up with her, his hand closing on her shoulder, tugging her back into their yard.

"Where are you going?" he said.

"For a walk."

"You're not going for any walk," he said, gathering her toward him. "You're staying right here."

He was like a fisherman on the deck of a boat—he had that sturdy, balanced look, as if a hurricane could beat down upon him and he wouldn't stir—patiently reeling her closer until she was in his arms. Then he just held her there. Held her and held her until she found herself releasing the weight of everything she'd been holding in.

"Tell me," he whispered.

"I can't," she said, hearing a sob escape from her throat.

"Tell me," he said again.

Now she was the one who whispered: "I'm afraid."

She was afraid, she meant, to tell him. And she was also simply afraid.

"Don't be afraid," he said softly. "I'm right here."

But everything she could imagine saying to him was so dark, so terrifying, that she felt if she even began he would instantly take off screaming for the hills. How could she tell him that she imagined a great black worm consuming her insides until there was nothing left? That she worried that thinking a single less-than-victorious thought would be like feeding fertilizer to the voracious black worm? That she fantasized, if she veered quickly and inexorably toward death the way her mother had, about filling her pockets with stones à la Virginia Woolf and jumping off the George Washington Bridge?

Better to be silent, a tack that often implied strength. When her mother died, Lisa was so composed—so "good," according to her father and her aunts—that everyone just naturally began relying on her to make the phone calls and organize the out-of-town relatives in for the funeral and shepherd the younger children through the wake. The adults had been hesitant at first, but she had reassured them she was all right, and her behavior confirmed it. Lisa is amazing, they said.

Of course, there had been moments when she'd fallen apart. A month after her mother's death, grocery shopping for the family, she noticed that all the early summer fruits and vegetables—the strawberries, the sweet cherries, the slim new asparagus—had arrived in the store, and it hit her that here was a new season her mother would never see. Her mother, who did nothing *but* smell the roses, would miss this fresh round of sensual pleasures, as well as all the rest to come. Right there in the store, she'd been astonished to find herself hemorrhaging tears. She'd had to run out into the parking lot and hide in the car until the sobbing and the sadness passed.

"Lisa," Tommy said. "I know."

She froze. "I don't know what you're talking about."

"Yes, you do. They called here this morning when you were in the shower, asking about a surgery date."

She felt her face turn hot. She felt as if she were standing on the rail of the bridge at this moment, and she could tell him everything, right now, everything that had been laid out by Dr. Kaufman as well as everything that was in her heart. She could tell him about the scan that showed the spot on her liver, the surgery that would have to be performed in the next month, the grim statistics she had surveyed on the Internet when he was at the dealership and the kids were at school. And of course, he would have to know some of this. But maybe just a small piece—a piece as negligible as she hoped the spot on her liver would turn out to be.

"You're getting all worked up over nothing," she said breezily.

"Lisa," he said, his face turning red and his voice sounding almost angry. "Why in God's name won't you let me in?"

"And why won't you let me handle this myself, my own way?" she shot back. "You were totally content to leave me on my own to plan the wedding, to make it through my pregnancies, to get up in the middle of the night with the kids when they were babies. Why won't you leave me on my own now?"

He raised his eyes and lifted his hands as if appealing to God, and then let them slap down in seeming defeat onto his thighs as he looked hard into her eyes. "I love you," he said, his voice low but filled with intensity. "I don't have any other better explanation than that, Lisa. *I love you.*"

"Yeah, but I know what that means," Lisa said, trying to sound tough but feeling as if she might, if she let down her guard for even one minute, begin to cry. "You love me, the blonde energetic tennis-playing mom who whips up cocktails for a hundred. You don't love some fucking cancer patient."

She saw with satisfaction that Tommy seemed to have been silenced by that proclamation. Just as she suspected: it was true. And who could blame him? She didn't love herself as a cancer patient either, didn't even want to admit that into her self-image.

But now Tommy, like some unstoppable monster in the horror movies she had taken to watching on the days when the Internet medical sites and *Leeza* and *Montel* weren't gory enough, started speaking again.

"I wish you would let me help you, Lisa," he said.

"All right," she said, "you want to help me? Okay, then you can do this. I want to have the next moms' dinner here, with all my good dishes, my favorite recipes, a real blowout. You can help me by doing some of the shopping, taking care of the kids while I cook."

He nodded slowly. "Sure. I can do that."

"The night of the dinner, maybe you can take the kids somewhere so the moms and I can be alone."

"Sure," he said. "Of course." He was shaking his head yes, but impatiently, as if this were just the warm-up and he was waiting for her to get to the really important request.

"And Tommy?" she said. "These things you think you know, about me and my so-called health problems? I don't want you to say a word to anyone about them, not even to Anne or Deirdre or Juliette. Do you understand?"

He stopped nodding. He wished, she could tell, he could say no. But then he nodded again, a quick mechanical bob of his head.

The kids were careening back up the hill now toward them, Daisy in the lead. They were like a storm: you saw them first, lovely and silent, and then you heard them, frightening as gathering thunder. Lisa stepped away from Tommy, and for one instant, she felt the relief of having pulled off another escape.

CHAPTER 26

The April Dinner

It was the most beautiful table she'd ever set. She had unfolded the starched white linen tablecloth with the wide crocheted bands from its archival tissue. If it got stained, she decided, she was just going to throw it out. Or donate it to the Vietnam Vets. And this time, she wasn't going to let herself worry about the tax deduction. Tax preparation had always been her job, and once it became Tommy's, like all the other jobs, it was not going to get done that meticulously anyway. He probably wouldn't even sift through the box of receipts, would just dump them on some poor accountant's desk, or worse, throw them out and make up the numbers. So what became of the tablecloth wasn't important: its sole purpose on earth was to look perfect tonight.

In every other way, she also pulled out all the stops. She used Tommy's mother's Limoges china, and his grandmother's silver, the set with the scalloped spoons. The etched crystal wine-glasses they'd gotten for a wedding present that she'd kept stored away all these years. The Irish linen napkins and the ornate sterling candlesticks. At Homewood's fanciest florist, the one that charged three times more than anyone else, she bought the good tulips, the ones with the heads as big as avocados, in her favorite color, the tender pink of a child's lips.

And the food: all the most elaborate dishes from her most secret recipes, everything she'd made for dinner parties and holiday bashes over the years. And not only the things everyone else raved about, but also the things she loved most herself. The broiled mushrooms stuffed with crabmeat and garlic butter. The Caesar salad with the dressing that took all day to steep to garlicky perfection. The gorgonzola sauce and mashed potatoes like fragrant clouds; the apple and cherry upside-down pie and the handmade caramel ice cream. This might be the last time she got to eat these favorites.

She might have put these recipes in the book. Every once in a while, an idea for the book still flitted across her mind. But there wasn't going to be any book now.

Tommy and the kids were banished from the house for most of the day while she cooked, and he was happy to go, grateful to see her excited about something again. All she'd told him was that she was hosting the moms' dinner this month, and he hadn't asked anything further. He hadn't asked, for instance, about the three stacks of plates and linens and jewelry and clothes and even her secret recipes in the living room, each waiting to be given a new home.

True, they were in a far corner of the living room, behind a chair and a table. The plan was not to thrust them upon her friends as soon as they walked in the door but to work up to their presentation. Lisa saw the giving of the piles, of the gifts, as the climax of the evening and planned to orchestrate everything to build to that event. The giving, and then her announcement.

She had written out, as was her custom, a schedule for her work so she wouldn't forget everything and all the dishes would be ready at the proper time. But she was only on step twenty-seven of the forty-five involved in preparing the meal—peeling Yukon Gold potatoes while still wearing her khakis—when the doorbell rang. She wasn't expecting anyone, an hour before the dinner was set to begin, and couldn't imagine who she'd find at the door.

Deirdre. Standing there all dressed up in a tight red shirt and short black skirt and big hoop earrings.

"Oh," she said, looking beyond Lisa into the house, where the kids' soccer ball and cleats were still scattered in the front hall. "Am I the first?"

"Everyone's coming at seven, Deirdre. It's only six."

"Oh," Deirdre said. "I just thought, since we were eating here instead of going out—"

"It's seven." Lisa kept standing there, blocking the door. She hated having her preparations thrown off schedule, especially tonight, when she was determined everything was going to be perfect.

"Well, that's okay," Deirdre said, moving closer. "I'll just help you get ready. I know I can always use as much help as I can get the hour before a dinner party."

Lisa had no choice but to step aside as Deirdre swept into

the house. Stay positive, she cautioned herself. Think of this as an unexpected bonus.

"Oh, you've already got the table set," Deirdre said. "I would have loved to do that."

Over my dead body, Lisa thought grimly. While she could try to make the most of Deirdre's early arrival, she was determined to keep the creative pleasures of the evening for herself.

"You can help me peel potatoes," Lisa said firmly.

"I'll peel the potatoes by myself," Deirdre said, "if you mix me a drink."

Another rule broken: Lisa never allowed herself even one sip of a drink until the first guest arrived. The wait made her more excited about the start of the evening and provided a clear demarcation between the preparation and entertaining parts of a party.

Oh, what the hell, she thought. I could use a drink myself.

"I was planning on Cosmos," she said, retrieving the vodka from the liquor cabinet.

"Cosmos! Oh, no no no," Deirdre cried, dropping her peeler and joining Lisa at the liquor cabinet. "Cosmos are so over. How about that drink they made at that restaurant we went to in New York the night of the snowstorm. It's called the Bionic Babe."

"But I like Cosmos," said Lisa.

"Well, then you're going to love the Bionic Babes," said Deirdre. "You sit down and I'll do this."

A month ago, two months ago, Lisa would have put up a fight. A year ago, she might have thrown Deirdre out of the house. But now she just didn't have the energy. She sat back on her stool, ignoring the potatoes. Deirdre can mix the drinks *and* peel the potatoes, she decided.

The drink was delicious, she had to admit. She didn't even want to know what was in it. I'll just have this one drink, she told herself. Just one drink and then I'll get back on schedule.

"God, it's so great to be here again," Deirdre said merrily, picking up the peeler and tackling the potatoes. "Now that I'm back, I can't believe I ever dreamed of leaving."

"But you wanted to sing so badly."

"Oh, I can still sing, I'm just not going after the major shows and gigs in New York," Deirdre said. "I think I'm learning to appreciate moderation—the nice husband, the comfortable house, the okay career." She lifted her cocktail glass and, to Lisa's amusement, drained the entire thing into her upturned throat.

"Are you sure you're not settling?" Lisa said.

"I have to make sure that I'm not," said Deirdre, pouring herself another drink. "But no, I think I'm growing up."

Lisa wanted to be as happy for Deirdre as she seemed to be for herself, but she couldn't help feeling it was unfair that Deirdre was just getting around to growing up. Why should Deirdre get to have a thirty-five-year childhood, while that was longer than Lisa's entire life span?

"You better pour me another one too," Lisa said, sliding her glass across the counter.

Where was that list of things to do anyway? Twenty minutes had passed and she was dimly aware that she had more than twenty steps to complete before the other women arrived. But the list seemed to have vanished under the mounting pile of potato scraps beside Deirdre. She'd look for it as soon as she finished this drink.

"So are you up on all the happenings?" Deirdre asked.

"What happenings?"

"I didn't think so," Deirdre said. "We've all been calling and calling, and you never call us back. I don't think you even look at your e-mail anymore, do you?"

No, as a matter of fact she didn't, since her penis was already long enough, thank you very much, and she had no wish to correspond with anyone she knew. God, these drinks were *strong*. Maybe she should have asked what was in them. What was the question again?

"Juliette!" Deirdre cried. "Anne! I can't believe you haven't heard the big news."

The big news? Other than her own big major earth-shattering if not quite death-defying news?

"I guess I mean the big newses. Newsi? Anyway, Juliette's not pregnant, but Anne is. Can you believe that? It's Damian's, but she's not telling him. And Juliette has left Cooper, actually kicked him out of the house, and is in love with none other than Nick Ruby."

This did not compute. "*Your* Nick Ruby?"

"Apparently not." Deirdre laughed. "Anyway, it seems he's been after her since the very beginning." Deirdre sniffed the air. "What's that smell?"

Smell? Yes, there was something acrid in the room. It smelled exactly like . . . oh my God . . . burned mushrooms.

Lisa rushed to the oven and flung open the door, releasing a cloud—it actually resembled a mini-mushroom cloud—of smoke.

The mushrooms that were supposed to be the centerpiece of her hors d'oeuvre selection were charred to turdlike little crisps.

"Shit," she said, feeling almost as despairing as when the doctor showed her her liver scan. She looked at the clock. Only fifteen minutes until everyone arrived; no time to start on anything new. And she wasn't even dressed.

"Never mind," said Deirdre, swooping in and grabbing the cookie sheets, sliding the mushrooms neatly into the garbage. "You go get ready. I'll take care of whatever needs to be done down here."

"There was a list," Lisa said, beginning to root around in the potato peels.

Deirdre leveled her with a look. "I'm not dealing with one of your fussy little lists—step thirty-eight, mince parsley. Just tell me the broad strokes and I'll take over."

"Okay, put the cream and gorgonzola on the stove at a low boil. Get the potatoes into cold water on a hot flame. Heat the oven for the beef; I'll slide that in when Anne and Juliette get here. And make the Caesar salad. The dressing's already done and all the other ingredients are in the bowl labeled CAESAR."

"You label your bowls?" Deirdre asked, sounding horrified.

"It helps me stay organized."

"There's such a thing as being *too* organized," said Deirdre. "Never mind. Go take your shower."

God, Anne pregnant. She must be due in the fall sometime, Lisa calculated as the hot water hammered onto her neck. I'd love to see her with another baby; I wonder whether I'll still be here then. Maybe that could be something to aim for, she decided. That and Christmas.

She was in the bedroom, scrambling to dry herself, when she heard Deirdre calling her name from downstairs.

"Just a minute!" she sang out, searching for her underwear.

But then the door of her bedroom shot open and there stood Deirdre, staring at her standing there naked. Well, this was no big deal. They'd been in the locker room together at the pool, in the communal dressing room at Loehmann's.

"There were no anchovies in the Caesar salad bowl," Deirdre said.

"I don't use anchovies."

"Oh. I didn't know that."

They both kept standing there.

Then Deirdre said, "What's that scar?"

Her hysterectomy scar, along her bikini line. She'd stopped noticing it herself, but to Deirdre, who didn't even know it was there, it must look red and enormous.

"Oh," Lisa said, trying to keep her voice casual. "That's from when I had my thingie."

"You know, you never really told us what thingie you had," said Deirdre. "Or what's going on with you now."

The doorbell rang. Anne. Juliette. Both with far more urgent things to talk about than she.

"We can talk about that later. I don't want to spoil anyone's dinner. Will you get the door while I finish dressing?"

By the time she came downstairs, Deirdre had poured everyone fresh drinks and put out little bowls of nuts and olives. The kids' peanuts and some dried-up olives in the wrong bowls, Lisa noticed as she helped herself to a third cocktail. Well, who cared? Wasn't the important thing to have a wonderful time?

"What's this fabulous news I hear?" she said, kissing the newly round Anne on the cheek. "I'm so sorry I've been out of touch. It's been so crazy around here. Juliette. How are *you?*"

Juliette, in contrast to Anne, looked slimmer than ever, her cropped hair and skinny-hipped jeans making her look like a sexy teenager.

"I'm good," Juliette said. "Really good. I just never knew getting divorced was so much *work.*"

"Tell me about it," said Anne. "It's like a second career."

"So the divorce," Lisa said, "you're still going through with that, even though. . . ." She gestured toward Anne's rounded stomach. "And Damian, Deirdre says you're not telling him about the baby. But how . . ."

"How am I going to hide it from him?" Anne said. "The first part of my plan is to get the divorce agreement hammered out and push it through the courts before I start showing. And then once we're officially divorced I'll just let him think I went to a sperm bank, or got knocked up by another guy, or something. I won't be obligated to answer any of his questions then."

That sounded risky to Lisa, but it was hard for her to get worked up about these kinds of problems anymore. Have a baby on your own or share custody with your ex? However it turned out, you still had a baby. You were still alive.

After making the sympathetic sounds she knew were expected, Lisa ducked into the kitchen to make sure Deirdre had gotten everything ready. The salad sat waiting for its dressing in the right bowl, and the potatoes and gorgonzola sauce were bubbling away. Now she just had to tuck the roast into the hot oven, which would cook it to bloody perfection in half an hour, and hurry back to her guests.

"I already have an offer on the house," Juliette was saying.

"You really don't want to stay there?" asked Anne.

"God, no. That was always Cooper's place. I want something much smaller, two bedrooms, that's it."

"Do you think you'll move into the city?" Deirdre asked. "Live with Nick?"

"Since I hope to be going to school downtown, and Cooper already bought a loft in Tribeca, I think the city might make the most sense for both of us to get maximum time with Trey. And there's a school downtown that would be one of the best in the country for him. But I'm not sure about living with Nick—my lawyer has advised me not to even see him yet."

"How's Cooper been with working out a settlement?" Anne asked. "Damian's giving me such a hard time. He wants all this money, wants me to sell the house, pay him alimony. . . ."

"That's terrible," said Juliette. "I don't want anything from Cooper."

"You're crazy!" said Deirdre. "You *earned* that money!"

"That's what my lawyer says. I figure I'll take what I can get, keep what I need for Trey and myself while I'm in school—*if* I get accepted. Whatever's left over, I'll give to those nuns in Newark who take care of the abandoned babies and to Planned Parenthood and to my mother, who was always more interested in Cooper's money than I was."

Lisa gently nudged everyone toward the sparkling dining room. Sitting at the head of the table, she was aware of the pain starting to assert itself in her abdomen and the exhaustion that seemed to plague her earlier and earlier each day. But she also felt energized by being with her friends again.

"This reminds me of when the kids were babies, when we used to meet every Friday morning at one another's houses," Anne said, sighing contentedly, salad poised over her plate. "I thought I'd gone to heaven when I joined this group, when everybody laid out their best dishes and their cloth napkins, and baked a real cake even though it was just us, no men in sight."

That had been Lisa's idea when she organized the group, that they should treat themselves and one another to one fabulous morning a week.

"Yes," said Juliette. "It was the only time I ever used all that antique gold-rimmed china and the sterling from Cooper's family, but at least our meetings made it seem like all those things had some place in my life."

"I was so intimidated by you," said Deirdre, "by your big house and your Waspy Wall Street husband."

"Are you kidding?" said Juliette. "I was intimidated by *you* —you were so creative, with your pottery making and your mural painting, and you seemed to be able to feel and say things the rest of us kept wrapped up inside."

"I was intimidated by all of you," said Anne. "Especially you, Lisa. You all seemed to be so comfortable with the mom thing when I was struggling to keep my career going and figure out what I was doing with Clementine every night. I don't think I ever let you all know how much trouble I went through at work to get those Fridays off."

"I never told you how alienated I felt from Cooper," said Juliette.

"That we sort of guessed," said Deirdre. "I guess I always told everybody how dissatisfied I was with everything. But maybe I never told you how much you all meant to me."

Deirdre flung her hands out for emphasis with that last statement, and that's when it happened. She knocked over her glass of red wine.

"Oh, my God, I'm sorry, Lisa!" Deirdre cried, jumping up, snatching away her plate and atttempting to clear the table so she could pick up the white linen tablecloth. "We need cold water. Or is it club soda?"

"Soft Scrub," said Lisa. Saturating stains with Soft Scrub was one of her favorite tips. But now she was going to leave all that nonsense behind. "It doesn't matter. Sit down."

"No," said Deirdre, still fumbling with the tablecloth. "I know this is one of your favorite things." Anne was on her feet now too, as was Juliette, methodically unsetting the table.

"Please," said Lisa, panic rising in her throat. "I don't care about the tablecloth. Let's eat. How about that? I'll go get the roast. We'll just eat it with the salad. The tablecloth is going to get dirtier anyway."

"You'll never get that stain out if you don't do it now," Juliette said, continuing to move one dish after another from the table onto the sideboard. "And then the cloth will be ruined."

"I don't care if it's ruined, don't you understand?" Lisa cried. "I'm just going to throw it in the garbage can anyway."

Leaping to her feet, banging one dish atop another and grabbing the entire stack, Lisa stalked into the kitchen and slammed them down onto the countertop beside the sink, feeling the bottom one crack in her hands. Fuck it. Fuck it fuck it and fuck it again. Lifting the top dish from the pile, the gold-rimmed cream Limoges that Tommy's mother had had shipped in straw all the way from France, she raised it slowly above her head. She thought about how much it was worth, how carefully she'd preserved it for all these years, what was going to become of it if she washed it gently and set it back in the glass-fronted china cupboard yet another time. With a rush of fury, she brought her arm down, flinging the dish onto the floor, where it shattered with a thunderous noise, shards flying in every direction.

Now there was no stopping her. One by one she lifted the plates and hurled them to the ground, getting more inventive as she went, sailing one across the room into the pantry, lobbing another into the stove.

When the plates were all broken, she spied the roast sitting on its platter on the stove. Grabbing it, she upended the platter so that the meat fell with a thud into the garbage can. Then Lisa brought the platter itself down on the edge of the can so that it broke like a giant cookie right there in her hands.

She looked up. Anne and Deirdre and Juliette were huddled in the archway between the kitchen and the dining room, staring at her, shock transforming their faces. She hadn't realized they were even watching.

"Are you okay?" Deirdre said finally.

"Am I okay?" Lisa laughed. "What do you think? Does this look like I'm okay?"

She reached into the oven and, without even using potholders, grabbed the casserole of mashed potatoes, relishing the burn of the ceramic dish against her skin, and pitched it onto the floor. A gob of hot gooey potato landed on her leg and stuck there.

"How about this?" Lisa said, pushing past her friends into the dining room, where the table that had been so beautiful such a short time before stood in disarray, the wine stain like an enormous maroon birthmark sprawling across the once-pristine white linen. "Does this look okay?"

She began lobbing what dishes remained toward the fireplace and out into the hallway. Then she started on the glasses, watching with fascination as the dark wine arced through the air and splattered the walls, the ceiling, the beige carpet beneath her feet, her own silk blouse.

It wasn't until she lifted the carving knife that had been lying there in wait for the roast and started to hack at the tablecloth that the other women moved in.

She felt Juliette, surprisingly strong, pin down her arms while Anne snatched the knife from her hands. Lisa let out a breath that felt as if it had been suspended within her for years, and then, at the same moment, Juliette released her while Deirdre gathered her in her arms.

"It's all right," Deirdre whispered. "Let go."

And that's exactly what she did, letting herself collapse into Deirdre's embrace.

"I'm dying," she said into Deirdre's shoulder.

Gently, very gently, Deirdre edged back. She kept her grip on Lisa's shoulders and was trying, Lisa could tell, to look in her eyes, but Lisa kept her head down.

"What did you say?" asked Deirdre.

Lisa looked up then, looked them each in the eye.

"I'm dying," she said clearly, feeling it become real as she heard her own words. "I'm going to die."

"What are you talking about?" said Deirdre.

Lisa stepped back then, so that Deirdre had to let her go. She wanted to be sure they all knew she was serious, and that this was not some insane delusion connected to her tirade.

"I had a scan," she said, "after that night in the city, the night of the blizzard. The real reason I had to leave that night was because I didn't feel well. I hadn't been feeling well for a while."

Lisa looked at the chaos all around her and thought about how much she hadn't told them, how much they didn't know.

"I had cancer," she said, "when I was in the hospital in January. Cervical cancer. I had a complete hysterectomy then, and they thought they got everything. That's why I didn't need chemo. But now they've found a spot on my liver."

Deirdre frowned. "Liver. That's not good."

"That's really not good. If it's spread to the liver, it could be anywhere. I have six months, tops."

Until now, this information had been something she'd only let roll over her while she was sitting by herself in front of the computer, reading the statistics, calculating probabilities.

"Is that what Dr. Kaufman said?" Juliette asked finally.

"No, none of the doctors will come out and say it," said Lisa. They were all so cautious, warning her not to jump to conclusions. They'd have to see what they found once they got in there. The cancer might well be contained, they might be able to cut out all of it, and then the healthy liver would regenerate itself. This time she would get the strongest possible blast of chemotherapy, in an attempt to zap any cancer cells that may be travelling beyond the liver.

But she could read, and she knew it might not, probably would not, work out like that. It might be, it probably would be, throughout her liver and beyond, just as it had been for her mother. She could have the most thorough surgery, the most aggressive chemo, and still be beyond help. And then, just like her mother, she would be dead within months. Weeks.

"But it's time to face reality," Lisa said briskly. "My surgery is Monday, and I wanted to be sure I had everything squared away with all of you before then."

This was the moment, the moment she'd created the entire evening around. She led the way into the living room and could feel the other women following her.

"I thought a lot about what I wanted to leave each of you," she said, moving the chair out of the way. She found she was excited now about the presentation, calmer after her outburst and relieved to have arrived at what she'd planned to be the high point of the evening. "It was fun, actually, thinking about who had admired what, who would look best in which clothes. I typed out all the recipes, but you should read them over this weekend in case you have any questions so I can answer them before I go into the hospital Monday."

Anne's pile was first. It was too big to lift all at once, so Lisa gathered just the top half and turned to give it to Anne.

"I put my favorite gray cashmere sweater in here," Lisa said. "Don't send it to the dry cleaners, just wash it in cold water."

She looked up with pleasure at Anne only to find Anne staring at her with a horrified look on her face.

"I don't want this stuff," Anne said, refusing to take the pile from Lisa.

"What?" Lisa said, shattered. Maybe she shouldn't have included her old clothes—nobody wants somebody else's old clothes. "Why not?"

"Because I don't believe you're going to die," said Anne.

"Oh," said Lisa. "Trust me. I'm going to die."

Anne folded her arms across her chest. "If you die," she said, "whatever you leave me in your will, I'll treasure forever, but until then, all I want is you."

Juliette folded her arms too. "I'm with Anne," she said.

Exasperated, Lisa turned to Deirdre. "Come on, Deirdre," she said. "You're the realist here."

"Well, if you think believing you're going to die is realistic, then I'm not with you," Deirdre said, lining up next to Anne and Juliette. "Although if you've got that lemon squares recipe, I'll take it. Paul loves your lemon squares."

"Deirdre!" Juliette cried. "You will not take the lemon squares recipe!"

"The lemon squares recipe isn't important," Deirdre said. "What's important is that Lisa gets a more positive attitude to face whatever happens, and that's what we have to help her with."

"I'm so fucking sick of being positive," said Lisa, sinking down onto the sofa, letting the clothes and napkins and CDs and books she'd been holding tumble to the ground. "All I've been is positive, all I've been is together, and look where it got me."

She covered her face with her hands then and sobbed, and while she sobbed she felt one hand after another reach for her—

a hand on her back, one squeezing her shoulder, another smoothing her hair.

"Listen to me," Deirdre said finally. "We're not going to let you do this. We're going to be there when you have your surgery and we're going to take care of your kids and we're going to take care of you until you get better."

"You don't really want to do that," Lisa said through her tears.

"Yes, we do," said Deirdre. "We're your best friends, for God's sake. What did you think?"

What had she thought? "I thought you'd be grossed out. I thought you wouldn't like me anymore."

Deirdre shook her head. "I don't like you," she said. "I love you."

"I love you too," said Juliette.

"Me too," said Anne.

She knew it was her turn, that she was supposed to say that she loved them too. But what she really wanted to say was: now? You love me *now*?

CHAPTER 27

Deirdre

"Paul?" Deirdre said. She was sitting in bed, wearing only a black tank and panties, eating ice cream directly from the carton. The numbness around her gums from the first round of root planing—which was something between cleaning and periodontal surgery—had just about worn off, and while she didn't feel as sore as she was afraid she might feel, ice cream was all she was up for eating for supper. It was the first seriously hot night of the year, the weather having progressed from the flash blizzard through a lavishly floral spring and then to a suffocating blast of summer in six weeks. Jersey weather. Over at the bedroom window, Paul was straining to position the air conditioner correctly so it would cool down the room enough to sleep.

"Just a minute," he said, pushing the heavy appliance to the left until it slotted into place against the window frame. He stepped back from the window, shining with sweat, and collapsed into himself with the effort. "Ugh."

"Do you need some help?" said Deirdre. Usually, they did this job together, but the root planing had earned her semi-invalid status.

Paul dusted off his hands. "No. I think I got it." He plugged the air conditioner into the heavy-duty extension cord, pressed the on button, and stood back as it stuttered to life. A stream of frosty air hit Deirdre's legs and she yanked the sheet over them.

"Maybe I should turn the air conditioner off," Paul said. "I liked looking at your legs."

"Don't you dare," said Deirdre, smiling at him but feeling nervous. They'd made love only a few times since she'd been back. Not to say she wasn't happy to be there. She had found a voice teacher, a young mom who'd just moved out from the city, right here in Homewood. She'd started singing with an all-female a cappella group. She found, more than ever before, that she was relishing her time with her children, who seemed to have become both more independent and more fun over the months she'd spent in the city. It was even nice to be with Paul again.

But she still didn't want to have sex with him.

"I wanted to ask you about Lisa," Deirdre said, eager to find a subject more compelling than her legs. "Whether you think Lisa's going to be okay."

Deirdre had been spending a lot of time with Lisa, driving her for tests and to doctor's appointments, helping her with the kids and with the house. Now Lisa was in the hospital. Her liver surgery, eight hours long, had been two days ago. It had gone well: they'd found only the one spot on the liver and they'd managed to remove that. They believed she was cancer-free now and that the healthy part of the liver would regenerate, and if the cancer didn't pop up anywhere else—the cancer in her liver was technically cervical cancer, renegade cells escaped from their original location, and who knew where else they might be lurking, though the liver was usually the first catchment area—she would be fine. Assuming she didn't get hit by a bus.

Paul sat on the bed and sighed. "I'm a family doctor, Deirdre, not an oncologist."

"Yeah, but what do you think? Seriously."

He sighed again, more deeply this time. "Liver cancer has a terrible mortality rate," he said. "But I think this is a best-case scenario. The lesion was contained. Lisa is otherwise young and healthy. So if anyone can make it through an illness like this, it's her."

Deirdre shook her head. "Being with her, I feel like such a baby, complaining about my stupid dental woes."

Paul smiled gently and took Deirdre's hand. "You can complain about your dental woes to me."

"It's just that Lisa is still so amazing," said Deirdre. "She was in her hospital bed today, tubes coming out everywhere, ordering the kids' swimsuits."

Paul laughed. "That's Lisa. Blue, red, green, and pink?"

"No, it's weird, but since she got sick, she's completely given up on the color-coding thing. She said it never made sense in terms of hand-me-downs, anyway. She actually let the kids pick out their own suits."

"Anarchy!"

"Yeah, Lisa was a little worried because Matty insisted on a purple and yellow flowered surfer suit."

"Better she's worried about that than whether she's going to die," said Paul.

Hearing that word, *die,* spoken out loud in connection with her friend made Deirdre shiver, even though the idea of it was always lurking in her mind. She was conscious of it in terms of the reality of Lisa's illness, of trying to help Lisa get the best care and help her family cope with the uncertainty. But Deirdre was also aware of how the possibility of death had become a lot more vivid in her own life, influencing her decisions and her feelings about the choices she'd made. This is it, she kept reminding herself. You better be sure you're doing what you really want to do.

"It's so mind-blowing, the way everything's changed," Deirdre said. "I still can't believe it: Anne and Juliette both getting divorced, Lisa lying in a hospital bed. It's so ironic that of all of us I'm the only one whose life is basically the same as it was six months ago."

"Why is that ironic?" Paul asked.

Looking at his trusting face gazing back at her, Deirdre realized that of course Paul would have no idea what she was talking about. He hadn't been there at the dinner six months ago when she declared that she hated him; he hadn't known about her nonmusical fantasies about Nick and a more exciting life.

And now, she thought, now that she was home and no longer dreaming of leaving him in search of some more thrilling destiny, should she tell him the truth? She wanted, sincerely, for things to be better, more solid and more honest, between them.

But did that mean she had to confess all her sins of the past? Couldn't she just vow to do better from now on?

"I was the one who wanted to shake things up, who wanted to sing," she told Paul, hoping she wouldn't be struck down by lightning. It was the truth, even if it wasn't the whole truth. "Everybody else was more or less satisfied with the way things were."

"Maybe you were just the one who talked about it," said Paul. Paul was frowning and shaking his head. "I think it's pretty evident now that none of them were that happy either."

"What about Lisa?" said Deirdre. "She didn't choose to get cancer, to have her life undergo this radical change."

"She did, though," said Paul, energy filling his voice. "She may not have decided to get cancer, but she did decide to change her life after she did."

"True," Deirdre said. "But here's the thing that's bothering me. Do we always know what's best for us? I mean, we change something, but maybe it's a totally other thing that needs to be different. Like I went off to try and make it as a singer, but maybe what I really should have done is gone to nursing school or something. We could set up a practice together, right here in Homewood."

Paul patted her hand and grimaced. "You tried the helping professions, sweetie," he said, "and I think it was pretty clear that wasn't the right career direction for you."

Deirdre wasn't really listening, though. She was thinking about how she had fantasized about changing her love life by changing men, when what she really needed to do all along was to change her relationship with Paul. Except she had no more clue than she'd had before she left how to do that.

"I'm glad I came back," she said.

"You are?"

That much she knew, wholeheartedly, was true.

"I want you to know this, Paul," she said. "I'm here because I want to be."

"Really?"

"Really."

If she, like Lisa, thought she might have only six months or a year to live, would she still choose to come back home? She'd always thought, before her excursion to New York, that if she knew she was going to die she'd spend what little time she had left on earth jumping out of airplanes, circling the globe, having all the adventures she'd always been too scared to pursue.

But now Deirdre believed that the thing she most wanted, and also the thing she was most terrified of, was to stay right where she was and love her family. To try and fall in love with this man she loved with all her heart.

Paul gathered her close and held her. She felt her heart beating against his chest, her breath hot against his neck. Then his hands moved down and cupped her behind.

"Do you want this too?" he whispered.

She nodded so that he could read the movement of her head, though she could not bring herself to agree out loud.

As he moved against her, slipping his hands beneath the elastic of her panties, pressing himself against her thigh, she closed her eyes and did what she'd always done: she began to fantasize about Nick.

But then she forced her eyes open, an emphatic "no" echoing through her brain. This wasn't right. It wasn't fair to Paul, to their marriage, to *her,* and she didn't want to do it anymore.

"I'd like you to touch me," she whispered.

And he touched her, between the legs, but clumsily.

"No," she said, taking his hand to guide it. "Like this."

But then first his finger was too rough, then so light she could barely feel it.

She wanted this to work, she wanted this to change, she knew that getting angry or being too demanding would only backfire, yet she also knew she could no longer lie there with her husband but in her own world, enjoying something that wasn't even happening in the bed.

"I know," she said, a distant memory asserting itself.

Where had she hidden it? Somewhere Zack and Zoe wouldn't find it, somewhere Paul wouldn't find it, which also meant it was somewhere so obscure she had trouble finding it herself. But finally, not in the underwear drawer, not with the nightgowns, not under the socks, and not in the antique wooden box with the passports, she found—yes, that's right, stowed carefully beneath the silk lingerie she'd worn on her wedding day and never again—Lisa's long-ago gift to all of them: the Pocket Rocket. Of course, Lisa had already armed it with the kind of battery that held its charge the longest, and when Deirdre swiveled the base it whirred to life.

"What's that?" said Paul from the bed.

Deirdre held it up, grinning.

"What is it?" he asked again.

"Don't worry," she said, pulling her tank over her head, stepping out of her panties as she climbed into bed. "We're both going to love it."

CHAPTER 28

Lisa

Lisa stretched out on the blanket as the sun, finally and luxuriously warm, beat down on her face. She supposed she should be more conscious of things like sunscreen now, but she felt irrationally immune. She'd survived cervical cancer and liver cancer—correction: cervical cancer of the liver, weird as that seemed, especially since she no longer had a cervix at all—and she just figured she was not now going to get walloped by skin cancer. Next month, she'd worry about sunscreen. Next month, she'd worry about everything. But right now, she just wanted to relax.

Somewhere in the yard, she heard the buzz of Tommy's Weedwhacker. Through her days in the hospital and the weeks of recovery at home, punctuated by a round of chemo, Tommy had taken a leave from the car dealership but spent all his time tending to Lisa and the children and the household essentials, ignoring the yard. Paul had finally showed up and mowed down the thick spring growth, but two weeks later it was up to the kids' shins again, the garden weeds gone haywire. But this morning, Tommy had finally had the chance to go outside and cut the lawn down to a fine green stubble, ticklish beneath Lisa's back even through her shirt and the blanket, and now he was tackling the weeds at the edge of the driveway. He was, Lisa knew, in heaven.

She kept her eyes closed and listened to the babble of the kids nearby. They had their paints out, along with enormous sheets of paper, and Tommy had let them wear their swimsuits. "That way when they're done painting, they can just run through the sprinkler and they'll be clean," he said. This was the kind of thinking Lisa's mother had always favored, the kind of thinking that had always driven Lisa crazy. But now, in her new surrendered state, it made her smile.

She felt shade cross her face and when it didn't pass after a few moments she opened her eyes just enough to see Henry standing there, staring down at her. He was breathing through his mouth and holding a long thin paintbrush, a blob of red paint hovering from its bristles, over her face. The paint fell with a splat to her cheek.

"That's all right," she said quickly, hoping to short-circuit any possibility of tears from Henry.

He resumed the mouth-breathing and staring.

"Was there something you wanted, honey?"

He spoke so softly she had to ask him to say it again.

"I said—can I paint your head?"

She had to think about that for a minute. It was one of those sentences that, while simple and straightforward, one never expected to hear in one's lifetime, and so took a moment to comprehend. Her head? She reached up and realized the bandana she'd taken to wearing knotted pirate-style over her bald scalp had fallen off. Of course, she thought. Who could resist a canvas like this? Who, finding himself in possession of a paintbrush, wouldn't feel the desire to paint it? And why not? She could hardly look worse than she did bald.

"Well, of course, my sweetie," she said to her son, sitting up so he would be able to reach it better. "I'm sure you're going to make me look gorgeous."

Very slowly, he bent down until his lips were micrometers from her ear.

"Does that mean yes?" he whispered.

She laughed. "Yes," she said. "Yes."

"She said yes!" he crowed to his brothers and sister, who had obviously been waiting for the verdict. It was only in this month that Lisa had realized that while Henry seemed to be the shyest and most sensitive of the bunch, he was actually the bravest in many ways too, the one the others pushed forward to make difficult requests or to plead a disputed case. Henry's combination of directness and naked emotion made him a compelling and often irresistible advocate.

Now all four children crowded giggling around her, paintbrushes at the ready. The first touch to her scalp felt cold and wet and creamy, like lotion, and the bristles on the paintbrush were soft and stimulating as hair. She closed her eyes and let herself sink into the feeling.

In the brief period after her mother got sick, but before it became clear that she was going to die, her mother had embraced her illness the way she'd approached most of life, as an opportunity for pleasure. She'd lie propped up by pillows while the children, with Lisa in the lead, brought her bowls of chocolate ice cream and rubbed her shoulders and her neck. "Mmmmmm," she'd say. "Isn't that the best? Aren't I the luckiest mother in the world?"

Thinking of this now, Lisa felt tears gather behind her closed eyelids. This was the side of her mother she rarely let herself remember, the side she had loved and missed so desperately, then and still. If Lisa had gotten sick and her mother had been alive, she would have felt no hesitation about telling everything. Lisa's mother would have held wide her fleshy arms and Lisa would have climbed onto her capacious lap and whispered every feeling, every fact, until the only truth that mattered was that Lisa was loved, and safe.

"Why are you crying, Mommy?" Henry said.

"Oh," said Lisa, wiping her cheek, not aware that she had been, "I was just thinking about my mommy."

Henry plopped down behind her, his wet paintbrush trailing down her clothes.

"Who was your mommy?"

"Well," said Lisa. "Her name was Margaret."

"That's my name!" Daisy crowed. "Margaret Mary Reed, Daisy for short!"

"That was my mother's name, too, except she was called Peggy, not Daisy, and her last name wasn't Reed, it was Maloney."

"Maloney baloney," Matty said, laughing.

"Baloney faloney," said Will.

"Quit it, guys," Tommy said. "Your mom's telling you something important."

He had turned off the Weedwacker and was smiling down at her.

"Yes," said Henry, plopping heavily into her lap. "Tell."

"Well," said Lisa, trying to think of what she could say that would not scare the kids. "She loved ice cream. She liked to spend the whole day cuddled on the window seat in the living room with me and my sisters and brother eating ice cream and playing games."

"Just like you, Mommy." Henry grinned up at her.

That was how he saw her? That was what she'd become? Considering it, she couldn't have been more pleased.

"That's right," she assured him. "Just like me."

Henry gave her a hug, and then Tommy said, "So who's ready for the sprinkler?"

"I am!" cried Daisy, running out into the middle of the lawn.

Henry catapulted from Lisa's lap, and the other boys joined their siblings as Tommy turned on the faucet. The water rose up in a joyful arc as the kids ran screaming in circles beneath the tiny rainbows made by the sun.

Tommy came and sat beside her, looking somewhere above her forehead and grinning.

"What?" she said.

He raised his eyebrows.

"Tommy! What?"

He burst out laughing. "I'm sorry. Your head."

"Oh God," she said, running a hand quickly over what was now the dried mud feeling of the paint. "I nearly forgot."

"No," he said. "It looks cute."

"Adorable, I'm sure."

"Gorgeous," he said. He leaned over and kissed her.

She was sure this was a lie, but she was grateful for it. Even if she'd become more comfortable with the truth, that didn't mean she didn't still appreciate the artful evasion, the well-chosen fib.

He sat down on the blanket, and she settled back against him, so she could feel his solidity but couldn't see his face.

"How are you feeling?" he asked.

She nearly said her usual automatic fine, but checked herself. She'd been practicing, over the past month. With each small revelation, she waited anxiously for Tommy's response. And each time it was clear that he didn't hate her, that he wasn't going to leave her now that he'd gotten a look at the real—make that realer—her, she felt a little more willing to pull back the curtain next time.

"I'm tired," she said to him now. "It feels wonderful being out here in the sun, but I feel depleted. Like I don't know what's left now that they've finished."

The chemo had just ended and they were going to take a break now and see how she did. See whether she got better, or worse.

"From now on you'll just get stronger," Tommy said.

She pulled in a breath. She knew that positive spirit was just him, a big part of what had attracted her to him in the first place. Even as they drew closer, even as they became more honest, that was still there. And she needed it, to some extent. But not if it iced over the truth.

"Maybe," she said. "That's what I hope."

Then they sat there in the warmth as the children careened around them. It felt so natural, so normal, yet had they ever done this before? Lisa couldn't remember a time. Beautiful weekend afternoons had always been filled with hiking in a park or building a path in the garden, with preparing a barbeque or painting the shed. Never just with sitting in the sun.

"Hey, whatever happened to your book?" Tommy said. "Now that I'm on leave, are you going to work on that again?"

Lisa laughed. "I don't think I can really tell anybody how to live anymore," she said.

"Oh, yes you could," said Tommy. "You might even know more about it now than you did before."

She might have dismissed what he said as more sugarcoating, but then she thought: that could be true. Now, for the first time in her life, she knew how to simply be, how to love her husband and her children and to feel happy or even miserable in the moment, rather than cementing over every experience with a whirl of activity.

She might know more, she thought, but when it came to filling a book, there was so much less to say.

How to Live: Breathe in. Breathe out. Be happy now.

CHAPTER 29

Anne

Anne sat on the old steel glider on her front porch, waiting for Damian. She'd asked him to come out here to talk about their settlement. She'd sent Clementine away, to play at Deirdre's house, and was wearing a big sweatshirt over leggings. In work clothes, he might have noticed the new roundness to her figure, and she didn't want him even getting curious before the terms of their divorce were settled and the papers were signed. First she had to ensure there was no way for him to grab Clementine; then she would worry about making certain the new baby was beyond his reach. Plus, the sweatshirt was handy for hiding the tape recorder she would use to document their conversation.

From half a block away she heard his footsteps. For so long, the sound of his approach had filled her with anticipation and joy, but now she felt so anxious it was an effort to keep herself rooted on the glider. Take a deep breath, she told herself, wiping the wetness of her palms on the sweatshirt. You're ready for this.

He didn't even bother smiling when he spotted her, just let himself into the screened porch and sat in a wicker rocker across from her. She willed herself to keep gliding and to wait for him to speak first.

"So you told me on the phone that you were ready to settle," he said finally.

She nodded.

He smiled a little then. "You know my terms," he said. "The proceeds from the house, the savings accounts, the monthly payments."

"The alimony," she said.

He scowled. "Call it whatever you want."

She gripped the sides of her sweatshirt and cleared her throat. "See, the thing is," she said. "There's not going to be any alimony. Or anything from the savings account or the house."

"What are you talking about?" Damian said.

"There's nothing there," she said. "I quit my job, Damian. They were downsizing anyway. I probably could have waited a month or two, volunteered for a buyout, but I said no, I wanted to leave right away. The big opportunity was now."

"I don't understand," said Damian.

"My restaurant!" Anne cried. This was actually more fun than she'd anticipated. Her palms weren't even sweating any-more. "Somehow, you never could remember that I wanted to do that. A restaurant in town came up for sale—Cleopatra, that French-Egyptian place I went once with the moms, it didn't last long—and I realized I had to leap."

"Bully for you," Damian said dryly. "I still don't see how that changes anything."

"You see, there's no chance of alimony anymore, because I no longer have an income. And there are no savings anymore either, Damian. I invested all the money in the restaurant. The retirement money too."

"There's a simple remedy for that," Damian said. "I'll sue."

"You could sue," Anne agreed. "I don't know how far you'd get, given all the money we plowed in your films over the years. It seems only fair that I should get a tenth as much for my business."

"There's still the house."

"Actually, I refinanced the house. I needed the money to buy a liquor license." That had been a real coup; she couldn't help grinning.

"You think this is funny, Anne?" Damian said. "We'll see how funny you think it is when I win custody of Clementine."

"I don't think you have grounds for that suit any longer," Anne said calmly, "given that I'll be home full-time now, working only in the evenings, right here in town."

Damian scowled. "We'll see how confident you feel when I take Clementine to England with me."

"Oh," said Anne, happy that her corporate training had taught her to anticipate and prepare a response for every potential problem, "I don't think that's going to happen. I've already had a conversation with the immigration authorities, and Clem is on a list of minors whose parents have threatened to kidnap them and leave the country."

"I haven't threatened anything," Damian said.

"In fact, you just did. I have it on tape."

"You bitch," Damian spat. "I won't sign."

"Ah ah ah," Anne said. "More threats."

Damian glared at her and she made herself meet his stare until, suddenly, his expression seemed to soften. "When did you start to hate me so much?" he said.

It was such a plain question, the first purely true thing he'd said to her in longer than she could remember, that she answered him with the truth. "I never hated you," she said. "I just knew I had to leave you, and I loved you so much that I had to pretend I hated you to make leaving you less painful."

His dark eyes softened even further, and he looked at her with what she had once interpreted as love. "Do you still love me?"

And she could tell that he wanted the answer to be yes. That if the answer had been yes, there might still, even now, be a chance that they could get back together and forget all the animosity that had grown up between them.

But the truth was that while she didn't hate him, she didn't love him either, not anymore.

"No," she said.

He sighed. "I deserve that. I screwed up, Anne, I really did."

When she didn't reply, he said, "I regret it, you know. I don't suppose that makes much of a difference to you now, but I do regret it. I miss you."

And again, she spoke the truth: "I miss you too."

"But not enough," he said.

"No, not enough."

"I suppose that's it, then. We'll make it official, sign the papers, and go our separate ways."

She felt almost shocked, that once it was clear she had him, he had backed down so completely.

"So you'll sign?" she said.

"Yes, I'll sign."

She sat there and watched as he surveyed the first page, initialed it at the bottom, then turned to the second page and did the same. It was only on the last page of the document, where the terms of visitation were outlined, that he hesitated.

"Ummmm," he said, his pen levitating above the paper.

"It's the same schedule we've been using all along," she pointed out. She restrained herself from saying: the one you insisted on. The one you refused to vary by so much as five minutes. At this point all she wanted was for it to be over.

He put the pen in his mouth and chewed. "I'm going to need this to be different now," he said finally.

"What changes do you want?" she asked, her mind already spinning with what compromises she'd be willing to make: maybe he could have Clementine one evening a week in addition to every other weekend, or for three weeks in the summer as opposed to two. The important thing was that she retain custody, and it seemed he'd already caved on that.

"See, the thing is," he said, "it looks like I'm moving to LA. So it's going to be impossible for me to see Clem as often as I have been. As often as I'd like."

"Really?" she said, the only word she could manage to squeeze out.

"Yes, quite soon, I'm afraid. You see, *Bride for Hire* has found a Hollywood distributor. And so now it looks as if *Lakeisha for President* is going to be green-lighted any day—

with Queen Latifah starring, not Whoopi Goldberg, I'll have you know—so my base really has to shift to the Coast."

"Damian," she said, searching for a neutral word. "That's . . . amazing."

Amazing that he'd pulled it off, after all these years, just now. Amazing that he hadn't told her until this moment. He was actually willing to go ahead and extort the maximum possible from her when he was sitting on a multi-million-dollar deal of his own.

Don't get angry, she reminded herself. Look at the positive side: he'll be far away, and I'll be left to begin my new life on my own. With my child, she thought. With *both* my children.

"You've been working toward this for a long time," she crooned, one of her reliable old refrains. "I know how much you deserve it. What would work out for you?"

"I was thinking some concentrated period of time between shoots, say a week every three months or so, would be best."

Anne nearly choked. That was it? For herself, she was delighted to have so little interaction, but she knew Clementine would be disappointed.

"And of course," Damian was saying, "if business takes me to New York, I would hope you could be flexible enough to let me see her for an occasional evening."

"I think that could be arranged," said Anne.

She began writing in the changes, secure that the tape was still recording their conversation, should there be any discrepancy later. She made sure to write out Clementine's full name— to not refer to her as merely "the child," which might be interpreted to mean the child to come—in every reference.

There had been legal cases where noncustodial fathers, fathers who hadn't even known they were fathers, had sued for parental rights over their biological children. Some of the time they had won. But Anne didn't intend to let Damian know this baby was his, and didn't think he'd force a DNA test to find out. Why would he be interested in this baby, since he didn't even seem that interested in the child he *knew* he had?

"So that's it," he said when she initialed the changes and slid the paper back to him to sign.

"That's it," she said, watching as he wrote his name.

He took a deep breath, slapped his thighs, and stood up. "A good-bye kiss," he said, "for old time's sake?"

She smiled but did not move toward him. "Good luck, Damian," she said.

And watched him walk away.

CHAPTER 30

Juliette

She hesitated just once—on the steps outside his building, right before she rang the bell. It seemed as if she were about to go through or maybe over a divider in time—she thought of it alternately as a permeable glass wall, and as the very sharp peak of a mountain—that separated her past from her future. She faltered not because she was unsure about whether she wanted to go forward, but because she wanted to honor the moment, which offered a rare opportunity to notice her own life shifting as it happened. She was leaving behind all the things she was supposed to have and all the ways she was supposed to be and all the moves she was supposed to make. And she was moving toward what she really wanted.

Taking a deep breath, she pressed the buzzer, and immediately, as if his hand had been poised at the button, waiting for her ring, it sounded back. As soon as she was inside the building's hallway she heard his footsteps and looked up the stairwell to see him running down to meet her as she ran up. He was faster, and she hadn't even reached the second floor when she was in his arms, and he was holding her so tightly her feet lifted from the steps. When he finally set her down, he took her hand and they walked upstairs silently, side by side. The clean smell of his shirt overpowered all the other smells—the damp and the smoke and the onions on the fry—that mingled in the hallway.

The only other time they'd been alone together was outside for everyone to see, kissing on the stoop. Touching him, the heat of his skin was new, and the rough pads of his fingertips, and the pressure of his powerful arm against hers. He was so much taller than she was, which was unusual in itself, and so much larger than Cooper. He must have just gotten a haircut—his hair was shaved so close he was practically bald—and she noticed the pointed indigo edge of the tattoo that spiked from the neck of his T-shirt across his jugular. She felt thrilled to finally be with him, and strangely comfortable, even in her self-consciousness.

It had been right to hold off for all these weeks, she thought, so that now she could come to him free of ambivalence, through with the agonizing process of ending her marriage. All the angry words had been exchanged, the details hammered out, the tears cried. Now she felt truly single again. Now she felt truly ready to be with Nick.

Once they were inside his apartment and the door was bolted, they stood facing each other for a moment and then she raised her arms above her head like a child, letting him know she was ready for him to remove her shirt. It was her decision, but he was in the lead. It had never been this way with Cooper, who had always held all the power in their relationship, but whom she had never, she felt now, really trusted.

Nick slipped her thin cotton ribbed shirt smoothly up and over her head, tossing it across the room. Then he gathered her into his arms and she curled in upon herself so that she could feel him enveloping her. What was funny, for a love affair that had developed almost completely on the phone, through their voices, by sound and not by sight, was that now they seemed to have no desire to talk.

She kissed his chest, hard beneath his soft charcoal T-shirt, her lips moving slowly, kiss by kiss, across to his left shoulder, and then back to his right shoulder, hungry and then hungrier for the warmth she could taste beneath the fabric. He groaned, his head dropping back, his knees beginning to buckle.

"God, I love you," he said.

She stopped her kisses, stood up straight, looked at him.

"I love you too," she said.

"My turn," he said softly, bending down and tenderly kissing each bare nipple, and then moving his lips in an arc across her breasts in an exact copy of what she had done to him.

"You're matching me," she said.

"I will always match you." He had fallen to his knees now and did not stop kissing.

She ran her fingers over the stubble of his hair. "Even if I'm mean."

He looked up at her. "You could never be mean."

"I could," she assured him, thinking of how steely she'd made herself, telling Cooper that she wanted a divorce.

"I don't believe it." He resumed kissing, moving lower down her belly, unsnapping her jeans. Her fingers dug into his scalp.

"Ouch," he said.

"Told you."

"Come here."

He led her to the bed and they got into it together, she still in her jeans and he fully dressed, and pulled the covers over them.

"You're not leaving," he said.

"Not till Sunday, when I have to get Trey."

He hesitated. "So you're really going to leave him overnight? I know how you feel. . . ."

She put her finger to his lips. "Cooper's spending the weekend with him in Homewood," she said.

Juliette had been surprised, after the separation, by how much Trey missed his father, and further surprised by how energetically Cooper had pushed for full visitation rights. He'd done more to get close to his son in the weeks since the separation than he'd done in all the years before.

"I think Cooper's finally learning to be a good dad," she told Nick. "And besides, he's got Heather there to help him."

"We're staying in this bed until then."

She laughed. "Won't we need to eat?"

"I've stocked up."

"Don't you need to go somewhere and play some music?"

"I've called in sick."

She thought for a moment. "What if I don't want to stay in bed all weekend?"

"Then we won't," he said. "What do you want to do?"

She nestled into him. "I'll think about it."

What she felt with him was that she was home. She felt that when they talked on the phone, she felt it when she was in this apartment without him, and she especially felt it now that they were together. How amazing that she should experience this for the first time with a man she barely knew, in a place she'd rarely been, and not with her mother in the house where she grew up or her husband in the house where she lived throughout her years of marriage. It was as if the real Juliette had always been hidden inside the Juliette who had been moving through the world, and it had taken Nick to set her free.

She closed her eyes and breathed his heat in deeply, feeling drunk on it, as if it were a potion that would make her delirious. She lay there, feeling as if she could sleep, while he raised himself and eased off her pants. Then her underpants.

She was on her back, her eyes still lowered, when he moved down under the covers and kissed her first on one side of her belly, in the tender spot just inside her hipbone, and then on the other side. His lips moved lower until his mouth was between her legs. She tensed, remembering how Cooper had always used this as a not-very-smooth segue to other probings she did not welcome, but Nick felt nothing like Cooper, his tongue at once more gentle and more sharp than her husband's.

How could the same act feel so different with the alteration of just the man? She knew, of course, that this was supposed to be so, but she was still unprepared for the experience. It was as if she was aware that in all cases she was moving from one place to another, but before she was crawling through mud and now she soared, wind against her skin, through the clouds.

It was happening so fast though, there was no time to analyze. Juliette kept trying to step back and think about what she was feeling, but at the same time she realized she had to choose between thinking and feeling, that she wouldn't be able to have them both, and so she surrendered, frightening as it was.

When she found herself pushing against Nick's mouth and trying to pull him up and into her, reaching down frantically to undo his zipper, he made her stop.

"No," he whispered. "Not that way."

He got out of bed and undressed gracefully while she watched, and then slipped back into the bed, lying on his back.

"You on top," he said.

"I can't."

"I think you can."

He helped her. He held her up there with his large calloused hands and then he moved her back and forth until she didn't need any more help. It was as if he had something there, between his legs, that she had to have as she thrust against him, hearing herself cry out but unable to help it. And at the same time he was encouraging her, arching against her so that each little movement made her less and less self-conscious, and more and more excited.

And then finally there it was, the thing she'd never felt before but knew with certainty that she was feeling now. She seemed to pulse against him, a pinnacle and a release more exquisite than anything she'd imagined, all the times she'd imagined it. Do you feel this? she wanted to cry out, not only to him, but to everyone. Do you really feel this, all the time? Of course they did, she knew. It was the reason sex was sex in the first place, the reason everybody in the world seemed to want to do it again and again.

Slowly, she stretched out her limbs and eased down beside Nick.

"I've decided what I want to do," she told him.

"Oh yeah?" he said. "What's that?"

"Stay in bed with you," she said, grinning.

"All weekend?" he said.

"No," she said. "For the rest of my life."

CHAPTER 31

The June Dinner

In May, for the first time in nearly seven years, the moms did not meet for their monthly dinner.

Anne was too busy working on her new restaurant, stretching out in a jumbo booth whenever the sleepiness of early pregnancy overwhelmed her and she needed a nap. Damian had vanished into the land of make-believe and Anne found that, while life as a single mother was lonelier, it was also, with Consuelo's help, often easier than life as a married mother had been.

Juliette sold her house and was spending all her time before the closing—all the time she wasn't in bed with Nick—disposing of the vast quantity of items Cooper had amassed but left behind when he moved to a Tribeca penthouse his decorator said required all new furniture.

Lisa was lying low following the chemotherapy that followed her eight-hour liver surgery. While her friends visited her frequently, these get-togethers did not involve food.

Deirdre was busy too, though she refused to tell the other women what she was working on. You'll see, was all she'd say: You'll find out when we get together in June.

They finally met on the night before opening night, the dress rehearsal of Anne's new restaurant. Where Cleopatra's had been now stood Mom's, the kind of homey place she'd loved during her small-town southern childhood. The decor was all about comfort; but the real attraction of the place was the food: meat loaf and chicken gumbo, barbequed ribs and lobster rolls, blueberry pie and homemade chocolate ice cream, with excellent beer on tap.

Anne came out of the kitchen, her long white apron knotted above her blossoming belly, nervously surveying the room. They weren't open to the public tonight, but she'd asked the staff to invite everyone they knew, and she'd done the same, including everyone from Clementine's teacher to the guy— extremely cute—who installed her bedroom air conditioner. And of course Deirdre and Juliette and Lisa would be there, her most honored guests.

She took a deep breath. All afternoon, she'd been in the kitchen with the chef, showing him how to construct her own recipes and working with him on adapting his specialties for her place. Now, her wait staff—not groovy-looking kids but actual moms whose kids had flown the nest and overstressed or down-sized executives looking to change their lives—were lined up along the creamy wainscoted wall.

"Everybody ready?" she asked.

They nodded, and she moved to the best table in the place, with a round banquette—the exact spot, she realized as she straightened the black-and-white checkered napkins and polished a big water tumbler—where the four of them had sat back in November. Everything was right. Untying her apron, she moved to the front door and unlocked it.

She was stunned by how many people had been waiting outside the freshly painted red door. Clementine practically knocked her over with an enormous hug, before she took a seat with Consuelo and her husband. Friends and strangers alike kissed her and congratulated her. Even more exciting, she knew everyone would be even more enthusiastic once they tasted the food.

"This reminds me of these great old places in the Upper Peninsula, where I used to go on vacation when I was a kid," said Lisa.

"No, no," said Juliette. "It's like a little Parisian bistro, only American."

"I don't know," said Deirdre. "It kind of reminds me of Fisherman's Wharf. Or some funky little place in one of the coast towns north of San Francisco—Inverness or Point Reyes."

"So now we have one place where we can have all our moms' dinners, right?" Anne said.

"Absolutely," said Juliette. "Are you going to let us contribute dishes? I could do a tarte tatin."

"I'll give the bartender the recipe for my version of Bionic Babes," said Deirdre.

"Lemon squares," said Lisa.

A young man, powerfully built, with a round face and sawdust in his sandy hair, shyly approached their table.

"Excuse me," he said. "Annie?"

She smiled up at him.

"Did you want that pull on the top cupboard at the waiters' station in the middle of the door or the bottom?"

"The bottom, definitely," she said. "Ray, these are my friends I was telling you about—Deirdre, Juliette, Lisa."

"You look familiar," Deirdre said.

"He used to work in the hardware store, uptown," Anne said. "He's the one who built this whole place."

When the women had complimented his work and he'd retreated to attach the cupboard pull, they all turned to Anne, who could feel herself blushing.

"Annie?" Lisa said. "I've never heard anybody call you Annie."

Anne smiled. "I'm liking it."

"So are you seeing this guy?" Deirdre asked. "Ray."

"We're having a flirtation," Anne said. "I want to keep everything extremely low-key, until the divorce is final, which should be any day. But God, it's hard. Do you girls remember being this horny when you were pregnant?"

They all looked at one another, then burst out laughing and chorused, "No!"

"How are you feeling?" asked Juliette.

"Despite the horniness, or maybe because of it—great," said Anne. "And I just got the results of the prenatal test today. Everything's fine, and it's a girl!"

A girl. Juliette was trying her hardest not to be jealous, just to be happy for Anne, but a girl. How she would love to have a baby girl.

With all the sex she and Nick had been having—undoubtedly more sex in the past two months than she'd had in her entire life—she still wasn't getting pregnant. After the first few weeks, they'd stopped using birth control. It was so fast, they recognized, but they also knew they both wanted to be together, they both wanted a baby, so why not see what happened.

The problem was, nothing happened. Nick, unlike Cooper, was happy to go to the fertility doctor with Juliette, but Nick didn't have a problem. Juliette, it turned out, did. The diagnosis was incomplete, the prognosis uncertain, and given the newness of her relationship and the upcoming start of her occupational therapy program, she'd decided not to pursue treatment. Not now, anyway. Maybe, the doctors said, she'd get pregnant on her own. And if she didn't—she'd make sure to tuck away the proceeds from a few of Cooper's cast-off antiques in case she wanted to go through treatment down the road.

"A girl," she said to Anne. "You have to promise to let me spend lots of time with her."

Anne smiled. "She'll be free most evenings and weekends, when I'm here."

"It's a date," said Juliette.

"But wait," said Lisa. "Aren't you moving to New York?"

That had been the plan, what she'd told everyone. But Nick had changed her mind.

"We found a place out here," she said, a grin spreading over her face. "I signed the lease today, and we're moving in next week."

"We?" Lisa said. "You mean you and Trey?"

"Me and Trey and Nick," said Juliette. "I couldn't believe it either, but he convinced me he really wanted to be in Homewood."

"My my my," Deirdre said, shaking her head. "Nick Ruby in Homewood, New Jersey. That should shake a little life into this town."

"Does Cooper know?" asked Anne.

Juliette nodded. "It turns out he's living with someone too. Not only that: he went to the Dominican Republic for a quickie divorce so they can get married."

"Who is it this time?" asked Deirdre. "Some New York heiress? Or wait, I know, his secretary."

"Close," said Juliette. "It's Heather."

"Heather, your *nanny?*" Lisa gasped.

Juliette grinned. "One and the same. He hired her to help him with Trey on the weekends he was finally forced to be a parent, and realized very quickly that he couldn't live without her."

"What nerve!" said Lisa. "Are you upset?"

"Are you kidding?" said Juliette. "I'm delighted. I know that Trey's well taken care of when he's there, and it leaves me free to marry Nick."

"You're marrying Nick?" asked Deirdre.

It was the first time in a long time that Juliette had detected anything like jealousy from Deirdre about her relationship with Nick. But now her friend's face had undeniably paled, and she was biting her lip.

"You said yourself that you couldn't imagine being in a relationship with him," said Juliette.

"I know, I know," said Deirdre. "But now I guess this means I'm going to have to stop fantasizing about him too. He's going to be a husband. Neutered."

"I hope not," said Juliette, laughing. "I'm assuming Anne's old role of irritatingly sex-crazed member of our foursome."

"That was irritating?" said Anne.

"Yes!" they cried in unison.

"I'll try not to be too graphic. But what I really want to say is: can we have the wedding here, Anne? We were thinking early next year, maybe even—and I know this is putridly romantic—Valentine's Day."

"But of course!" Anne said. "The baby will be three months old by then so I'll do all the cooking myself. You'll have to let me know which of these appetizers you like best."

A waiter had just set two enormous white platters bearing the full complement of the restaurant's appetizers on their table.

"And," said Anne, biting into a Pig in a Blanket, "I have this great Red Velvet cake recipe I can make in a heart shape."

"That sounds fantastic," said Juliette. "And I want you all to be in the wedding. I'll have three best women. That's all right, isn't it? You'll all be there?"

Well, Lisa thought, maybe not me. February was eight months away, and she might only have six months. Or four. Or, on an outside chance, much much longer, maybe even some semblance of a normal lifetime. They just didn't know.

This was the kind of uncertainty that used to drive Lisa out of her mind. She'd push for a deadline, a resolution, an answer, even if she knew it would be less favorable than it might be if she eased up and stepped back. But then she'd been concerned with such issues as what teacher Matty was going to get for first grade and how much the interest rate would be for the refinance. They had seemed life and death at the time; now she couldn't imagine taking these matters even close to seriously.

But if these day-to-day problems seemed unimportant to her, they might be vital to the person involved. Henry still cried when the pre-k bully picked on him, Matty still worried if he got less than 100 on a math test, Tommy came home downcast when he didn't make his sales quota. The old Lisa—always too busy for weakness—hadn't taken much time to sympathize. Now it was almost as if her heart had been the part of her body that had been prodded and sliced and opened to the world.

"Of course I'll be there," she told Juliette, who looked so beautiful tonight, pared to her essential self, as if removing all that hair and makeup, the glasses and the big clothes, had finally revealed her happiness. In fact, why had she never noticed before how incredibly beautiful all her friends were: Anne with her paleness and angles made pink and plump by her pregnancy, Deirdre ripe in her bare black dress, her auburn hair curling wildly around her head in the humid June night?

"You're getting hair," said Juliette.

Lisa ran her hand over the top of her head. So she was. It was very fine, the down of a newborn baby chick, invisible in most light. But she'd felt a prickling in her scalp the past few days she thought might be portentous and had stopped wearing her head scarves to encourage any theoretical growth.

"When it comes in," she told Juliette, "I'm going to keep it short, like yours."

"I was thinking about shaving mine in solidarity," said Deirdre.

"I've been throwing up in solidarity," said Anne. "Though I think it's stopping."

"You guys have been great," Lisa said. And they had been, taking her kids on outings, dropping off food, stopping to chat. Deirdre had even tried to clean the kitchen once, but she'd finally given up and sat on the bed talking to Lisa, which made them both more relaxed.

"So what does the doctor say?" asked Juliette. "They got it all, right?"

"They got it all in the liver," said Lisa.

"So what happens now?"

"As soon as school's out, Tommy and the kids and I are going out to Michigan to visit my family."

"Like—" Anne started, but then stopped herself.

"Like this, you mean?" Lisa said, running her hand again over her nearly bald scalp. "Yes, like this. I think it's time I told them about my"—say the word, she told herself—"cancer."

Tommy had talked her into it. Yes, they'd be upset. Yes, it would mean she'd have to let them know she wasn't omnipotent and immortal. But there were good things, Tommy said, about choosing to be human. Things that had proven alluring even for plenty of gods—and goddesses.

"It'll be easier now," Deirdre said, "now that everything's over. I mean, they might be freaked out, but at least you can reassure them that you're okay."

Lisa hesitated. She hadn't worked out exactly what she was going to say to her family about this, though Tommy was lobbying for the truth. "If they're going to lose you, Lisa, if we're all going to lose you, we deserve a chance to say good-bye."

But what if nothing was for sure? Wouldn't it be better to live as if you *were* immortal, the way most healthy people lived every day?

"I can't reassure them," she told her friends, who were all looking at her as if they were the ones who wanted to be reassured. "I hope I'm okay, I hope it's over, but the doctors just don't know. And it's going to be a while before anything is clear."

There was no response to that, no possible argument against it or reassurance that everything would be all right. They all just sat there together, breathing. But there were compensations, Lisa thought, as an intense wave of happiness—at the beauty of the night and the place and her friends, at their good news that helped balance her uncertainty—washed over her. I know that this, this moment, is all I'll ever have, she thought: it's all any of us can ever be sure of.

Deirdre had to blink hard and breathe down deep into her stomach to keep herself from breaking into huge racking sobs and hurling herself into Lisa's arms. God, she'd always thought Lisa was strong, and fearless, but the woman had entered another dimension. She was now officially Deirdre's new role model.

No one at their table was able to speak, but then their waiter appeared, whisking away their picked-clean appetizer plate and setting down a selection of entrées.

"I thought we'd all just share," said Anne, breaking the silence.

There was roast turkey and grilled trout, fried shrimp and barbequed chicken, meat loaf and Anne's famous lobster rolls, plus heaping bowls of buttermilk biscuits and onion rings and mashed potatoes with melted butter. And there was a pitcher of beer *and* a pitcher of margaritas.

Lisa ate more enthusiastically than any of them, which helped everyone else to relax and dig in too. Then after dinner there was a strawberry and rhubarb pie and a caramel cake and chocolate ice cream, washed down by iced tea and more beer. Finally, it was getting dark outside, the sun so reluctant to go down on what was nearly the longest day of the year.

Across the table, Deirdre caught Anne's eye, Anne raised her brows, Deirdre nodded, and then stood up.

"Okay," she said. "Now I can tell you all what I've been working on." She took a deep breath. "I've got a new singing act. And nobody better laugh."

"Why would we laugh?" said Lisa. "*You* were the one who made so much fun of poor Mrs. Zamzock when we were here last fall."

"Okay," said Deirdre. "Fucking touché."

"Listen," said Anne. "I have a surprise too."

She waved at Ray, who seemed to have showered and changed into regular clothes, and Ray ducked into the kitchen, coming back into the room with Paul and Zack and Zoe, who hugged their mom and then ran to sit with Clementine.

"If I'd known I would have told Tommy to come down with the kids," said Lisa. "He's dying to get a look inside this place. Well, maybe not *dying* . . ."

"Don't worry," said Anne. "I thought of that, too."

Ray summoned out Tommy and Lisa's four children, who ran to sit with the twins, all except little Henry, who climbed into Lisa's lap.

Deirdre looked at Juliette, all alone, but then Juliette said, "I have a surprise for you too."

She stood up and walked over to the kitchen herself, emerging with Trey by one hand, and Nick by the other.

Paul and Nick, finally in the same room. There was nothing to be done about it but to try and keep breathing, as Paul kissed her right cheek while Nick kissed her left. Paul was actually taller, Deirdre noticed with surprise, and his lips felt sweeter against her skin. It was an interesting moment, but one she was glad had finally passed.

"I'd like to back you up, Deirdre," said Nick, "if that's okay."

"But you don't know the numbers I'm going to do."

"Oh, yes I do," said Nick, throwing a smile Paul's way. "Paul told me."

"I introduced them," said Juliette.

"It was my idea," said Anne.

Lisa shrugged. "I pretended I was surprised."

Deirdre patted her shoulder. "You did that very well."

Deirdre squared her own shoulders then and straightened the black silk dress around her hips, tilting her chin up and looking squarely at Nick.

"We're not going to play 'Misty,'" she said.

He smiled. "Wouldn't dream of it."

"Or 'Moon River.'"

"I actually like 'Moon River.'"

There he went, disagreeing with her again. She would simply not pay any attention; as a soon-to-be husband, he could finally be ignored.

"I may be a lounge singer in New Jersey," she said, taking his hand and beginning to walk toward where Anne had set up a microphone in the corner of the room, "but I still have my standards."

He was sexy, she could still give him that, but she was happy that in the end she realized that the love of her life was Paul, who was beaming at her from across the room, looking as if he was already about to burst into applause. And while she was thrilled for Anne, she was very glad that she wasn't the one who was pregnant. As for Lisa, Deirdre was grateful she was finally getting a chance to know her friend, and all she could do was hope that she would continue to know her for years to come.

Nick wheeled his bass out from Anne's office. Ray made sure the microphone was working. Deirdre congratulated Anne to a roomful of cheers and introduced Nick and herself. And then she closed her eyes, and spread her arms, and opened her mouth and her heart, and there was only her song.

Up Close and Personal With the Author

BABES IN CAPTIVITY IS A CURIOUS TITLE. WHAT DOES IT MEAN?

Despite the whole Yummy Mummy trend, I think a lot of women still put their babehood—the flamboyant, sexy, out-in-the-world side of themselves—under wraps when they get married and have kids and move to the suburbs. Continuing to be a babe seems selfish at that point, or unseemly, or disloyal in some way to your family. So you hunker down and devote your energy to the considerable task of setting up house and raising babies. And then when your youngest kid hits full-time school you look up and say, What about me?

The four women in my book each have a different view of being a babe, and each is bound by a different kind of captivity. Deirdre, the character whose dissatisfaction sets the story in motion, feels as if she sacrificed her sexuality along with her singing career on the altar of a safe but unexciting marriage, and now she wants to break back out into the wider world. Juliette traded her beauty for the security of a rich husband, but discovers that, since he's the one with all the money, he also thinks he's got all the power. Anne, who keeps her powerful sexuality hidden under her conservative business suit, is a captive of her love for her husband. And Lisa, a bundle of energy and efficiency who seems to have held fast to her babehood, turns out to be imprisoned by her notion that life can and should be perfect.

ARE THESE FOUR WOMEN BASED ON WOMEN YOU KNOW?

The individual women, their personalities, families, situations, stories, are entirely invented. What is drawn from life is the power of their friendship. Most women today have female friends who are central to their lives and it was this relationship that I wanted to write about. It changes form over time: You might be on a field hockey team in high school, in a sorority in college, have a kind of *Sex and the City* group of close friends when you're single. You segue into a moms' group once you have kids, and then perhaps a group based on work or on mutual interests—I'm part of both a writers' group and a reading group, for instance—once the kids get older. But the closeness of the group and the value of the friendships stays the same.

FOUR WOMEN, INDIVIDUAL PLOT LINES, REGULAR MEETINGS OVER MEALS—HOW MUCH IS THIS LIKE *SEX AND THE CITY*?

I didn't see the connection until toward the end of the two years I worked on this book. I saw it more as part of the long tradition of stories about groups of women, from *The Group* to *Valley of the Dolls* to *Divine Secrets of the Ya-ya Sisterhood*. I love the HBO show, but this book is more like *Sex and the Suburbs.* These women are certainly a lot less forthcoming about the details of their sex lives with their husbands, because the sexual performance of husbands tends to be off-limits in a way that boyfriends are not. At the first twinge of dissatisfaction, the *Sex and the City* girls seem to pick up and change their lives. But these women are much more deeply dug in. Even when they begin to admit they're not happy, even when they pinpoint a solution to their problems, it's not so easy to launch a career or have a baby or get a divorce when there are long-term marriages and huge mortgages and most importantly the welfare of young children to consider.

DEIRDRE SEEMS TO BE THE ONLY DISSATISFIED CHARACTER AT THE BEGINNING OF THE BOOK. WITHOUT HER AGITATION, DO YOU THINK ANY OF THE OTHER CHARACTERS WOULD HAVE GONE THROUGH WHAT THEY DID?

No, maybe not, but that doesn't mean they would have been better off. I think there's a tendency among women friends, once they're married and living settled lives, to challenge each other less, to shy away from revealing their true feelings and problems and be reluctant to rock the boat. You get together with your girlfriends for coffee or dinner, you laugh a lot and blow off the stress of your kids or your job, but it's rare that someone says, as Deirdre does at the beginning of the book, "I hate my husband."

But it can also be refreshing when one person takes the risk of telling the real truth. It can encourage everyone else to be more honest with each other, which then can take the friendships to a deeper, more satisfying level. Not every group, not every relationship can survive this kind of honesty, but the ones worth hanging onto can. Without Deirdre's provocation, Juliette might never have told Cooper she wanted to have another baby, Anne might not have nudged Damian toward letting her have her turn at satisfaction. While this would have spared them a lot of upheaval and pain, I don't believe they would have been ultimately happier. Lisa's problems, of course, weren't voluntary, but without her three friends she might never have chosen to go public with them, which would have left her lonelier and more isolated in her difficulty.

WHICH OF THE FOUR WOMEN DID YOU IDENTIFY WITH THE MOST?

I truly felt like I identified with whichever one I was writing about at the moment. One of the best things about writing this book was getting to jump around from one woman's viewpoint and life to the next. Each time I'd draw toward the end of a chapter, I'd be reluctant to let that character go, because she'd come to feel like "me," and then as soon as I got into the next character, I'd think, "No, *this* is the one who's most like me."

I tend to be mercurial and impulsive like Deirdre. In groups I've been part of, I'm the one who's usually most likely to stalk in late to a dinner, announcing, "I hate my husband." And then to proclaim I love him again the next day. I identified with Deirdre's artistic ambitions and temperament, and I admired her guts in pursuing her unlikely dream, even if it meant doing something unconventional like sometimes leaving her kids overnight.

I've worked throughout my years of motherhood, so I identified with that side of Anne. And since both my parents died long ago and my only sibling died during the writing of the book, I very much felt Anne's cosmic loneliness. Anne's discovery toward the end of the book—I don't want to ruin the plot surprise for readers who might not have gotten there yet—was something I added in a later draft. I felt very happy for her.

With Juliette and Lisa, I identified with different aspects of their experience as mothers. That feeling of Juliette's, of loving her son fiercely and craving another baby, no matter what, is one that's vivid for me. And with Lisa, I related to that experience of having a child who insists on claiming the amount of love he craves, which forces her to open her own heart. It's so hard for Lisa to show her true self; she feels that she won't be loved if she's anything less than perfect, though she discovers it's quite the opposite. I've made that same discovery myself, getting closer to friends.

YOUR LAST NOVEL, *THE MAN I SHOULD HAVE MARRIED,* IS TOLD IN THE FIRST PERSON AND FOCUSES ON ONE MAIN CHARACTER. HOW WAS IT DIFFERENT WRITING THIS BOOK?

It was easier in some ways, because I didn't have to rely on one character's voice and observations to carry the whole narrative. But it was much more complicated working out the overall plot—who told what to whom when, as well as figuring out the trajectory of the group—as well as devising the women's individual stories. After I wrote the first draft, I created an enormous chart that I taped to the wall of my office, with each character's scenes on a different color of sticky note, and the dinners on yet another color, so I could get an overview of the entire book. That helped me construct a more cohesive second draft. Then, when I wrote the third and final version of the book, my friend and fellow novelist Christina Baker Kline suggested I write each woman's story in sequence—that I do all the Deirdre chapters, for instance, and then all the Juliette chapters—finishing with the dinner chapters. And that was a brilliant idea, because it forced me to spend concentrated time with each character and so strengthen the individual stories, and because it also made the process, going into it for the third time, a lot more interesting.

THREE DRAFTS! HOW MUCH DO YOU CHANGE EACH TIME YOU REVISE?

A lot, which isn't unusual, judging from the experiences of the novelists I know. It's more unusual when something emerges graceful and fully formed from your computer the first time around. In this book there are only four chapters or scenes—one for each character—that arrived as if on the wings of an angel and survived more or less intact through each draft. Those are the chapter when Anne blows off Damian at the bus station, the one where Deirdre confronts the agent, the chapter in which Henry insists on climbing into the bed with Lisa, and Juliette's final scene, with Nick in his apartment.

Juliette's name changed. She was originally called Gaby, until I realized she was anything but. Nick was Dick in the first draft, but that's my husband's name, and I decided it was just too weird to give my fictional hunk the same name as my real-life one. In earlier drafts, there was no "good-bye shag," as the pithy Clare Conville called it, between Anne and Damian, and no resulting plot twist. Anne also was without her restaurant ambition, and Deirdre was a lot more determined to sleep with Nick. Damian kidnapped Clementine. Instead of tall and thin, Paul was short and fat. And Lisa never lost her hair *or* broke any dishes.

HOW DO YOU MANAGE TO BALANCE MOTHERHOOD AND WRITING?

Like most of the characters in this book, my youngest child is in school full-time now, which makes the whole thing easier. When they were younger, I always had babysitters but my work day was shorter and I wrote mostly magazine articles and nonfiction books, because I needed to focus on what paid the bills. Now, my husband does the early morning breakfast and kid chores, so I can wake up at 6:30 or 7, grab some coffee, and head directly to my desk. Ideally, I work on fiction until noon, reserving the very first part of the day for my most creative work. Then I usually switch to journalism: I'm the coauthor of eight successful baby-naming books and I also write for *Parenting* and *Glamour* along with other magazines. When my kids come home from school late in the afternoon, I usually stop working; that's when I cook dinner, do laundry, go food shopping. If you try to wedge those chores into your work day, you'll never get any writing done.

Like what you just read?

Then don't miss these other great books from Downtown Press!

Scottish Girls About Town
Jenny Colgan, Isla Dewar, Muriel Gray, et al.

Calling Romeo
Alexandra Potter

Game Over
Adele Parks

Pink Slip Party
Cara Lockwood

Shout Down the Moon
Lisa Tucker

Maneater
Gigi Levangie Grazer

Clearing the Aisle
Karen Schwartz

Liner Notes
Emily Franklin

My Lurid Past
Lauren Henderson

Dress You Up in My Love
Diane Stingley

He's Got to Go
Sheila O'Flanagan

Irish Girls About Town
Maeve Binchy, Marian Keyes, Cathy Kelly, et al.

The Man I Should Have Married
Pamela Redmond Satran

Getting Over Jack Wagner
Elise Juska

The Song Reader
Lisa Tucker

The Heat Seekers
Zane

I Do (But I Don't)
Cara Lockwood

Why Girls Are Weird
Pamela Ribon

Larger Than Life
Adele Parks

Eliot's Banana
Heather Swain

How to Pee Standing Up
Anna Skinner

Look for them wherever books are sold or visit us online at www.downtownpress.com.

down
town
press

Great storytelling just got a new address.

PUBLISHED BY POCKET BOOKS

10403